## PRAISE FOR *THE CONSEQUENCE OF LOVING COLTON*, BOOK 1 IN THE CONSEQUENCES SERIES

"*The Consequence of Loving Colton* is a must-read friends-to-lovers story that's as passionate and sexy as it is hilarious!"

—Melissa Foster, *New York Times* bestselling author

"Just when you think Van Dyken can't possibly get any better, she goes and delivers *The Consequence of Loving Colton*. Full of longing and breathless moments, this is what romance is about."

—Lauren Layne, *USA Today* bestselling author

"Absolutely brilliant! Laugh-out-loud funny, with the perfect amount of tenderness and heat to keep me captivated to the very end."

—J. L. Berg, *USA Today* bestselling author

"The tension between Milo and Colton made this story impossible to put down. Quick, sexy, witty—easily one of my favorite books from Rachel Van Dyken."

—R. S. Grey, *USA Today* bestselling author

"From the very first page you will be hooked! Milo and Colton's story had me laughing out loud, swooning, then back to laughing. It was an amazing ride that I didn't want to end. Rachel Van Dyken outdid herself with this one!"

—Kelly Elliott, *New York Times* bestselling author

# the consequence of seduction

*The Redemption of Lord Rawlings*

*An Unlikely Alliance*

*The Devil Duke Takes a Bride*

## London Fairy Tales

*Upon a Midnight Dream*

*Whispered Music*

*The Wolf's Pursuit*

*When Ash Falls*

## Seasons of Paleo

*Savage Winter*

*Feral Spring*

## Wallflower Series

*Waltzing with the Wallflower*

*Beguiling Bridget*

*Taming Wilde*

## Stand Alones

*Hurt Anthology*

*RIP*

*The Dark Ones*

# the consequence of seduction

## THE CONSEQUENCES SERIES
### BOOK 3

*RACHEL VAN DYKEN*

**SKYSCAPE**

**SKYSCAPE**

Published by Skyscape, New York
www.apub.com

Amazon, the Amazon logo, and Skyscape are trademarks of .com, Inc., or its affiliates.

ISBN-13: 9781503953017
ISBN-10: 1503953017

Cover design by Jason Blackburn

Printed in the United States of America

*This series would not have even happened had the Rockin' Readers fan group not decided to jump in and help do a group beta read. What started with one book has now turned into four. Thanks for being down for anything and for being the best fan group in the world! Love you girls and David (our one male member, who's pretty amazing).*

# PROLOGUE

## REID

I was told the nurses swooned when I was born, something about being the most beautiful baby they'd ever seen. It was my jumping-off point, and in a way it set the course for the rest of my young life, making me believe that if you were good-looking and well liked, you held the world in the palm of your chubby, chocolate-covered hand. In hindsight, it probably wasn't the best idea that my mom told me their reaction. It caused me to expect a certain amount of attention everywhere I went, attention that, no matter where we went—grocery store, doctor's office, school—I always had.

Things got progressively worse as I got older, because when I wasn't on the receiving end of admiration, it upset me. Girls adored me, and in return, from a young age, I adored them. I was immature and rarely rejected, so it never occurred to me that I needed more than good looks, nice eyes, and a killer smile to get by. I used my charm on everyone from my own parents to schoolteachers. If someone told me no, I helped them understand why they should change that to a yes, and usually I was successful. Eventually my mom noticed she had raised a spoiled monster, so when I turned sixteen she tried to keep me in check by talking my teacher out of changing a bad grade. I may have flirted with said teacher, I may have sat on her desk, and I may have slightly come on to her—then again, she was really young and I was desperate to pass the class. My ear still burns when I think about my mom pulling me out of the principal's office headfirst.

I learned an important lesson that day, one that stuck with me. She said looks would fade, but you were stuck with a personality forever.

•   •   •

As the whiskey seared its way down my throat, I winced, swallowed, then poured myself another shot.

Then another.

And another.

And another.

My chest still hurt. I rubbed the spot where my heart was trying to put itself back together again.

"Reid," my mother's voice whispered in my head. "Girls are going to love you, and you're going to love them, but there will come a time in your life when you have to choose one."

"But I don't want to choose one!" I said, absolutely horrified at the prospect. Would it be like choosing a best friend? Or picking out my favorite G.I. Joe? How did people survive making those types of choices? I mean, when Dad asked if I wanted orange juice or milk, I hid under the table and cried!

"Honey." Mom rolled her eyes. "Believe me, by then you'll be a grown man, mature. You'll know your own mind. Trust me on this. You'll know."

I laughed bitterly and tilted my head back, pouring another shot down my throat.

Older.

Wiser.

More mature.

Not true. Not at all. Because when it finally came down to picking one girl, I'd hit a little . . . snag. Yes, let's call it a snag. I mean, to call it a mistake makes me look bad, and I'm not the bad guy in this scenario. Believe me, if there ever was a villain to name all villains? A monster kids talked about around the campfire? Whispered about in front of a mirror?

Look no further than Jordan Litwright.

I took three more gulps straight from the Jack Daniel's bottle, hoping to erase my own memory.

My story starts like a lot of people's do: with a bad decision.

Followed by several more bad decisions.

And then guilt.

Shame.

Remorse.

A few tears . . . not on my end. Please, I'm a guy; I don't cry. Hell, my eyes may . . . fill with water, but I have bad allergies.

The thing about picking one girl? The thing about growing up and knowing that it's time to retire your college sweatshirt and grab a tie?

Well, it sucks.

It makes a man feel trapped.

And when men feel trapped, they do stupid shit.

When men like me feel trapped? Well, we say yes when we should say no.

I said yes.

And now I'm sitting in my penthouse apartment in New York, alone.

A shrill bark interrupted my pity party.

The dog didn't count.

He was hers.

Didn't belong to me.

Just part of the bet, part of the ruse, part of the seduction, if you will. I'd taken that bastard in just like I'd taken the princess—made an honest dog out of him—and when it came time to bail, she left the little monster with me.

"Come on, Otis, let's go."

The shit zoo—hell, who names a dog breed after crap? The shih tzu, whatever—ran circles around my legs, pink leash in its mouth, waiting to go outside.

"Lucky bitch," I grumbled, reaching down and patting his head. "I do everything for you, feed you, clothe you, love you, and in return, what do I get?"

The dog whimpered and then began to pee.

Otis had a tendency to show his approval via bodily functions.

"Yup." I sighed. "That's about right. I get pissed on."

Jordan would have liked that. But she wasn't here to see it. Not anymore.

But that's the end of the story.

I need to start at the beginning.

Actually, let's start before the beginning. With the first bad choice.

Which, of course, was . . . listening to my brother, Max.

# CHAPTER ONE

## REID

"You're like a fish out of water, man. A dog without a bone. A mermaid without her—" Max turned and looked to his fiancée, Becca.

"Merman?" she suggested. I rolled my eyes. Great, just give Max more ammo.

"Yes." Max snapped his fingers. "By God, you're brilliant."

She rolled her eyes. "It's why you keep me."

"Oh." Max put his arm around her. "And here I thought I kept you for sex. My bad."

"Clearly your sex isn't enough to keep the woman trapped," I offered in a condescending voice. "She needed diamonds too."

"Nobody asked the Reid gallery," Max snapped. "And we weren't talking about me, we're talking about you."

"My favorite subject." I winked at Becca.

Max threw a chip at my face. "Put sunglasses on those things before she throws her bra at you. I don't want my fiancée launching herself across the table because you don't know how to train those eyes. Feel me?"

"Do it again," Becca whispered.

"What's Reid doing?" Milo asked, plopping down next to me with Colt and Jason in tow. We were having our weekly meeting at our favorite bar in the city.

I still wasn't sure how it had happened. Four months ago I was invited to Jason's wedding. The plan was simple: break up the bride and groom. The bride in question just so happened to be an ex from hell. The type of ex you order a hit on just because the mere fact that they're alive and breathing offends the shit out of you.

I would never go as far as to do something like that . . . but I did try to break them up. In doing so, I experienced some of the most traumatizing moments of my life at the hands of an eighty-six-year-old woman who truly had the strength of ten men.

I'm not exactly sure what happened, because I was high most of the weekend on antianxiety pills Max crushed into my drinks, but there were ants, trees, at one point I think she rubbed Bengay on me, and when I opened my eyes one fateful Sunday afternoon, the woman had no top on.

She was also putting on a Superwoman wig.

But that's not the point.

The point is that somehow, that experience had bonded me to everyone around the table. Jason was a local police officer and had had more than his fair share of bad luck when it came to relationships. Milo, his sister, had recently married Colton, his best friend since childhood. I wasn't sure how that didn't affect their friendship, but they all seemed completely okay with the fact that Colton was sharing Milo's bed at night. I glanced to the right. That left my brother and his fiancée. Damn, a lot had changed in the last year. One weekend was all it took to transform my otherwise normal life to one where I scream when I smell Bengay and hide under the table whenever an elderly woman walks into the room.

"The eyes!" Becca explained to Milo. "He was doing the eyes again."

"Damn your eyes!" Max exploded. "This night is about an intervention."

I raised my hand.

Max swatted it down.

Sighing, I waited for his speech. Max never did anything halfway. His explanations were always—and I do mean always—long. And they usually involved lots of pictures, props, and hand gestures, all of which were more than likely illegal to use in public areas.

"My intervention six months ago was about getting my head out of my ass," Max said thoughtfully as he tapped his fingertips against his chin.

"Hear, hear." I lifted my glass in the air and smiled.

Max's eyes narrowed. His intervention actually included more than getting his head out of his ass. We had signed him up for a reality dating show on which he got attacked by goats and sea life on a daily basis and nearly got clawed to death by twenty-five available and desperate women. Judging by the tic in his left eye, I imagined he was taking a stroll down memory lane.

"Continue." I sipped.

Max shook his head as if returning to the present and pounded the table with his fist. "Reid's intervention is about *getting* ass."

Whiskey went flying out of my mouth before I could stop it— landing on Jason's cheek and nose. Cursing, he wiped his face off and stumbled backward, landing on one of the waitresses.

Chips and salsa went sailing into the air.

Joining the whiskey on Jason's face.

We waited in silence for Jason to set himself to rights. I ordered another whiskey. Milo yawned. Colt took out a few more napkins "just in case," and Jason finally rejoined us at the table smelling like a Mexican fiesta gone wrong.

We often waited for Jason. He was so accident-prone that Max actually ordered giant-size bubble wrap for the guy as a birthday present.

Jason hadn't been amused.

I'd laughed my ass off.

Also earning myself a black eye to match the one Jason had at the time.

"I get plenty," I explained once Jason joined us again. "And why are you concerned?"

Max tilted his head, then covered my hand with his. "Bless your heart, you don't even know."

"Know?" I repeated.

"Your balls." He nodded. "They're getting old."

"They are not!" I jerked away from him. "I'm twenty-eight!"

"Next stop forty," Max said under his breath. "Should we pick out your coffin? I'd go with oak. It's always so nice—soothing, really."

"Funny, I'm a fan of the darker woods myself," Milo piped up.

"I'm *not* dying!"

"Shh," Max whispered. "It's okay."

Patience. Patience. Patience. Oh, and just in case you were wondering, when Max was born? No praise. In fact I'm pretty sure the doctor said, "Sorry, ma'am, we did everything we could." He'd been a pain in my ass since birth. When he was an infant he did nothing but cry; even then he knew how to push all of my buttons, repeatedly.

Jason sat down on my other side. Smart move, since I was a few seconds away from committing fratricide, and at least now Jason's body blocked me from getting a direct shot to Max's head with my fork. "Honestly, he's right. I mean, it's time to settle down."

My eyebrows shot up. "This, coming from the guy who almost married Satan last year and since then hasn't been able to go on a date with anyone under the age of fifty?"

"Leave Cecil out of this!" Jason defended his elderly companion, with whom he had Friday-night dinner on a biweekly basis.

"What?" I snorted and glanced around the table. "You guys all have a clock or something?"

"It's called biology," Max said slowly. "Don't you read?"

"Do I—" I licked my lips and looked down. "Max, what's this about?"

He shrugged. "Ever since Grandma."

I started shivering in my seat. Jason wrapped his arm around me.

"Don't touch him!" Max yelled. "That makes it worse."

I nodded.

Jason held up his hands in surrender while the waitress set my whiskey on the table. Everyone waited while I threw back the entire thing. Max scooted his drink toward me and nodded.

So I took his drink.

And then Milo sent hers.

And really, I lost track after that, but at least I wasn't thinking about Grandma again.

"So . . ." My vision blurred. "What's this about ever since . . . her?"

"You've lost your game." Max shook his head. "All you have left are the eyes and, let's be honest, those have made their fair share of misfires this past week."

"What? When?" I picked a chip off Jason's shoulder and popped it in my mouth.

"Thanks, man," he mumbled.

"Can we get some salsa up in here?" Colt yelled.

"Dude!" Max's eyes widened a fraction of an inch as he leaned in; the group followed. "The mall."

"The mall?" I repeated. "What did I do at the mall?"

"You gave the eyes to a puppy, man. Not cool."

"It was a badass puppy!" I said defensively.

"There are ways to look at puppies, Reid, and there are ways to look at puppies. Feel me?"

"What? No! You're crazy!"

"I'm only saying this because I love you, but the puppy started crying when you looked at it, Reid. What does that tell you?"

"I don't know!" I rubbed my face. "I scared it?"

"Nature . . . is off because you, my friend, are off. You need to get back on the horse. Forget about Bengay. Use the power"—he pointed to his eyes—"for good. Stop staying in on the weekends! Don't drink by yourself! And for the love of God, you don't need to pack a gun. Jason's grandma isn't coming for you! All right? Now, I have a plan."

I slammed my fist against the table. "Prison. Death. Choking." I pointed to everyone. "Those are what your plans entail. Do I need to reference the last time you guys all had a plan? Or an idea?"

"Black eyes," Jason added.

"Community service, damn it," Colt muttered, grabbing a chip from Jason's other shoulder.

"I can't control the world!" Max lifted his hands in the air. "Jeez, I'm not God and I'm not president." He beamed. "One day, but not now. No, it's too soon."

Beside him, Becca rolled her eyes. How the hell did she put up with his bullshit all the time?

"We'll start slow." Max shrugged. "Slow and steady wins the game."

"Says no athlete—ever," I sang.

"Shut it, Reid! I'm doing this because I love you!" Max turned away from me and toward the crowd. "We'll start with a plain one and then move on from there once you've done your time."

"Time as in prison?"

Max ignored me. "I see her now. Brown hair, brown eyes, not too skinny, not fat, just right."

"We picking out a puppy?" I joked.

"You and puppies!" Max gave me a look of complete disappointment before scowling. "Stop being weird! Now walk up to her, do the eyes, and seduce her."

"What?"

"Seduce her." Max smiled. "It's easy. Watch."

He turned to Becca and nodded his head. "How you doin'?"

"Oh, dear God." I rubbed my face with my hands, wishing I could teleport to my apartment without having to ride back in the car with my brother.

"Trust." Max gripped my hand. "Don't you want to expel Grandma from your brain? From the very blood that flows through the Emory veins?"

"Hell, yes," I growled. Another drink was set in front of me. I tossed it back.

"That's the spirit!" Max shouted. "Now, go seduce the girl! Give her the eyes, be a man!"

"On three." Colt held out his hands. "Manhood!"

Max counted, "One, two, three, *manhood!*" We all cheered and I stumbled toward the bar.

Let's pause here for a second and do a little counting, shall we?

One drink when I started the story.

Another drink.

Three more drinks, considering I also drank Max's, Colt's, and Milo's.

And another, all before I made my way toward the bar.

Five drinks. Five drinks in less than fifteen minutes.

Carry on.

Like I said, it all started with listening to Max, so as I got up on shaky legs and made my way over to the bar, I had no idea I'd be sealing my fate.

No clue that the plain girl twisting the straw between her pretty little fingers would destroy me.

Or that there'd come a time when I'd go through drunken hell on a daily basis if only she'd give me another chance.

# CHAPTER TWO

## JORDAN

It was a two-drink night. Possibly a three-drink night if I could get the bartender to give me at least five minutes of his attention. Instead, he was pouring free shots, which I'm sure were frowned upon by the establishment, and trying to get some hot blonde's phone number.

I sat back and watched in rapt fascination.

She twirled her hair.

He leaned closer.

More twirling.

He tilted his head.

And then she arched her back, which made his eyes focus on her perky breasts before he shoved another shot in her direction. I sipped what was left of my rum and Coke, irritated that the drink was already gone. Okay, so maybe it was a four-drink night. I could always call a cab, right?

The girl laughed loudly. It wasn't an attractive laugh either. I imagined it was the exact sound turtles made while getting it on, an almost guttural groan that emitted from her tiny body before she plastered her long fuchsia nails across his forearm and rubbed.

Her nails were getting tangled in an abhorrent amount of forearm hair.

It was like watching a really horrible dating show.

Damn, I wished I could hear the dialogue better.

"Beautiful," he whispered looking down at the mating dance of her nails with his body hair.

She blushed.

On demand.

But no way was that girl a virgin.

Neat trick.

I cleared my throat and waved in his direction. As entertaining as it was watching fake boobs seduce the hairy bartender, my drink was gone, and I was having a hell of a day—or week was more like it.

He ignored my raised hand.

I flipped him the bird.

He ignored that as well.

That was the problem with being me. I was the in-between girl. I wasn't knock-your-socks-off gorgeous or ugly. If I were ugly, at least people would stare long enough to give me some attention.

No, I was invisible.

The one men passed over, not because I was an eyesore, but because in a sea of faces, mine was literally the last one to be noticed.

When I was little, I thought it was because I was shy.

As I got older, I realized people just didn't see me.

In third grade when we were asked to do self-portraits, I presented mine to the class only to have my teacher give me an F for drawing a complete stranger.

I used my own picture. I kid you not.

I was continually sat on in the fifth grade. The bus driver eventually had me sit up front with the extra backpacks because it was becoming a problem.

High school was just as bad. During my freshman year, I guess I was too close to the gym wall, because when the janitor was painting it he painted me too. He said he didn't see me standing there.

In my bright pink shirt and yellow shorts.

My thighs were Charger red for two weeks.

Sigh.

I twisted the straw between my fingertips again and winced.

My feet ached from wearing my heels all day, my tight pencil skirt felt two sizes too small, and my white oxford shirt was wrinkled from sweat.

So maybe it was good I was invisible, because there was nothing attractive about the way I looked right then. My red lipstick had been chewed off hours earlier, and my eyes never did that sexy thing where they kept on eye shadow for longer than five minutes.

It was amazing—I'd leave the apartment excited about my makeup only to take a bathroom break a few hours later and realize it had disappeared from my face.

It was as if a magical makeup-removing unicorn had come and licked it off my face during my coffee break, leaving me pale and lifeless. Damn unicorns.

I slumped in my seat and stared into my empty glass, where two ice cubes remained.

"Rough day?" a deep voice rumbled behind me. Now, I'm not one to exaggerate, but I could have sworn in that moment my ovaries stood up and cheered as my body tingled with awareness only a voice like that could stir. Immediately I regretted my reaction. After all, my relationship with men was just as bad as my cloak of invisibility. If a man did notice me, it was usually to point out something that was wrong with me, making me wonder if it was even worth being noticed in the first place. My personal favorite was when a man approached me only to ask me to move to the left so he could hit on the girl behind me. On rare occasions when I lucked out and was the object of their attention, they were gay and loved my shoes, which usually meant at least I'd have a decent conversation.

I sighed and glanced down at my heels. I really did have great taste in shoes.

With that voice, my money was on the latter.

"Vince Camuto," I said in a bored tone. "Last season, though I'm well aware they look like this season, thus the pairing with the pencil skirt. And no, the skirt isn't Chanel, it's Burberry."

And . . . silence.

See? This is what I mean. He was probably talking to someone else, or thought I was someone else and was so embarrassed he hightailed it out of there. Chill, dude, I'm not going to throw myself at you and insist you have my babies. Even if your voice sounds like smooth caramel on crack.

A warm hand grabbed my shoulder, scaring the crap out of me. With a yell, I jerked my hand, causing the ice to topple out of my drink and down my white shirt.

I was too busy trying to get the ice out of my bra to look up.

"Wow, that's new. Can't say I've ever caused a woman to dump ice on her own shirt before." The voice just got sexier by the minute, didn't it?

"Aha!" I pulled out the almost completely melted cubes and dropped them to the floor, then looked up. I blinked to make sure I wasn't hallucinating. And then I turned around like a complete loser.

Nobody sat behind me.

Damn, I guess I'm back to the gay thing.

"Sorry." I turned back around and forced a smile. "Long day."

The man had crazy hypnotic eyes. They were an aqua blue that I could have sworn full-on shimmered after I stared at them too long.

Note to self: don't look directly in his eyes for fear that clothes will spontaneously pull themselves off my body. I cleared my throat and narrowed my gaze.

His wavy auburn hair fell perfectly parted to the side, revealing a shaved section on the left right above his ear. It was trendy, sexy.

Full, bow-shaped lips curved into a smile. "That's all right." He pulled out a bar stool next to me and sat.

What was I supposed to do with my hands? Panicking, I grabbed my empty glass and clenched it so tight I wouldn't have been at all surprised if it shattered in my hands.

The bartender finally made his way over. Bastard.

"What can I get you?" He placed a napkin in front of the hot and mysterious stranger.

"What she's having?" He pointed a long, gorgeous finger in my direction.

A confused frown marred the bartender's face. "Er, you just get here?"

I fought back a growl. "No. Been sitting here for a half hour now."

"You sure?" Did he really have to press the issue?

I gritted my teeth. "Pretty sure."

"Hmm, maybe Keith helped you then."

It hadn't been Keith.

"Rum and Coke," I grumbled, wanting him to go away so I could stare at the pretty man candy next to me.

"Diet?" the bartender asked.

"What?" I felt my face flush. "No, regular Coke."

He paused, giving me a once-over, and then shrugged and made my drink. In that moment, I had a very vivid daydream that involved a malfunctioning nutcracker.

"Double," said Handsome on my left. "Make both of ours doubles. Hell, maybe give her a triple."

"Ha." I tapped the counter with my fingertips. "Getting drunk on a school night is frowned upon."

The mesmerizing aqua eyes darn near bugged out of his head.

"Relax." I smirked. "I have a fake ID."

He clearly didn't understand I was joking. With a curse, he stood to leave.

I burst out laughing. "I'm kidding. I'm thirty, I promise. I'll even show you my ridiculously obnoxious photo on my driver's license." I nodded. "There was a storm that day."

He flashed a smile and sat again. "I'm sure it's not that bad."

"I call chicken," I announced, then jerked my ID from my black Coach clutch and thrust it in his face.

"Damn." He shuddered. Yup, I'd just made a hot stranger shudder in disgust. That's how awesome I was at picking up men. Then again, he was gay, so the poor guy was probably horrified at the sweatshirt I was wearing in the picture.

"Yeah, well." I put the ID back just as our drinks arrived.

Handsome Stranger paid for them, then took a large sip.

"So." I twisted the two straws in the drink with my fingers. "Where's the lucky guy?"

"Lucky guy?" His eyes narrowed as he took another drink. "I'm confused."

"You're gay," I announced in a defeated voice.

Rum and Coke sprayed all over the counter. Handsome Stranger proceeded to choke on what I could only assume was an overly large tongue as he continued to cough and then finished his entire drink, slamming the glass back onto the countertop.

"Did Max put you up to this?" he rasped.

"Ah, lover boy has a name." I winked. "Max. Sounds . . . flimsy. He the chick in this relationship?"

"Holy hell, I'm going to kill him." He shook his head. "See, this is what happens when he tells me to take a chance!"

"To be fair"—I gave him a polite nod—"he was probably trying to encourage you to live a little."

He glared. "I live just fine . . . in a penthouse."

"Didn't ask." I held up my hands in defense.

"With floor-to-ceiling windows."

"Awesome." I started to scoot slowly away.

"Oh, no you don't." Mr. Handsome hooked his foot into my stool and jerked it toward him. I nearly collapsed into his lap. "What did Max tell you?"

"Is this a game?" I whispered. "Because I don't think I know how to play."

"Game." He bit down hard on his full bottom lip. "If it was a game, I'd be losing."

"O-okay." I tried to inch away again, but this time his hand came down on my arm, holding me still.

"I'm not gay."

"Then who's Max?"

"My brother."

"Whoa." I laughed. "Okay, that's a little too much crazy for one night. Thanks for the drink, but I think I'll . . ." I held up my hands and waved into the air. "I'll pass on whatever game you and your lover are playing. Have a good night."

"But—"

"See ya!" I grabbed my coat and darn near collided with a wall in order to get away.

The minute I walked outside it started pouring rain.

I tried to hail a cab and only succeeded in getting drenched from head to toe. Hanging my head, I finally decided to walk back to my apartment. Was it wrong to wish to get mugged? Because that would at least prove to the universe that I wasn't invisible.

Or that the only people that hit on me were either gay or crazy or—lucky me—both.

# CHAPTER THREE

## REID

"So?" Max barked into the phone. "How'd it go?"

I stared blankly ahead as the sound of the TV filled my large apartment. "Just tell me why you did it."

Max sighed. "I seriously have no idea what you're talking about, but could you please get there faster so I can go have sex?"

"Too much information."

"Then talk faster, bitch!"

I must have been a real bastard in another life to get cursed with a brother like Max, one who would try the patience of ALL nuns, not just one of them—all of them. Even the old senile ones with hearts of gold.

"She knew I was hitting on her."

Max was silent, then whispered, "Isn't that the point?"

"No," I roared. "She was in on it! You planted her!"

"I did no such thing!" Max argued back. "Why the hell would I do that? I wanted you to get on the horse, go for a ride, slap the pony, get yours—"

"I get it." My temples throbbed.

"So, what would lead you to assume I planted the ass I wanted you to tap?"

"You kiss your fiancée with that mouth?"

"I do more than kiss her. Last night, I—"

"I'm sorry I asked," I interrupted. "And the girl you planted accused me of being gay!"

Max burst out laughing.

I growled.

"Oh." A few more chuckles. "I'm sorry. I was laughing with you, not at you."

"I wasn't laughing."

"Why the hell not? It's hilarious!"

"Good-bye, Max."

"No, wait!" Max laughed louder. "See! This is what I was saying earlier! Your charm is misfiring. It's like you've discovered the unlucky penny. You have to get out there and settle down. It's time, man. At least the universe proved it to you so I wouldn't have to."

"Whatever." I licked my lips. "I've got an early call time in the morning, so I'm going to bed."

"Did you at least get her number?"

"Dude, she ran away from me."

Silence.

I waited. "Max, you still there?"

"It's sad when your balls start to work against you by rejecting all traces of females in your vicinity. I'll add them to my prayer list."

"Please don't pray for my balls at the dinner table."

"Silly, we pray for them in bed."

"Good night, Max!"

"Night, Reid! Remember, get on the horse!"

"Right."

I pressed "End" and threw the phone against the black leather couch. Max was the confused one, the deranged one. I was happy! I was just fine living the high life of a bachelor!

Hell, I was an actor, well known on Broadway and soon to be all over the media, especially considering I'd just been cast in the film role of the century playing opposite A-lister Mona James.

I didn't need a woman.

I wasn't off the horse, therefore there was no need to hop back on and ride it. Riding had never been the issue. I did just fine with one-night stands—no need to add a relationship to the mix.

And I hadn't lost my touch with women. So what if I'd had a few bad dates in the past month? It wasn't my fault my last date accidentally set herself on fire. To be fair, the candles had burned a bit out of control, but candles were romantic. I was setting the scene, damn it!

And the other two girls? Well, they just lacked—something. I wasn't sure what, which was exactly how I'd worded it when I took them both out to a fancy dinner the night before my flight out to LA. I didn't have time to separate the dates, and it wasn't like we were serious. I couldn't even remember one girl's name, but when you're in bed, does it really matter? I received wine in my face from one and a swift knee to the balls from the other, which meant I spent the majority of my five-hour flight with an ice pack on my crotch.

I refused to believe it was bad luck.

Bad luck was seeing a black cat and then getting hit by a semi, not going on bad dates with overly emotional women who got pissed because I refused to commit.

I flipped off the lights in the living room and made my way to the bedroom.

Sleep—that would cure everything. Besides, I was meeting with my new PR company in the morning. My manager was adamant that we use the best company in the business, considering this movie was going to either make or break my career. I hated that it was a necessity, but

I wasn't going to say no even though it was so expensive I wondered if each publicist came with their own private jet and small island.

Ridiculous that in this day and age I needed to have a glorified babysitter because I couldn't be trusted on my own. Now, if it was Max, I'd get it. But I'd never had a problem being in the public eye. I'd just have to make that crystal clear when I met with them. Hell, I'd probably be the easiest client they'd ever had.

"Sleep," I repeated to myself.

After all, tomorrow was another day.

# CHAPTER FOUR

## JORDAN

As luck would have it, I was late for my nine a.m. meeting. It wasn't my fault. I was one of the "lucky" people in my apartment building who suffered from a freak power outage.

I was midrinse when the lights went out in my bathroom and the shower turned frigid.

Which meant no hair dryer.

Making my normally smooth and at least semiglossy brown hair the current obsession of at least two poodles, both of which tried to hump my leg on the short walk to work.

It didn't help matters that I'd had to put my makeup on using a tiny mirror and sunlight from the window.

Lipstick did, however, manage to make it on my lips and I think I managed to draw a semistraight line on for eyeliner. Though by the odd looks I was receiving from people walking down the street—people who seemed to be giving the crazy lady a wide berth—regardless of how straight the eyeliner, it wasn't helping.

The only bright spots in my morning were the Starbucks in my right hand and the promise of a promotion if I was able to make the next client as squeaky-clean and shiny as a new toy.

I was one of the best publicists at my firm.

The other star students were all glossy haired and perfect. The women had magic faces that kept makeup on even into the wee hours of the morning and the men had chiseled jaws and killer smiles. So basically I was the evil stepsister of the firm, or it sort of felt like it. Then again, I wasn't a horrible or jealous person, so maybe I was just the ugly duckling?

My heel caught on the sidewalk, and as I moved to brace myself, my coffee flew out of my hand.

"Nooo!" I could have sworn it happened in slow motion, my athletic body flying through the air while I reached out to grasp what was left of the only good thing in my day—nay, my life—and missed. My body collapsed against the stairs, scraping up my palms as my hands braced for the impact.

And honest to God, tears welled in my eyes as I glanced down at my venti mocha with extra whipped cream.

And like Cinderella's pumpkin carriage, my cup was squashed under the heels of busy New Yorkers as they made their way into the same building.

Nobody offered a hand.

Because this wasn't a fairy tale.

And I was no Cinderella.

Instead, my cup was shredded to pieces.

Sticky coffee stained my bloody hands.

And what were at least cute shoes—though not glass slippers—now missed a very vital part—the heel.

With a sigh, I pushed to my feet, my body aching, hands stinging, and hobbled into the building, clutching my purse to my body. My

Gucci was now my armor as it shielded me from anyone and anything that would and could push me down.

Finally, I made it to the elevator and squished in between a woman who smelled like too many one-night stands and a man who clearly had onions on his bagel, with a side of hummus.

I breathed through my mouth.

My floor dinged.

"This is my floor." I pushed through the throngs of confused faces and wasn't surprised at all when I heard someone mutter. "Who's that?"

"Only been riding the same elevator for the past eight years, but no sweat," I muttered under my breath, hobbling toward the glass doors of Platt Publicity.

"Jordan!" Ren, my boss, flashed a pearly white smile and then frowned. "Did you get in a car accident?"

"Don't own a car," I said through clenched teeth.

"Did you get run over by a taxi, then?" He opened the door for me, and his concerned expression choked me up a bit. He was nice and the only man who noticed me. Then again, he was like sixty and married with five kids. So there was that.

"No," I huffed. "Just a rough start to the morning." I stopped at my office and tossed my things onto the nearest chair. "Tell me they're late, Ren. Tell me I have time to change clothes and tame my hair and—"

"They're here!" Ren's assistant rounded the corner and ushered us toward one of the meeting rooms. I was half-tempted to dig my broken heel into the ground, but knew it was pointless. I was going to meet one of the biggest clients of my career looking like roadkill.

"Just smile," Ren said under his breath.

I smiled.

He winced. "Less aggressive, more . . . friendly."

I tried again.

He patted my hand, his kind brown eyes looking me up and down with pity. "Why don't you just let me do the talking?"

"Fine," I grumbled. The silver-haired fox of a boss could charm anyone and anything with a pulse, so it was probably best he did the talking anyway. After all, it was his company, and I was just one of his favorite publicists.

At least I could do something right.

I averted my eyes as he'd instructed and made my way to my usual chair, only to find it occupied.

I blinked, my gaze narrowing on an athletic, lust-inducing body that definitely knew how to fill out an Armani suit.

The body was attached to large hands that looked strangely familiar.

I continued my appreciative stare all the way up his broad chest and stopped when my eyes zeroed in on his mouth.

It was a nice mouth.

One I wouldn't forget.

Even after the oddness of the night before.

"Handsome Stranger?" I blurted.

His eyes narrowed. "Don't you mean Gay Handsome Stranger?"

I smirked. "How is Max?"

"You two know each other?" Ren asked.

"Yes," we said in unison while I continued sizing him up. I wondered if it was a bad sign that he recognized me after the chaos of the morning. Why even try, am I right?

"Good." Ren took a seat. "That will make things so much easier, don't you think, Ella?"

"Yes!" Ella, who I recognized as an agent, reached for Ren's hand and squeezed. "So good to see you."

They were of similar age.

And started talking about their kids.

While I took a seat next to the handsome guy and tapped my chin. "You look . . ."

"Handsome? Not gay? Take your pick."

"Bummer, I was going to say sober." I smiled sweetly.

He rolled his eyes. "For the last time, I'm not gay. It was a mistake; if you knew my insane brother, you'd understand."

I held up my hands.

"So does that work out?" Ren asked from the front of the table.

"Er." I cleared my throat. "Absolutely."

Handsome Man narrowed his eyes. "Sorry, I wasn't paying attention. Care to reiterate the conversation?" This he directed at me.

I felt myself flush from head to toe.

Ren slid a folder across the table. "Everything should be there. The contract isn't your usual, Jordan."

I wasn't sure if that was a good thing or a bad thing.

"Jordan." Mr. Handsome rolled my name around on his tongue like he wanted to take a taste. I shifted in my seat and shot him a glare. Total self-preservation move. "Isn't that a guy's name?"

"Reid." Ella coughed from her end of the table.

I smiled sweetly. "Reid, hmm, what an interesting name." *Isn't that something that grows out of algae-infested water?* That's what I wanted to say, but because I needed him as a client, I refused to comment further. Not that it mattered, since it seemed like he could read my thoughts.

His lips twitched with a suppressed smirk.

"Ha-ha." Ren laughed uncomfortably, breaking the silent staredown Reid and I were having. "So we'll just let you two discuss the details of the contract. I assume you're able to do that now, Jordan, or did you want to reschedule?"

What? Because I looked like I'd been the unlucky recipient of swine flu? No, thanks. This was my job, and regardless of how I looked, I could do my job.

I nodded as Ella and Ren exited the room.

"So, you're my client," I said blandly. "Can't say I'm surprised. You look the type."

Insulting the client wasn't part of the plan—in fact, the entire plan went to hell the minute my brain recognized the guy from the bar the night before. He didn't seem like he'd be a diva actor who needed babysitting on the weekends because he'd decided to fly to the South of France for the weekend, get drunk, then miss his call time. I pressed my lips together. He didn't seem violent either, or aggressive, but then again, what did I know? I'd had to lie plenty of times to protect my actors from the press. If I was paid for how many times I said, "They're being treated for exhaustion," I'd be a millionaire.

"So." Reid leaned his forearms against the table, his muscles glistening under the fluorescent lights. How was that possible? "What type is that?"

"Arrogant self-absorbed actors are my specialty."

"You forgot gay."

"So now you admit it."

He rolled his eyes. "I was joking."

"I didn't get it." I sighed and opened the folder. "Okay, so this is how it's going to work. I make sure you keep an impeccable reputation during filming, show you how to make the people love you—and I do mean love you—and if I do a good job, which I will, we'll renegotiate for higher pay, which you'll happily agree to, so we'll sign on the dotted lines and be a match made in PR heaven. Questions?" I was being harsh, which was not normal for me. I usually started meetings with compliments and by the time we were finished signing the contract the actor was convinced that they couldn't so much as breathe without me. I was torn between wanting to prove to Reid that he needed me versus it being the other way around. I'd never been in a situation where my client made me feel defensive, like I needed to wrap myself in body armor to keep myself safe.

"One," he whispered. "What really happened to you this morning?" He leaned forward and sniffed. "And why do you smell like chocolate dog?"

"Aw, you're such a charmer. We'll have to work on that." I patted the folder and pulled out my business card. "From here on out, I'm your girlfriend, your wife, the best friend you never had, your sister from another mister. I am your world. Stick with me, keep it in your pants, and make sure all big decisions happen before midnight and without the aid of alcohol, and I think we'll do just fine!"

He took the card and gave me a blank stare. "Who are you?"

"Right now?" I stood on wobbly feet and inhaled sharply. "I'm your ticket to being the biggest A-list star Hollywood has ever seen."

Clearly it was time to sell him, since his blank stare didn't exactly exude confidence in my abilities.

"Tom Williams." The name alone used to inflict fear in publicists around the world. He was a nightmare. A stuck-up man-child who was known more for his nightly conquests and arrests for drug possession than his acting chops.

Reid's eyes narrowed. "He won an Academy Award last year."

"He did." I nodded smugly.

"Claimed his life was changed after seeing a bright white light after nearly getting hit by a car."

"He was high." I rolled my eyes. "And the car was electric. It ran over his toe and he collapsed, but I was sick of his crap, so I made up a story about how he should have died and was clearly spared so that the world would be a better place . . . gifted." I rehearsed the speech all over again word for word as I locked eyes with Reid. "Gifted with the voice of angels and the heart of a saint, this is your wake-up call to be the best actor in the world. Are you going to take it?" I wiped a fake tear from my cheek and gave him a smug grin as I leaned back in my chair and crossed my arms.

Reid stared at me, dumbfounded. "Clearly they gave the Academy Award to the wrong person."

I examined my chipped fingernails. "Like I said, I'm the best."

He grunted. "I'll believe it when I see it."

"My track record is pristine," I said in a clipped voice.

"Even if your appearance is—" He waved a hand in front of me.

"Awesome?" I added.

"I was going to say lacking." He scrunched up his nose. "Seriously, though, what's that smell?"

I rolled my eyes. "My mocha spilled and I may still have some shampoo in my hair because the electricity went out in my building."

"No, no, that's not it." He leaned forward, his nose almost colliding with my neck as he inhaled deeply. "You smell like . . . cinnamon?"

I rejected my body's natural reaction—the same reaction that had me wanting to lick the side of his neck to see if it tasted as good as it looked. *Down, girl.* "It, uh—I always put cinnamon on my whipped cream."

He jerked back and grinned, his full mouth making me dizzy with desire. "Do you now?"

I stood on wobbly legs. "I'm off-limits, just so you know. Flirting with me will get you nowhere. In fact, I'll probably just end up charging you more because you piss me off."

Reid leaned his muscled body back against the chair. "Why are you the best? Really? You don't look the part—no offense."

Rejection slammed into me as I lifted my chin in defiance. "I'm the best because none of my clients can charm their way into my pants. I'm the best because I take my job seriously. I'm the best because I have an obsession with expensive shoes and purses and really need a paycheck in order to get them. I'm the best because I am. It's as simple as that. If you have a problem with me, then there's the door." I slammed the contract back on the table and leaned forward, chest heaving. I hadn't meant the all-out verbal attack, but by his stunned expression it must have worked.

Reid gulped. "Okay. I can work with that."

Relieved, I almost collapsed against the chair. I really did need him to sign with me. I wanted that promotion so bad I could taste it. I deserved something after spending countless hours answering three a.m. phone calls and working fourteen-hour days. I loved my job, but getting a promotion meant I could finally relax rather than bust my ass like I had been since getting hired. I needed to prove myself one last time. "Fine, I'll get your information from Ren and meet you on set later this afternoon."

Reid stood and shoved his hands in his suit pockets. I had a brief fantasy of doing the same. Not to be weird, but he had nice hands and the pants were getting all the touching. "Maybe fix your shoes before then."

"Fine."

"And your hair." He pointed.

I huffed.

"A little makeup . . ." He eyed me up and down. "Or a hat, a hat might work."

I gritted my teeth and let out a growl. "Anything else?"

"Yeah." He flashed a beautiful, heart-stopping grin that I was 99 percent convinced would be plastered all over teen girls' walls six months from now. "I'll take a grande latte, two raw sugars."

"I'm not your personal assistant."

He shrugged and made his way toward the door. "I figured you'd want another coffee since yours spilled, and you'd want to be polite, right? Isn't that what a good publicist teaches? Manners?"

Manners, my ass. Steam was probably billowing out of my ears. I'd fought hard to climb my way to the top and I didn't need a spoiled Hollywood actor making the last rung on the ladder difficult.

"Fine," I snapped. "Anything else, Reid?"

"Shouldn't it be 'sir'?"

"Ask me to call you 'sir' and see what happens."

"Tsk, tsk." He frowned. "So violent. Oh, and also." He moved back into the room and touched my face. His finger came back with a dollop of whipped cream. With evilly seductive eyes, he dipped his finger into his mouth and moaned. "You've had this on you since the beginning of the meeting."

"That was mine." Right. That's what I was going with. The whipped cream he'd just tasted off my face was mine. At least I was semi owning the situation, right?

Reid smirked, biting down on his lower lip. What was with him and his plump lips! "Oh, sorry, I can always give it back." He leaned forward.

My body rejoiced while my mind went on complete lockdown.

"Oh, no, you don't." I pushed against his chest. "This relationship is professional. No seduction allowed. Besides, it doesn't work on me."

He shrugged. "Really? Are you saying you're immune to my charms?"

"Yup." Was he flexing? The "Hallelujah" chorus really needed to stop chiming in my ears.

"I always love a good challenge."

"I'm not waving a red flag in front of you, Reid. I'm just being honest. Now get back to set before you get fired."

"See ya later." He stepped back and winked.

I didn't react.

I stayed immune to his charms while I watched him walk all the way down the hall and out of sight.

And when I was positive he was gone . . .

I sank into my chair and let out a little whimper.

# CHAPTER FIVE

## REID

Theater camp had been forced on me at a young age. Both my brother and I had no choice but to spend the entire summer spouting Shakespeare while normal kids got to go to actual camps where things like s'mores and campfires were allowed. Theater camp was all about the competition, about being better than everyone else. Agents attended our summer finale, and that's how I ended up on Broadway.

It was fun.

Until the schedule started stressing me out.

And then the movie offers very slowly started rolling in. I rejected most of them until this one caught my eye. I was always a sucker for contemporary Shakespeare remakes.

And this one was a personal favorite.

*The Taming of the Shrew.*

Mona, the actress who starred opposite me, was anything but a shrew. In fact, she was probably one of the nicest women I'd ever met. Too bad she was happily married with three kids.

I grabbed my script for the day and hurried down to set. My meeting with the PR firm had gone longer than I thought, thanks to my insane obsession with trying to make my new publicist blush or yell—really either worked for me. She wasn't one of those women that immediately caught your eye, but she had a silent beauty with her big full lips and perfect hourglass shape specifically designed to drive men wild, compliments of those damn pencil skirts she kept wearing.

Muttering a curse, I continued walking toward Central Park, where part of the filming was taking place. I could have sworn I passed at least a dozen women all wearing pencil skirts. Maybe that's what Max meant when he said the universe was plotting against me.

The only woman I had hit on in the past two months—and she just so happened to be off-limits.

Maybe she was one of those girls who had a hard-shelled M&M exterior, and I just needed to crack it. Or find another nut completely.

Wait, somehow she'd changed from a blue M&M to a nut. I really needed to get more sleep.

And stop fixating on her rejection.

My phone buzzed in my pocket just as the set came into view.

"What?" I barked into the phone.

Max sighed. "So, how'd the meeting go?"

"Are you really playing the concerned brother right now or are you just bored?"

He yawned. "Actually I'm in the bathroom and I thought, hey, what do I do when I want to cheer myself up? Call Reid."

"I cheer you up?"

"Absolutely." A toilet flushed in the background. "You always cheer me up. Wanna know why?"

"Because I'm awesome?"

"No, no, that's not it." Water turned on in the bathroom. "It's because your love life is so depressing. It makes any sort of bad day that

I have seem like a tiny blip on the radar. Tell me, how was that cold bed last evening? Did you cry yourself to sleep?"

I rolled my eyes. "I just got back to set, I don't have time for this."

He sighed heavily into the phone. "Look, I have an idea."

"Your idea got me rejected last night."

"No, this one's better."

"I highly doubt that."

One of the PAs waved me over. I held up my hand.

"You've always wanted that house in the Florida Keys, right?"

"Wait, what?" It was hard to keep up with him sometimes. "What does that have to do with your idea or my rejection or cold bed?"

"Everything!" Max shouted. "Do you not listen? What the hell is wrong with you?"

"Max, tell me the truth, are you drunk at work?" Max had recently taken over the Emory hotel empire and was literally bored to tears because it ran so efficiently that he said he needed to find a hobby lest he hang himself from the ceiling of his multi-million-dollar office. I had a sinking feeling I was the new hobby.

"Listen well, young grasshopper." His voice had taken on a thick indistinguishable accent. There was a reason only one of us was currently acting for a living. "The house was given to me. You got the one in Seattle. Our parents, bless their hearts, had no idea I hate Florida and you hate the rain. They would if they ever listened or read any letters I sent them, or even just, you know, attended family dinners on Easter, Hanukkah, Presidents' Day—"

"Max!" I yelled. "Get there faster!"

"Oh." He coughed. "Right." More coughing. "Well, we'll trade. I'll give you the deed to the Keys home, you give me the deed to Seattle . . ."

"What's the catch?"

"You."

"Huh?"

"One relationship that lasts longer than one month. I think that a secure, solid relationship might do you some good. Ever since Grandma—"

"We promised never to utter her name again," I said in a hoarse voice. "You promised!"

Max cursed. "Sorry, man, ever since *the incident.*"

"Thanks."

"Anytime," he said in a soothing voice. "You've been as jumpy as a goldfish in a tanning bed."

I pinched the bridge of my nose and made my way toward the PA. Max was famous for taking ten years to explain things.

"Anyway." Was he whistling? "One month. You stay committed to one girl for one month and the house is yours."

"One month?" I repeated.

"Thirty days, give or take a day," he explained. "Unless it's a leap year or February. Wait, is it February?"

I let out a groan. "September."

"Whatever." The phone line cracked. "I'm losing you. My office is like a freaking dungeon. I'll start sending the girls—"

"The girls?" What? He was sending who? "Max? Max, are you there?"

"Ha . . . fun!"

"Max!" I had a really bad feeling, the kind you get after getting hit on in prison by a bearded lady.

"Reid!" John, one of the many PAs on set, flagged me down again. "It's time for the wedding scene!"

"Shit." I shoved my phone into my pocket.

"Head over to wardrobe." He gave me another script. "And note the changes in the vow section."

"Got it." I quickly scanned the pages. "Oh, John, before I forget, my new publicist is going to be stopping by. Go ahead and just send her to my trailer when she gets here."

He gave me a thumbs-up and trotted off.

# CHAPTER SIX

## JORDAN

I brought his coffee. Don't ask me why. Maybe because in my mind it meant a fresh start. One that had nothing to do with him hitting on me or me being responsive to his charm. It was a coincidence we met at a bar first, but now it was all business. Maybe the fresh start was more for me than him. I needed some sort of symbol that what was between us was business and that I was completely capable of playing nice.

Coffee. It was a peace offering, as if I'd just walked into the UN building wearing a MAKE LOVE, NOT WAR T-shirt. I bring him coffee, offer a smile and a pat on the cheek, and suddenly we're best friends. Laughing at each other's jokes. I scratch his back, he scratches mine.

It made sense.

After all, he was a man.

Men are easy.

Taking care of a male actor? Even easier. It was like selling cake to a cake shop. As long as I stroked his ego, kept him well fed, and made sure he was in bed at the proper times, I really never had any issues.

My job was kind of like being a nanny to the wealthy.

Did you take your pills?

Did you eat breakfast?

Remember, you have a peanut allergy! And yes, there are peanuts in peanut butter.

Oh, I'm sorry, you're on a diet. No, cheese isn't a vegetable.

Nap times are encouraged, yes.

No, you can't stay up to watch yourself on Jimmy Fallon. Of course, I'd love to tape it for you!

See what I mean? Easy.

And Reid. Well, with his good looks, I could only imagine his brain, or lack thereof, was about as small as the rest of the men I worked with. How hard could it be? He was my meal ticket, my gold-crapping goose, my yellow brick road.

"Miss." Some geeky-looking techie charged toward me, alternating between giving me the stink-eye and talking into his giant walkie-talkie. "You can't be here."

I rolled my eyes. "I'm here to see Reid Emory. I'm his—"

"Oh!" The man held up his hands. "No need to explain." He blushed a bright red. "I'll just show you to the, er, rest of them, and he can, um, take it from there, I guess?"

"Sure?" Clearly the poor soul was overworked, but I wasn't one to judge considering the morning I'd had. I followed him wordlessly through the band of vehicles and trailers.

"Must say . . ." Nerdy guy coughed into his hand. "I've heard of actors really taking on roles in a serious way, but I never thought it would be this . . . intense, you know? Everyone's talking about it. On set, I mean."

"Talking about it?" The hairs on my arm prickled. "His devotion, you mean?"

"Oh, yes." Could the stars in Geek Man's eyes get any bigger? Reid was an actor. He hadn't discovered a new planet! "I mean, ever since this morning." He shook his head as his eyes welled with tears. "He's a legend, a legend in the making. Everyone thinks so."

"Right." I was starting to get a little uncomfortable with the hero worship. I'd had a few people on set stalk my actors, and it wasn't a laughing matter. Terrifying was more like it.

"And the women." Geek Guy's eyes went wide. "Well, they're crazy! I mean, no offense."

"On behalf of women everywhere, I accept your apology." I licked my lips and decided to take a sip of my coffee. I needed something to do, something to distract me from shaking the small man and asking him to walk faster and stop talking.

"Well." He held up his hands. "Here's the trailer. You'll have to fill out a form like the rest of them. Reid's cautious like that." He elbowed me in the side. "And I've been told by Max, Mr. Emory's personal assistant, that if you're in the running we'll get back to you in four to seven days."

"In the running?" My eyes narrowed in on the ten or so girls standing around the small trailer. "The running for what?"

"The shrew, of course." Geek Guy shrugged. "You know, for the taming."

"The—" I choked. "Taming?"

His eyes narrowed. "That's why you're here, right? To try out for the real-life part of Shrew in Mr. Emory's dating calendar? It's already hit all the big news stations. To think, he's taken it this far so that he can know the true emotion that goes into taming a woman."

"Yes," I said through clenched teeth. "Because that's what all women want, to be tamed."

Geek Guy nodded sympathetically. "It's not your fault you're mean."

Holy shit on a stick! I was going to fillet Reid Emory with a machete, then set him on fire! What? In the span of a few hours after signing his name on the dotted line, he's already doing his own messed-up PR stunt? I stopped walking. Wait a second. With a groan I pulled out my phone. I'd forgotten to put a Google alert on the guy. I furiously typed in his name. Rage washed over me. Twitter alerts popped up all over the place, along with TMZ, Fox News, *Kelly and Michael*. I placed a hand against my chest and told myself not to freak out. It, whatever it was, would blow over.

I clicked on the first article just as the geek guy spoke in hushed tones into his headset. He led me a few more feet, then stopped.

"I gotta run back to set, but Mr. Emory should join you shortly. Try to keep it to a three-question minimum. After all, you're technically trying out for the role of a lifetime. To think! Mr. Emory's real-life girlfriend! And it's all going to be documented on YouTube!"

"YouTube?" Reid was dead. So dead. Deader than dead. Pretty sure that meant the contract was now void, considering I no longer had a client and I couldn't exactly work for someone who was no longer breathing. Strangulation. That's what I was contemplating.

"See ya!"

I turned on my now stable heel—thanks to the shoes I kept in my desk for unlucky situations like this morning—and glared.

Ten women, all beautiful, all Botoxed within an inch of their lives.

"Get in line!" one of the girls spat. Ah, the shrew speaks.

Pretty sure I'd be grumpy too if I had someone poke my face with needles while I tried to stuff my curvy body into Spanx ten sizes too small for my body.

"Yeah." A short, blonde-headed witch turned in my direction. "We were here first, and Max said that . . ."

I was seriously going to find whoever this Max was and beat him with a baseball bat.

Max, why did that sound familiar?

Max, Max, Max.

"Max!" I shouted. Then I stomped my foot.

"Shit, what did my brother do now?" Reid said from behind me.

I was about to answer when the girls all but lost their minds and dignity and started shouting, "Pick me, Pick me!"

"This isn't kickball," I muttered under my breath.

"If it was"—Reid winked—"you'd be the ball, you know because of your hair—oh, wait, that's a frizz ball."

"Funny."

He grinned. "No, seriously, why are these women shouting?"

"For you." I patted him on the back. "Something to do with the real-life taming of a shrew? Oh, and tryouts." I looked down at the sheet the geek had given me. "And apparently we need to list our food allergies. I can't eat shellfish. That gonna be a problem?"

"What the hell?" Reid jerked the sheet out of my hand and scanned it, his face paling by the second. "Who knows about this?"

"Everyone!" one of the girls squealed. "I was at the gym on the elliptical—"

"Of course you were," I said under my breath.

Reid leveled me with a glare and cleared his throat.

"You were?" I said in a fake cheerful voice. "On the elliptical reading *Cosmo*, huh?"

"How'd you know?" She jutted out her bony hip, then pouted. "Anywaaaays . . ." She dragged out *anyways* like a pubescent teenager at a One Direction concert. "I was on the elliptical."

"She said that already," I whispered.

Reid elbowed me.

"When"—she clasped her hands in front of her—"I saw it on the noon news! 'Up-and-coming actor Reid Emory takes Method acting to the extreme!' I wasn't the only girl either. Tons of us started screaming when they gave us the location and what you were looking for, and honestly, I may look sweet, but I can be a real bitch. I mean, that's what a shrew is, right? And you're going to tame me . . ." She full-on purred the last sentence as she blinked heavily in Reid's direction.

"Something in your eye?" I asked sweetly.

Reid grabbed me by the elbow and led me away. "Just a sec, ladies." He hauled me around the trailer and cursed. "Do something!"

"Wait, what?" I jerked away from him, spilling coffee onto the ground. "I should kill you for this!"

"Please, that's what you do! You spill things!"

"How do you even know that?

"Chocolate stain, right corner of your shirt, near your ear."

"Why!" I yelled into the universe.

Reid held his hands up. "Look, I know this has been somewhat of a bad morning for you, but if we don't fix this . . ."

"We can't just say it was a practical joke, now can we?" I tried desperately to keep my voice even.

Screaming erupted. We both peeked around the trailer to see hair pulling and one of the girls banging her fists against her own chest. Her boobs were immobile.

"Huh." Reid frowned. "That's not normal."

"Nothing about this is normal," I hissed as one of the boobs in question made an appearance. "How is it that we've been working together for less than three hours and you're already a bigger pain in my ass than the clients I've had over the last five years?"

He smirked. "I guess I'm just that special."

The crying got louder.

Reid looked like he was ready to cry himself.

"Okay, okay." I handed him his coffee. "Drink this and I'll figure it out."

"If we don't pick one, I have a feeling we're going to be worse off." Reid shook his head, then took a long sip. "Oh, wow, you actually remembered."

"Best friends, you and me, until the six months of filming and postproduction are complete."

He held up his hand for a high five.

I flicked it away.

He jutted out his lower lip.

"I'm ignoring the pout." I closed my eyes so my treacherous body wouldn't lean toward him.

"Holy shit," Reid murmured. "They're rocking my trailer."

"It's like a Justin Bieber concert gone wrong." I nervously glanced around us as people started holding up their camera phones. The situation was going downhill fast. The girls were screaming, demanding that Reid return to their side of the trailer. Thankfully security was already standing in front of the women, keeping them from full on charging us. They would rip him to pieces if I tossed him out there, and even though that idea had merit, something told me he'd just make the situation worse by picking every last one of them and making my life even more of a living hell.

"Back off, bitch!" a girl wailed.

Reid gave me a panicked look. "Isn't this what you do? Fix things?" His look went from panicked to doubtful.

Irritated that he was challenging me when I should have home court advantage, I thrust out my chin and marched around the trailer. If he wanted me to fix it, I was going to fix it, all right. "He's made his choice!"

The girl first in line caught my eye. She was jumping up and down. At least her boobs moved. She'd do. And if she was nice instead of shrewlike, we'd simply tell everyone that she hardly needed any work and set her free. Problem solved.

Immediate silence.

I cleared my throat and pulled at my chocolate-stained collar. "He chooses—"

"The lovely . . ." Reid wrapped his arm tightly around me. What was he doing? Mind reading? Picking his own girl? "Jordan . . ." His eyes narrowed as his lips brushed my ear. "What's your last name?"

"L-Litwright." I stumbled over the word like I'd just learned how to spell out *cat*.

"Sorry, girls." Reid hugged me closer. "But she's the shrew for me."

My lips trembled behind a suppressed moan. Dead. He was dead to me.

"But"—Reid released me—"how about some autographs and pictures for the road?"

The squealing continued.

And I was left standing by the trailer, wondering how the heck I was going to explain to Ren not only that I was fake dating my new client but that my new title was no longer just publicist.

But shrew.

# CHAPTER SEVEN

## JORDAN

"How the hell did this happen?" Ren fumed from behind his large mahogany desk. Normally his office with its private stash of Twizzlers and floor-to-ceiling windows that overlooked the city was somewhat of a sanctuary for me.

My hand twitched for some sugar.

His deep-brown eyes narrowed in on me as he brushed back some of his silver hair. "Jordan, this isn't like you."

Reid was silent next to me.

"Is this . . ." Ren held out his hands, bracing himself against the desk. "Is this some sort of midlife crisis?"

"Hardly!" I snorted.

While Reid said, "Maybe."

I opened my mouth, ready to defend myself, but by defending myself I'd end up making Reid look bad, and the situation would appear even worse. I needed to either suck it up and make it look like it was all part of the plan or confess and take the chance that Ren didn't think I could handle Reid.

Ren sighed. "Jordan? What happened?"

Swallowing my pride, I tried a different tactic. "Look, Ren, it wasn't our fault." He didn't let me finish.

"Oh, good." Ren nodded. "We'll just tell that to the press. It wasn't our fault. I'm sure they'll be very understanding."

"Great!" Reid rubbed his hands together.

I groaned. "He's being sarcastic." I pressed my fingertips to my temples and rubbed. "Look, Ren, give me some time. I'll come up with something, I—"

Ren held up his hand, cutting me off, and turned his back on us to face the cityscape. For a few minutes I wondered if that meant we were excused. For some reason this reprimand in his office felt a heck of a lot like getting called into the principal's office. Not that I would actually know, since the one time I did get called in after the senior prank the principal accused me of going to another school entirely.

I'd showed him my ID badge.

He said it was a fake.

I'd asked why the H-E-double-hockey-sticks (yes, I actually said it just like that, I wanted to be semipolite) would I make a fake student ID?

His answer? To steal the mascot.

Facepalm.

"You'll do it." Ren turned suddenly, his face glowing. "We can spin this in our favor."

I sputtered, "You can't be serious! I thought you'd have a better idea than this one!" I jabbed my finger in Reid's direction, and he lifted his hands in surrender. Smart move, considering his idea was to smile and kiss for the camera. I'm pretty sure the final nail in my shrewlike coffin occurred a half hour later when I slapped him across the face in the middle of Times Square.

It had taken five minutes before we were trending news.

Me and my chocolate-stained shirt and Reid with his gorgeous, breathtaking smile. There was something so incredibly depressing about seeing yourself at your absolute worst, next to perfection.

Ten minutes later, Ren summoned me to his office, so I threatened Reid within an inch of his life—either he came with me to the meeting or I would push him in front of an aggressive taxi—or ten. He was done filming for the day anyway and wanted to stop by Max's office to give him hell.

"Ren, I can come up with something else." Anything. Else.

Ren shook his head no. "This . . . this can be good for us. We'll say the information was leaked before we were ready."

The headache moved from my temples down my jaw. "And how do we explain that I'm the—"

"—shrew," Reid finished.

"Helpful!" I clenched my teeth. My feet ached because I'd only left the cheap heels at the office, my stomach was growling loud enough for my grandma back in Washington State to hear, and I was having a very lifelike daydream of Ren tossing me a Twizzler only to have it disappear in front of my face. I needed food. And coffee. And a do-over, but I was pretty sure that last wish wasn't going to get granted.

Ren's grin grew. I didn't like that grin. It was an evil grin, one that nine times out of ten was followed by equally evil laughter. "You hate your new publicist, so you've decided to take it upon yourself to tame her rather than a random girl in the city. It makes sense. After all, you're going to be spending a lot of time together," Ren continued, smiling. "People are quite fascinated with this movie to begin with. Think of the publicity we can drum up by allowing the audience the fantasy that Reid's goal—no, his life purpose—is to find a woman he can tame and bed."

"Whoa, whoa, whoa!" Oxygen. I needed oxygen. "Nobody said anything about bed!"

"But that's the thing!" Ren smirked. "You don't have to. Imaginations will run wild. Think about it: they see you two get ice cream, a fight breaks out, Reid kisses you, and people assume you're going to go back to your apartment—"

"It's safe to say I know what they're assuming." I held up my hand. I shouldn't have come in to work that morning. Clearly the universe was trying to tell me something when I got shampoo in my eye and my Starbucks got trampled.

"I'm in." This from Reid.

I shot him an irritated glare while my internal anxiety tripled. How did I go from being behind the scenes to the main attraction? I might complain about being invisible, but it worked for me. I didn't know the first thing about being on camera and . . . I wasn't blind or stupid. Girls like me did not belong with men like Reid. I'd be a laughingstock. Insecurity washed over me, choking the air from my lungs.

"What?" He shrugged and walked closer to the desk just as Ren pulled out a Twizzler and handed it to him. "Candy?"

Somehow Reid managed to eat the entire thing in one big chomp. Mouth watering, I had to look away. Damn Twizzler-stealing slut!

Reid stole another Twizzler, then turned his aqua-blue eyes in my direction. "Want a bite?"

"Not hungry." I crossed my arms and looked away as my stomach growled in protest. I'd probably eat Reid's arm if he got too close.

"Jordan," Ren barked. "I imagine this won't be difficult for you. Simply do what you do best."

I was screwed, so screwed. I couldn't say no to Ren, and I had a sinking feeling going along with his plan wasn't going to end well, but what choice did I have?

"What does she do best?" Reid asked in an innocent voice I knew was all for show.

"She sells the idea and makes people believe it's the truth."

• • •

"I'd say that went pretty well, all things considered." Reid chuckled as we made our way into the Emory Enterprises building.

"What?" I snapped, I full-on snapped, to the point that a sweet old lady hurried past me, snatching her purse close to her chest like I was going to shank her.

Reid grabbed my arm.

I stopped walking and looked down at his hand.

The hand touching my arm.

The hand making love to my arm.

Oh, this wasn't good.

My body was a conniving whore! Quivering with the fact that a handsome guy was actually touching me and it wasn't to move me to the side or push me into oncoming traffic because a hotter, more stupid girl had managed to get her heel caught in the sidewalk vent and I was standing in the way of him saving her.

I closed my eyes. Really, it was my only option at that point. I could still feel his stare, though—so maybe my only option was to move away.

I stepped back.

And collided with a man making his way up the stairs.

"Sorry," I grumbled.

"I didn't see you." He frowned.

"Happens all the time," I grumbled as he maneuvered around us and made his way into the building.

When I looked back at Reid, his beautiful face was marred with an irritated frown. "What was that?"

"What was what?"

"He ran into you."

"Right."

"How could he not see you?"

"Because he wasn't paying attention?" I countered. "Look, I don't know, it does happen a lot, though. I mean, don't you ever get sat on in the subway?"

Reid burst out laughing. "Hell, no. I mean I don't actually ride the subway, but I'm pretty sure if someone sat on me it would be on purpose, know what I mean?"

"Ew." My left eye twitched.

"Why are you winking at me?"

Twitch, twitch, twitch. "I'm not winking!"

He pointed. "Yes, you are. Stop it! It's weird! I don't know if I should wink back or just stand here."

"It's a twitch! A nervous tic, you moron!"

"Aw, I make you nervous?"

"Can we just . . ." Breathe, Jordan, breathe. That's it, nice and slow. Hot dogs and butterflies, what does the man bathe in? He smelled . . .

"And now you're sniffing my shirt." He choked on a laugh. "Something you wanna say?"

"Just, um . . ." I jerked back. "Making sure I know your scent so I can track you down." I gulped. "Like a dog." My face heated with embarrassment. "Because, uh, that's what dogs do."

"They also pee to mark their territory. You gonna do that too?"

"So." I barely managed to keep in my embarrassed laughter and shoved his muscled chest like we were homies or something. "This is where the infamous Max is, huh?"

Reid ignored my inability to have a conversation that didn't revolve around my peeing on him and fell into step beside me.

"Yup." He exhaled as he steered us away from the main elevators toward a back hallway.

He swiped a card across a large metal door, which opened into a private elevator. The walls were bright pink. The music—Britney Spears.

"What is this hell?" I whispered once the doors closed.

"This, my sad, misinformed friend, is Max's idea of funny."

The doors in front of me were papered with old pictures of boy bands and a very revealing picture of Reid and some other good-looking guy singing with 98 Degrees.

"You were in a boy band?" I blurted out.

"I'll take it to my grave," Reid muttered under his breath. "Only Max and I use this elevator. Last year, he taped pictures of retirement homes inside and found a Bengay-scented air freshener."

"Um, why?"

The elevator finally dinged at the top floor.

"I may have fallen victim to a horny grandmother."

"Do I want to know?"

"No. And you'll never know, unless you volunteer to pay for another round of therapy."

I burst out laughing, then covered my mouth once he sent me a glare that was anything but amused.

The elevator doors opened up to a large lobby with modern decor. White leather couches were framed around a black coffee table with a few magazines scattered about. A tall black desk was directly facing the elevators as we stepped off and into the serene environment. It felt very Zen. Green plants lined the hall as we made our way around the couches and approached the desk. It was pretty, pristine, and totally unexpected after the elevator ride.

"Molly," Reid crooned in a low, seductive voice that had my ears perking up like someone had just shouted that Channing Tatum was naked and giving away free doughnuts.

Clearly, this Molly had a similar reaction. It didn't matter that she looked twice my age, with black hair pulled into a tight bun on the top of her head and bright red lipstick that flashed behind a blinding white smile. On closer inspection, it was almost impossible to tell her age. Her pencil-thin brows were pinched together behind black glasses that I'd bet money weren't prescription.

"What can I do for you?" Her lips curved into another toothy grin as she lifted one of her pens and started sucking on the end. Oh, please. "Sir?"

"She calls you sir?" I mumbled under my breath.

Molly's gaze snapped toward me. "Is she homeless?"

Eyes wild, I flinched, ready to jump over her desk and shove the pen into her Botoxed face.

"No." Reid gripped my wrist tightly and held me in place. "She's . . . my publicist."

Molly burst out laughing.

I forced a smile. "It was a rough morning."

"I'll say." She kept laughing in a totally degrading way that also happened to sound like fingernails on a chalkboard.

"Is my father in?" Reid asked, interrupting her cackling.

She held up her finger then scanned the computer. "Yes, he's in the building for the next two hours. Did you need him?"

Reid's grip loosened on my wrist. "Would you mind terribly asking him to meet me in Max's office?"

"Of course not!" Her ability to both scream those words and also make me take a step back was impressive. Ears ringing, I was tempted to pound the side of my head.

Reid winked.

Molly did a little jig in her chair.

And I tried not to gag. Her reaction made it even more imperative that I have absolutely no reaction to him. I got it. I really did. Reid was one of those guys that couldn't help but ooze sexuality everywhere he went.

The really grating part was that I knew even if he wasn't half as good-looking as he was, women would still be falling all over themselves. It was the way he carried himself, the confidence that was real, not fake arrogance. You wanted to be his friend. And you wanted to make him smile. And you wanted those damn eyes trained on you.

My eye started to twitch again.

"Do you have eye drops for that condition?"

I smacked the side of my head.

"Or that." Reid coughed. "You could just do that." He led me down a long hallway, where we stopped in front of two black double doors.

I reached for the handle, my eye really going on a crazy streak.

"You should probably get that under control before we go in." Reid pointed to my eye.

"I can't control it!"

Reid winced, his handsome face making even that look dead sexy, what with his five o'clock shadow and aqua eyes like laser beams. Maybe that was the problem—my eyes felt so insecure they started to twitch in his hot presence.

"He'll think you're winking."

I rubbed my face, not caring that makeup was probably going to come off on my fingers. "Why does it matter?"

"Trust me, it matters. You don't want those pretty things misfiring in his presence."

I ignored the way my heart did a little leap at the way he said *pretty* and *things*. I was the pretty thing. Or my twitchy eyes were. "You make him sound—"

"Not normal. It's Max."

"You keep saying that." I rubbed under my eyes just in case there was any leftover black eyeliner. "That means nothing to me!"

"Oh." Reid tilted my chin up like he was inspecting me. "It will soon, trust me." He frowned, then licked his thumb and rubbed it beneath my right eye. "There." He pressed his lips together, then patted down my hair, tucking it behind my ear.

I huffed, blowing air out of my cheeks. "Did you really just mom-lick me? Then pat down my hair?"

Reid patted my shoulder. "Hey, we're in this together. I just want you looking . . . presentable before I throw you into the fire. Then again, if you look like you just got run over, he might ignore what I'm about to do to him."

"Do?"

"Just follow my lead. Don't show weakness."

I rolled my eyes. "Fine, let's get this over with."

Reid opened the door and cracked his neck. What? Were we going to brawl or something? "After you."

# CHAPTER EIGHT

## REID

As expected, Max was sitting behind his excessively large mahogany desk, most likely plotting world domination. His red leather chair was turned away from his pristine desk, his feet up on the windowsill. It wouldn't surprise me at all if he actually wrote in his schedule: *Gaze over the city, mock the little people, work on evil genius laugh.*

"I've been expecting you," he said before I even opened my mouth.

Jordan's eyes widened as she looked from me back to Max's chair. Slowly, he turned, his arms behind his head like he was a normal, relaxed individual rather than—well, rather than what he was.

Words always failed to describe my brother.

He was an enigma.

The only of his kind.

And hopefully the last.

His deep-set dimples slowly appeared as he smiled at Jordan then back at me. Standing, he made a sweeping gesture with his hand. "I imagine you want answers."

"Max." I gritted my teeth. "What the hell were you thinking?"

"I saved his life once," Max acknowledged. "Actually, more like three times, but who's keeping track, right?"

"You are." I let out a heavy sigh. "You have tally marks on a chalkboard back at the apartment."

He waved me off. "So you must be the lovely shrew."

Jordan's grip on my arm tightened enough to cause severe blood loss to all my lower extremities, which was probably a good thing, considering she was ridiculously sexy when angry. Her hair seemed to continuously grow the more time I spent with her, like the stress fed the frizz. And her lips? Well, she bit them. Hard. All. The. Time. Which made them swollen and red and completely distracting.

"Why?" she croaked. "I'm supposed to be launching your brother's career! Not ruining it!"

Max nodded, his expression one of concern as he pressed his hands in a prayerlike motion in front of his lips. "I see, and when did you know you had this problem?"

"What?" Jordan blinked. At least her left eye had stopped twitching. She turned to me for help. "What are we talking about?"

"Exactly." Max nodded. "Well, it's worse than I thought. You both needed me, and I knew you were too proud to say something."

"What's happening here?" Jordan hissed under her breath.

Max went over to his desk and hit a button. The room fell dark and, much to my horror, a slide show of Milo and Jason's grandma started playing on the wall. There she was, toothless, smiling, beckoning.

I shivered, then hid behind Jordan like a real man.

"See?" Max clapped his hands. "You need me! You can't get back on the horse and I'm going to force it! It's not like I told you that your publicist had to be the one you rode."

Jordan raised her hand. "Just to be clear, there will be no riding. Of any kind."

Max pouted, hitting the button so the creepy pictures of Milo and Jason's grandmother disappeared. "But that's the best part."

"You?" She pointed. "You run a billion-dollar company?"

I'm sure she was trying to figure out how the hell he ran anything but his mouth, considering his desk was void of any sort of paperwork. All he needed was a computer. It was a bit terrifying how Max could do the work of ten men in less than half the time and with one tool.

"Yes." His shoulders sagged. "But it runs itself. I'm just biding my time."

"Biding your time?" She just had to ask.

"Until the presidency beckons."

Jordan burst out laughing.

I remained silent—because I knew Max. With his luck? It was bound to happen. I could see it now. Max in the Oval Office sipping whiskey, smoking cigars, his twitchy finger hovering over all sorts of red buttons of mass destruction. I shivered.

Jordan crossed her arms. "You can't be serious."

I held up my hand. "Don't get him started."

"Four score and six months ago"—Max thrust his hand into the air—"I was a sad, lonely bastard without any real direction in my life—"

"He's still a bastard," I pointed out.

Max glared.

"Sorry." I smiled. "Continue."

"And this one . . ." He pointed to me. I was the one. I wanted to duck, but what was the use? Plus, I had a plan, one even Max wouldn't see coming. "Saved me. I was on a dating show. You may know me as Bachelor Maximus."

Jordan's eyes narrowed and then bulged out of her head. "Holy crap! The guy who's scared of goats?"

Max flushed and tugged at his collar. "I'll have you know Hades and I have a very complicated relationship that I don't need to defend to anyone, least of all you."

I eyed the wet bar in his office and made my way over. "This may take a while. Jordan, you want a drink?"

"It's one in the afternoon," she pointed out.

My response: "It's Max."

With a quick nod in my direction from Jordan, I knew I had at least one person on my side against the terrorist that was my brother. Max yawned. "Whiskey, two cubes. Thanks, bro. So, Jordan, as his publicist I'm sure you're aware that most Hollywood actors fizzle out after a breakout role mostly because they aren't able to handle the fame and the pressure that comes with it."

Jordan opened her mouth and then closed it.

"I'm sure you're also aware that seventy-point-two percent of American viewers admit to liking a male actor not based on his acting performance but his dating life?"

She scoffed. "That isn't even a real figure and you know it."

"Fifty-two percent"—he just kept going—"of producers are more likely to hire an actor who's willing to try Method acting for a role. And ninety"—he adjusted his tie as I brought him his drink—"ninety-eight percent of producers are more likely to hire an actor based on his ability to stay in a committed relationship."

Jordan gulped. "So that last one may be true, but—"

"Tsk, tsk." He winked. "I helped him."

She tilted her head. "You think selling him out to the media without even telling him your plan is helping?" She took the drink out of his hand and knocked it back before handing the glass back to him. "I'm calling your bluff. You're just a bored, sad little man."

"Nothing about me is little." He smirked. "You'll have to get Reid to drop his pants to witness the definition of little."

I muttered a curse and poured myself another drink, then brought over Jordan's.

"Well!" She shrugged and downed her entire drink. She didn't even choke or wheeze. Impressive. "Good job, Max. Now we have to pretend we're in a relationship, and if it goes bad—if people find out that it's fake or that it was a setup by his evil brother—then Reid's finished. Done."

"I'm not worried about that." Max puffed up his chest. "Because by the way he's looking at you right now, and the way your breath hitches every damn time he looks in your direction, I did better than I thought. Didn't I?"

"How do you live with him!" Jordan threw her hands into the air, nearly hitting me in the arm as I handed her another drink, while I was still focused on the fact that she had trouble breathing around me. That was a good thing, right?

A knock sounded at the door.

Max frowned.

"What's wrong, Max?" I walked over to the door. "Not part of your plan?"

"You sneaky little whore." Max pointed an accusing finger in my direction. "What hast thou done?"

"Dad!" I damn near shouted, making my own father teeter on his heels. "You're here."

Our father wasn't a man of many words—he was black-and-white, old school. Which really begged the question, where the hell did Max come from? No, really. I'd like to know.

One time I asked my mother if he was adopted.

And she just laughed and said, "Oh, your father used to be just like him!"

My father wore the same color tie every day for forty years. I highly doubted it.

"What can I do you for, son?" Dad's hair was completely white and slicked back. He wore a black suit, white shirt, blue polka dot tie. Always. It never changed. He eyed Jordan and held out his hand. "Allen Emory. Pleased to meet you."

She shook it, then took a step back.

"Well . . ." I cleared my throat. "I'm the eldest son."

Dad nodded and sat down on one of the white leather couches in the corner.

"And Max inherited the company. He's doing such a great job, by the way." I winked at Max. He gave me the finger behind our dad's back while Jordan choked on what I assumed was my drink considering she'd tilted back both hers and Max's.

Max's eyes narrowed into slits. "Reid, what are you doing?"

"And I know how important image is for this company. I mean, Dad, you built this ship from the ground up. The good Emory name is known around the world. Because of you. I don't think"—I wiped a fake tear—"I don't think I've ever thanked you."

"Shit," Max muttered under his breath, then spread his arms wide. "Papa, we're so proud."

It was on.

"But"—I forced two real tears down my cheeks. *Beat that, Max!*—"I just feel like we're lacking. I mean, your name, our name, it's everything. And as the eldest I just, I don't know, I thought, doesn't it look bad that the youngest is running the company? The youngest is getting married first." I slammed my fist against my chest. "It kills me that I'm considered the disappointment."

"Son!" My dad stood and walked over to me, arms open. "You could never be a disappointment."

I put my fist into my mouth and let out a hoarse cry, the type that appears to be so painful you don't want to make an audible sound. "Oh, but I am. And I just . . . I just wish I could make you proud."

"Son, you make me proud."

I nodded wordlessly. "Can I be honest?"

"Of course!" Honest-to-God tears started to fill his eyes. Did I feel guilty? Maybe a little, but would it be worth it in order to destroy my brother? Hell, yes.

"It hurts my feelings that Max is getting married first. He's gotten everything in this family and . . . I just, I just wish I could be first."

"Uh." Max charged toward us, a small bead of sweat pooled around his left temple. "But Reid, you don't have any prospects, and come on, that's kind of silly. It's marriage. Since when have you cared about marriage?"

My dad's chest puffed up. "Marriage is the most sacred of all bonds!"

I nodded and wrapped my arm around my father. "It is, oh, but it is."

I could have sworn in that moment Max had a silent panic attack, where the insides scream but nobody can hear you but you.

His eyes frantically darted left to right and then zeroed in on me, his face impassive other than a small tic that started at his jaw.

"Dad, let me get married first. Let me bring the first Emory girl into the family. Nay, into the fold." I grabbed his shoulder and squeezed tightly.

"But," Max sputtered, "we just picked a date!"

"Well, I don't see the trouble with pushing the date back at least a few months. We were having issues with getting the whole family to Bora Bora on such short notice." My dad nodded, then patted me on the cheek. "Let me do this for your brother, Max. We can push your wedding back—after all, it's a destination wedding. Give your brother some time to settle down, at least a few months. That way, both of you are happy."

Jordan had no idea why this was a big deal.

I imagined she wished she had popcorn. As it was, she was watching the exchange with rapt fascination, and she wasn't even commenting, which I could tell, even in my short time knowing her, was totally out of character.

Though she was tilting the whiskey back like it was water—then again, that was a common occurrence where Max was concerned. You either drink or wish you had a drink.

"Will that be all?" Dad asked.

"Yes." I nodded, wiping my cheeks again. "Thank you, Father."

"Anything for my sons." He embraced me, then held open his arms to Max. My brother stepped into his arms and hugged him tightly before Dad excused himself and walked out of the office.

"You lie!" Max roared the minute the door closed. "How could you?"

Jordan cleared her throat. "What just happened?"

I smirked. "Max's fiancée asked him to make a promise. To make the wedding night more . . . special. Once they have their engagement party, no sex until the wedding."

"And?" Jordan stumbled toward me. "When is the party?"

"It was supposed to be this weekend." Max started tugging at the collar of his shirt. "Leaving three months without sex . . . but now—"

"Now," I said cheerfully, "she'll make you keep your promise, because what happened the last time you didn't keep your promise? Oh, that's right, she said, and I quote, 'Max, prove to me you love me. Keep this promise, just this once.'"

Jordan was full-on leaning against me. Too much whiskey—hell, too much Max—did that to a person. Laughing, she shrugged. "So what, Max can't have sex for a few months. Who cares?"

"Me!" Max roared. "I care!"

Jordan kept laughing.

"I'll get you for this, jezebel!" He thrust his finger at her.

"Whoa!" She held up her hands. "You started this, not me!"

Max nodded his head. "Too many uncontrollable factors . . . I should have taken Reid's shrewdness into consideration."

"So." I clapped my hands. "Looks like I have to start taming my shrew." I held out my arm to Jordan. "Shall we?"

"No," she yelled, then stomped her foot. "I hate you! I won't go anywhere with you, you horrible man!" She let out a drunk giggle.

"Oh, oh, shucks." I snapped my fingers. "Guess this is going to take longer than I originally thought."

Max glared. "I'll get you for this."

"Do say hi to your fiancée for me." I saluted him with my middle finger and walked Jordan out of his office.

# CHAPTER NINE

## JORDAN

I was tipsy.

The Britney-glammed elevator dipped, and I gripped the railing on the side and tilted my head as ". . . Baby One More Time" started playing. I could have sworn the Britney poster was moving. All I needed was a schoolgirl outfit and I'd be all set to star in my own music video. Then again, I'd probably end up getting arrested, because that was JUST the type of day I was having. I could see it now—Reid Emory's newest publicist arrested for pretending to be a teenage woman and hitting on a minor after chasing him down the street over a stolen doughnut.

*Whoa.* I swayed on my feet. How did I get from schoolgirl outfit to doughnut? Or taking advantage of minors?

"Hey." Reid elbowed me as the elevator finally rumbled to a stop. "You did good in there."

I nodded, not trusting my voice to be slur-free as I continued digging my fingers into the metal rail.

The doors opened.

I didn't move.

Afraid that if I did I'd puke.

Just how much did I drink up there?

"It happens." Reid gripped my arm and led me gently out the doors. "He has that effect on people."

"I have . . ." I cleared my throat and widened my eyes, thinking, *Surely if I go all owl-eye on Reid, I won't look intoxicated.* Right, because not blinking really sells someone on your sobriety, said no person ever. "No idea." I licked my dry lips. "What you're referring to."

Reid released my arm and very gently pushed my body with his pointer finger. I nearly toppled over—would have, had he not grabbed me again and sighed. "That's what I'm talking about. Don't blame yourself. It's the Max effect."

"But we won." I nodded. "Or actually, you won, with your quick thinking. Now we can just pretend we hate each other." I frowned. "No, wait, that won't work. We still have to date and convince the media that you're taming me." My head started to pound. "I'm starving. Are you starving?"

Reid said nothing and just held me closer to his body.

"You smell like—" I inhaled his shirt, my nose plastered against it like a hound ready to chase a coon across the country. "Sexy sex cologne."

"Oh?" Reid nodded. "Good, because that's what I was doing the whole time you were tossing back whiskey upstairs, having sex so that my natural musk would attract perfect strangers."

"You were?"

"Jeez, where do you live? I need to get you home."

It started to rain. "I live in a pond." I spread my arms wide, then toppled forward, my purse falling down around my wrist. I swung it around in the air like an ax. "Under the sea . . ." I giggled, then started wiggling my hips. "Under the sea, down where it's wetter, down where it's better, take it from me!" Somehow I'd taken on a very convincing accent. I was seriously hilarious. Why wasn't Reid dying of laughter?

Reid grinned. Then pulled out his cell and snapped a few photos. "That good, huh?" I winked, then nearly fell backward down the concrete stairs leading to the street.

"Yeah, Sebastian, words can't describe. So I took a picture. Might post it to Facebook later, tag you in it, add a few choice hashtags, like #sebastianlives, #savecrabseatshrimp, and #Girlsgonewildtheshrewedition."

I saw two Reids. My stomach plummeted, sinking to my feet.

"Ugh, I don't feel so good."

"Well, you look awesome." Reid grabbed my hand.

I curled my lips up at him in disgust.

"Especially that face—that one's my favorite. If I squint and tilt my head you resemble a pissed-off poodle. Tell me, does your hair have a name? Considering it's like a separate organism living off your body? Let's call it Parasite Bob."

"You're a parasite!" I yelled.

"Shh, Sebastian. We'll get you back to the ocean, just calm down."

"I'm not a crab!" I wailed, suddenly craving crab like none other.

"Of course you don't have crabs!" Reid countered. "Poor thing." He motioned his head toward curious onlookers. "It's a good thing our city cares for the homeless."

I dug my feet into the ground. "I'm not homeless, you bastard!"

"Then show me where you live so I can make you a pot of coffee and hatch out a plan that leaves Max out of our lives and keeps us from going to prison."

"Prison? Why would we go to prison?"

"Max. I may kill him. I've threatened him for years, but this may just be the one time I follow through." His face was serious; not a hint of humor marred his perfect features. Okay, so maybe it was safer for all parties if we got farther away from the building.

I nodded, suddenly realizing it was a very real possibility that Reid would turn around, jump on Britney, ride to the top, and kick his brother in the family jewels. "Fine, my house is . . ." I looked down the road, then up the road, then blinked up at the sun.

"Saturn?"

"No." I pushed on Reid's muscled chest. "I live . . . in Midtown-ish."

"Midtown—*ish?*"

"I think so."

"You think so?"

"Stop repeating everything I say!"

Reid held up his hands. "Fine, let's grab a cab and pray you at least remember your address so we aren't roaming the streets. I don't take you for the type who would actually survive overnight in the elements."

He hailed a cab, shoved me in—not very gently, mind you—and turned those aqua-blue weapons in my direction. "So?"

"Er, Koreatown, fifty West Thirty-Fourth."

"Koreatown," Reid repeated. "I should have known."

I rolled my eyes. "I'll have you know I live next to the Macy's flagship store. I'm within walking distance of Grand Central and—"

Reid held up his hand. "Not a tourist, you don't need to sell me on New York, Sebastian."

"Stop calling me that!"

"Sorry, Shrew."

I groaned into my hands and prayed it would take us only a few minutes to make it to my apartment.

It didn't.

Because, as I previously stated, I was clearly unlucky.

Twenty minutes later, the booze had worn off and I was left feeling itchy, sweaty, gross, and dehydrated.

I threw a twenty at the driver and basically launched myself from the car, hoping my catlike reflexes would startle Reid and cause him to stay in the car and disappear so I could wallow in shameful peace.

Clearly he wasn't easy to get rid of.

He gripped my wrist, got out of the cab, and slowly walked with me to the door.

The doorman tipped his hat as we walked in, which only made things worse. That same doorman had stopped me on multiple occasions, accusing me of stalking some of the residents. It probably didn't help that I'd gone on one date with my neighbor and when I refused to go out with him again, because he had a gross cheese fetish, he made a scene in the lobby.

Since then, I'd had three run-ins with Dwight.

He threatened to call security on me only once.

Since then we'd given each other a wide berth. I ignored him and he ignored me.

"Excuse me." Dwight cleared his throat and approached us just as I hit the button for my floor.

Gritting my teeth, I turned and crossed my arms, ready for a battle.

"Yes?" Reid answered.

Dwight looked down at the ground, then back up at Reid, his ruddy face flushed with excitement. I'd never seen the man so much as hint that he had a sense of humor or knew how to smile. He was in his midfifties, losing most of his hair except for a small patch I could only assume he refused to cut, right in the middle.

"I saw your show last year at least a dozen times."

"Oh, wow." Reid nodded. "Thanks, man, that means a lot."

"You are"—Dwight held out his hands, his eyes blurring with tears. Oh, dear Lord—"hands down the best Phantom this world has ever seen."

Lay it on thick, Dwight. I half expected him to burst into tears.

"We have to go," I snapped, ignoring the fact that my estrogen seemed to immediately triple in supply at the thought of Reid wearing a cape. Hot damn.

Dwight's eyes narrowed. "You sure you live here?"

"For the past two years," I said through clenched teeth. "Reid." I gripped his arm. "Come on."

His arm was so firm, strong. I glanced up.

*Cape, cape, cape!* my body freaking sang. Oh, man, I wonder if he kept the mask?

"Sir." Dwight shook his head. "An absolute pleasure."

Reid reached out and patted his shoulder. "For me too." He glanced down at the name tag. "Dwight."

Dwight gasped. Like a freaking schoolgirl. I shook the visions of a Phantom Reid out of my head and crossed my arms.

If Dwight fainted, I was going to purposefully knock myself out and pray that when I woke up this day from hell was nothing but a really horrible nightmare.

He didn't. Faint, that is, but he did fan his face and walk quite briskly back to his desk before he lifted his phone into the air.

A picture was snapped just as the elevator doors closed. I could imagine the caption now: REID EMORY INVITES HOMELESS CAT LADY INTO HIS APARTMENT FOR AFTERNOON TEA.

I winced as my own reflection flashed back at me in the shiny elevator doors.

Reid's eyes met mine in the reflection, and they were kind. His expression was one you save for old ladies while they buy discount bread at the grocery store just because it's on sale, then feed it to the birds. "It's true, you've probably had better days."

"My hair." I touched the top of my head. My frizzy hair just kept growing and growing, like an overwatered Chia Pet.

"It wouldn't stay down." Reid shrugged. "Believe me, I tried."

I rolled my eyes. "You licked your hand and patted it."

"Exactly."

The doors opened. I hurried past the other doors and stopped in front of mine.

Yellow tape.

Why, why was there yellow caution tape in front of my door?

"Uh-oh. Kill someone last night?"

"It's not crime scene tape, you ass!" I ripped the tape from my door like I was Xena, Warrior Princess, shoved my key in the lock, and stepped in.

The apartment was semidark.

I flipped the switch.

Nothing.

"You smell smoke?" Reid coughed and covered his mouth just as my tiny shih tzu barreled out of the bedroom and launched himself onto Reid's leg.

Reid looked down at the small rat. "Friend of yours? Funny, I expected you to be more of a cat person."

"Come here, Otis."

"Otis?"

"Yeah." I snuggled my dog close to my chest. "You know, from Milo and Otis?"

Reid's eyes scanned my small one-bedroom apartment. I knew it wasn't anything special. I didn't have time to decorate, and even my sad pathetic coffee table was naked, not even a coaster decorating the thing. But I'd always been of the mind that a woman doesn't need a coaster if all she drinks is wine.

"I know a Milo."

"Right. Okay." I dropped Otis onto the ground and went to another light switch. Nothing.

"Did you pay your power bill?" Reid asked, his tone completely serious.

My cheeks heated as I clenched my fists to keep from scratching his eyes out. "Yes. As I said before, my electricity went out this morning, but they promised it would be fixed within a few hours."

A knock sounded at the door.

I ignored it.

Already knowing what it was.

More bad news.

Because after today, how could it really be anything good?

Reid pushed past me and opened the door.

"You can't be here!" A stout man with a wiry mustache pushed into my apartment and clenched his fists at his sides like he was trying to keep his anger in check. "It's been condemned."

"Whoa, whoa, whoa!" I held up my hands. "Over the electricity?"

He sighed, looking at me like I was a complete idiot, before addressing the other male in the room. "She your girlfriend?"

"Something like that." Reid smirked. Hey, at least he semi claimed me, right? "Now, what's going on here?"

The man held out his clipboard, handing it to Reid, a relative stranger. Never mind that it was my name on the lease. All that mattered was that there was a man to explain things to rather than a hysterical lady with poofy hair. "The electrical is so old we've had to condemn the oldest apartments on this side, the ones not renovated or part of phase one."

My stomach sank. "I was told it was perfectly safe."

"Lady, that smoke you smell? Could have been you or your little fur ball had some pathetic squirrel not sacrificed itself on a power line this morning. You need to pack your shit and stay with friends. If you need help moving, I can give you some numbers, but you can't stay the night."

"But—"

"Lady." Seriously, if he called me *lady* one more time I was going to show him how much of a lady I could really be and slam his head in the doorway. "Stay with your boyfriend, I'm sure he won't mind."

"He would." I gritted my teeth. "Believe me."

The man left, slamming the door behind him.

And that's when I felt the familiar sting of tears. Nothing in my day had gone right, and now I really was homeless. All I needed was a cart and an END OF THE WORLD sign.

# CHAPTER TEN

## REID

I wasn't one of those guys—you know, the type that knew how to comfort other human beings well. I did the typical rough pat on the back and chin nudge. When I broke up with my last girlfriend, I patted her ass and said, "Good game."

It may have been because I was breaking up with her while watching SportsCenter, but she cried. Hard. Then shrieked and asked why she even put up with me in the first place.

I wasn't sure if it was a rhetorical question, so I ignored her.

Which just pissed her off more.

So tears—the kind I was about 99 percent sure were going to start flowing freely from Jordan's eyes—freaked me out.

"Er." I looked frantically around her sparse living room. Where was the wine? The chocolate? The cuddly teddy bear that I could chuck in her general direction to distract her enough so I could make a run for it?

"I'm homeless!" she wailed, wobbling on her legs. I took a tentative step backward and covered my nether region, in case she wanted to take out her bad day on the entire male gender, and not wanting to be the one she made an example out of.

"There, there." I coughed into my right hand while the left kept its protective goalie-like stance. "It will be all right."

She blinked her big brown eyes up at me. "If you pat my head, I won't be responsible for my actions."

Good thing she warned me, because I was just about to pat her head—like a dog—and possibly scratch behind her ear and ask if it made her feel better. I might be really good at flirting and getting a girl to fall for me, but I was shit at real emotions. I didn't cry over women— they cried over me. Plain and simple.

"So." I licked my lips. "It seems your hands are full here, so I'll just . . . keep in touch? Maybe we can do lunch tomorrow?"

"Do. Lunch," she repeated, her eyes widening into an expression that looked a hell of a lot like the beginnings of a toddler meltdown.

"Yeah." I gulped. "Food always makes me feel better, so . . . you know, now you'll have something to look forward to."

Somehow I was making the situation worse, if the red on her cheeks was any indication.

"Reid, I have no home. I have to move out of my apartment while trying to keep your sorry ass out of a media firestorm, and you expect me to do all of that how? If I lose my job and my home—" She blanched. "Oh my gosh, I can't, I can't lose my job!"

"I think you're overreacting," I said dryly.

Jordan flashed me another terrifying look that had me taking a step closer to the door. Almost there. Freedom. So close. I reached for the doorknob just as she said. "I know!"

My entire body felt like it had just been electrocuted. Looking back on this moment, I'd recognize it for what it really was—somehow she'd channeled whatever superpowers Max possessed and shifted the universe, deciding my future, my destiny, without ever asking my opinion in the first place.

"You." Jordan stalked toward me. "You have an apartment."

It was the perfect opportunity to lie. Really, I was an actor. I could make her believe I'd sold my penthouse within the last twenty-four hours because I wanted to live on the streets.

In a box.

Or a cart.

Hell, I could have said I was renovating, right? Joined the circus? But her face.

I was always a sucker for a pretty face.

And hers was more than pretty; it was pathetic pretty. Large brown eyes blinked up at me, their innocent trust making me feel all warm and fuzzy inside. Damn it! I needed to look away.

But I couldn't.

I opened my mouth.

Nothing came out.

She put her hands on her hips, which drew me in more, because damn, did the girl have some delicious curves on her. What was that smell? Her perfume? I was falling . . . oh, no, it was happening . . . she was using her feminine wiles on me. And I was a powerless bastard.

I needed someone to hit me over the head with a cement block.

Instead, she fluttered her eyelashes twice.

And I hung my head and muttered, "Grab a suitcase."

"Yes!" Jordan jumped into the air, then launched herself into my arms, nearly sending me flying backward. Her legs wrapped around my waist and suddenly she was kissing me on the mouth, then hopping down before my body had time to register that the gorgeous woman had all but pressed her goodies against mine. "You're the best!"

Wait! My body tightened. I should at least get sex out of the deal, right?

As a thank-you?

"At least first base," I mumbled under my breath.

"Pardon?" Her eyebrow arched, making me feel ten inches tall.

"Just, uh . . ." I scratched my head. "Sorry, it's a sports metaphor, you know, pass first base, the hardest base, and you're home free!"

"Oh." She shrugged. "For a minute there I thought you were asking for a sexual favor."

"Never!" Hell, yes, I was. Instead I broke eye contact and rubbed my hands together. "Let's grab your shit and go."

Jordan rolled her eyes and disappeared into the bedroom while I shakily leaned against the wall and wondered what the hell I'd just agreed to.

• • •

"Ground rules," I stated once we were riding the elevator up to my apartment. I was holding a suitcase and a plant she'd refused to leave behind because she'd kept it alive for three freaking years. Another mark against her, considering anyone who could keep a plant alive that long needed to get laid, or just find a hobby, any hobby that made their life look less pathetic. Checkers. I'd have more respect for her if she was in a checkers club.

But no, my new roomie-slash-shrew fake girlfriend had a plant fetish.

And she wasn't the only one having a rough day.

Otis let out a pitiful moan.

"Shh, Otis." Jordan rocked the small shih tzu back and forth like it was an infant, then kissed its head. "We're almost there."

I cleared my throat just as the doors opened, revealing the marble penthouse lobby.

"Holy crap!" Jordan did a little spin.

"Wait." I stopped her spinning and jerked my hand back just before Otis took a giant bite out of my thumb. "Ground rules, remember?"

Jordan rolled her eyes. Her frizzy hair had yet to calm down, and if anything it had doubled in size and was cheerfully growing to the tune of "Stairway to Heaven." Her big brown eyes were makeup-free, her complexion flushed but beautiful. Her round face only made her appear more feminine and enticing.

Which was the last thing I needed.

An attraction to my roommate.

And publicist.

And shrew.

What the hell kind of day was this?

Jordan peeked around me, her gaze on the large black double doors behind me. "Jordan, focus!"

"Sorry." She returned her gaze to me. "Ground rules. Yes."

I held up a finger. "One, you're only here until we can find a place for you to live where you won't get electrocuted."

She nodded.

"Two." I held up two fingers. "I like order, you know, clean lines, clean laundry, made beds, no dirty dishes—"

"Whoa." Jordan chuckled. "Are you saying you really are gay? It makes perfect sense!" She slammed her hand against her forehead. "The need for a good publicist, the whole taming of the shrew. Who is he?" She was already pulling out her cell, ready to do damage control.

"Chill." I held up my hand. "Not gay, just a type-A personality."

Her eyes narrowed.

"Fine." I sighed. "I'm settling this."

I went in, molding my mouth to hers, her protest dying against my lips as my tongue swiped her lower lip, once and then twice, before entering into the sweet velvet delicacy of her mouth.

Otis moaned.

Or maybe it was me.

Jordan wrapped a hand around my neck, pulling me closer.

"Drop the damn dog," I hissed against her mouth.

Otis fell to the ground with a thump and started barking wildly while I picked up Jordan by her hips and held her against my body.

Barking continued.

The kissing didn't stop. Who knew she had such talent? Her mouth was like a weapon. I was ready to suffer all the day long if that meant I'd get to taste her.

Jordan's cell went off.

I pleaded with the universe, *Just let her cell die!*

"My, my," a voice said from behind me. A very evil voice. "What do we have here?"

I jerked away and glared at Max, who leaned against the elevator doors. "You guys taking your work home?"

"Max." I gritted my teeth. "Not that it's any of your business."

He tilted his head. "Oh, it's always my business."

Otis barked and started terrorizing Max's feet.

"Aw, hey, little guy."

"Otis," I clarified.

"You guys already bought a dog?"

"No," we yelled in unison.

"It's Jordan's."

"And you, the lovely lady, and her dog are at your apartment because?"

I scratched my neck, as honest-to-God hives started popping up around the collar of my shirt. "We hit a . . . snag."

Max eyed Jordan up and down. "I'll say. Also, question: Is she aware that by this time tomorrow her hair's going to be in the 90210?"

Jordan growled. "Max, what did you need?"

His grin grew. "I live here. In this building. I was just coming up to see if I could talk my brother into reasoning with me about this whole wedding situation. But now? I don't think that's going to be a problem. Not with you two buying a dog and cohabitating. You'll either have sex or kill each other before the end of the week. My bet's on both."

"My electricity went out!" Jordan said defensively.

"You have to pay the bill, small fry." Max shook his head at me and pointed a thumb at Jordan. "She always this dense?"

Jordan lunged.

I grabbed her by the arm just as Max stepped out of the way, laughing and holding his hands up in surrender. "We still on for dinner tonight?"

"Shit!" I released Jordan. "I forgot!"

"Bring her." Max nodded to a very fluffy, aggravated-looking Jordan. "It seems we've finally found another friend we can bring around Milo."

"Milo?" she repeated.

Max gave a thoughtful nod. "Yes, yes, I think you'll do quite well together."

"Me and Milo?"

"No, you and Reid." He clapped his hands. "Keep up."

"But—"

I put a hand over Jordan's mouth. "Shh, don't question him."

"Until this evening." Max tipped his nonexistent hat and walked down the lobby to another door.

"Tell me." Jordan closed her eyes and pinched the bridge of her nose. "Tell me he doesn't live in the penthouse next door."

"Two penthouses in this building." I shoved the key into the lock. "We own both."

"Because?"

"Because we own the building," I finished, pushing the door open. "Oh, and don't think I've forgotten, we need ground rules."

Jordan tried to push past me. I stopped her halfway through the door. "Unless you want a repeat of that kiss—the rules need to be established."

"Fine," she snapped. "Then can I please take a shower?"

"You're being kind of demanding, all things considered, don't you think?"

"No." She crossed her arms. "What I think is that this is all your fault to begin with!"

"How do you figure!" I yelled, tossing my keys onto the granite countertop, where they slid across the smooth surface and fell on the floor. Otis barreled over and started sniffing them.

"It was a normal day for me!" Jordan's voice rose. "I was reporting to my job, not hurting anyone—"

"—except the eyes of the poor people who had to stare at you while you whistled your way to work!"

She let out a horrified gasp, and her hair actually seemed to grow with her anger. Seriously, she needed to get ahold of that hair before it took over the world. Max would be pissed if someone ruined his plans.

"You"—her nostrils flared. It would be cute if it weren't so terrifying—"are the reason I've had the day from hell! Because of you and your evil brother—"

"Thank you!" A muffled voice came from the far wall.

"How *thin* are these walls?" Jordan screeched.

"Enunciate!" Max yelled back. "And for the love of God, project!"

I shook my head and walked over to the fridge, pulling out two beers, both for me, and briefly contemplated hitting myself over the head with the second bottle once I finished the first.

"Fine." I held up my hands. "You win, it's my fault, but now that I'm sharing my multi-million-dollar paradise with you—we're even."

Jordan marched over to the counter and grabbed the other beer, hitting the tab off the top via the side of the granite.

She made it look cool.

Not that I would ever say it out loud, lest she never move out and make my life a living hell.

"Rules," I said for, oh, I don't know, the fifth time in the last fifteen minutes? "No bringing men home to my house—ever."

"Do I count?" Max yelled through the wall.

"Seriously," Jordan said in a hushed voice. "Who built this place?"

"Who do you think?" I nodded to the wall. "Max was in charge of this project and offered me the other penthouse."

Jordan shook her head. "Sneaky bastard."

"Thank you!" Max said again.

"Can we block him out?" she whispered.

"Talk louder!" Again Max.

Jordan smirked. "Oh, baby, right there."

I choked on my beer.

"That's it!" she screamed, slamming her hand against the countertop. "Oh, you know how to make a woman feel so good!" Otis started barking. I wasn't sure if that was a check in my favor or not as far as Max's listening was concerned. "Oh, oh, yes, yes, yes, yes!" Bonus points for screaming, and suddenly I appreciated her hair and the wild way it seemed to bounce with every scream. I could definitely be down with that . . . oh, I could do a lot of things with that. I squeezed the bottle harder, blood pumping to all the wrong areas.

"Yes!" She slammed her hand against the counter again. "You're so—"

Silence.

And then. "Guys?"

Otis barked.

"Guys?" Max yelled. "What happened? Since when has Reid ever gotten a girl to scream?"

"All the damn time!" I yelled back.

"Please," Max replied. "I live here."

"Really wish you didn't!"

"You love me!"

I turned to Jordan. "It was a nice try . . ." This time I patted her hand. "Really, you had me believing I was a magic orgasm-giving unicorn."

Jordan giggled, the beer teasing the edge of her lips. I wanted to take a step forward. Instead I backed up, nearly colliding with the fridge.

"So, I guess the only rules are . . . don't bring any guys back here. Ever. Keep it down until Max gets married and moves somewhere else, and well, try to keep the apartment clean."

Jordan set down her beer, and her teeth teased her lower lip as she slowly held out her hand. "You've got yourself a deal."

"Oh." I tugged her closer to my body. "And another thing?"

"Yeah?" she said breathlessly.

"You need to take a shower before dinner. I refuse to claim you and that thing on your head."

She stomped on my foot and walked down the hall.

"Second door to the left," I yelled. The door slammed.

It was worth it to see the fire in her eyes. "Well." I nodded to Otis. "What do you think, boy?"

His answer?

To lift up his leg and pee on my keys.

Fan-freaking-tastic.

# CHAPTER ELEVEN

## JORDAN

There were worse things than cohabitating with your client turned fake boyfriend, right?

I chewed the lipstick from my lower lip and shot a nervous glance at Reid. I hadn't exactly brought cocktail attire to his apartment, but I did own at least four Diane von Furstenberg wrap dresses. I threw on a white one and added my fake green crocodile heels and prayed that my hair would stay in the tight bun I'd fastened just above my neck.

I even added makeup.

A real effort took place!

I think it probably helped that Reid had some of the best bathroom lighting I'd ever seen. It was the type that made you look half your normal size as well as tan, something I'd never been accused of in my entire life. If anything, my paleness just made me more invisible.

"You look good," Reid muttered in a hoarse voice once we were walking toward the restaurant. I'd pretended to be busy checking my messages in the cab while he stared longingly out the window, probably wishing he could simply jump out of the car and be done with the whole charade. It's not like it had been a cakewalk for me either.

I was going to have to line up TV interviews, do a press release, and try to appear shrewlike while also enamored with him while filming. Just the thought of it had my head aching. Granted, it was my job, but he was adding a crap load more work onto what I usually had to do, and all he needed to do was smile and wave. To add insult to injury, I was going to be in the spotlight as well, and it's not like I was comfortable with it, not even a little bit.

I sighed. At least he was easy on the eyes.

But his personality left much to be desired.

"Thanks." I held my head high as he opened the door to Barbour, a high-end bar and grill in Upper Manhattan.

A couple exited the restaurant, nearly colliding with me in the process. I barely managed to sidestep them when someone else ran into me from behind.

"Sorry," I managed to croak out.

Reid frowned, then pulled me firmly against his side. "Seriously, people can be so rude."

I shrugged. "It's fine; it happens . . . often."

"What? People being rude to you?"

"No." Because at least then they would see me. "People not watching where they're going . . ."

He nodded and ushered me through the door. I stopped at the hostess booth, but Reid kept walking, so I followed him back. We walked through black velvet curtains and into a large room with a table set for eight.

Max was already seated, a beautiful girl with short, dark-blonde hair by his side, her smile captivating and fun. She was wearing a miniature black cocktail dress and had some killer leather wrap bracelets on her left wrist. I always noticed jewelry—thought it said a lot about a person.

Her jewelry screamed fun.

Not pretentious, or even psychotic, which was the most surprising thing of all, considering she was marrying Max.

As if reading my thoughts, he jerked his head to the side and made eye contact with me. "Well, well, well, the fake orgasm girl. Glad you could make it."

He stood.

A guy sitting next to him choked on his drink while a girl with blonde hair launched herself across the table and patted him on the back, spilling water in his lap. He screamed, then jerked away, only to bump his knee on the chair and fall to the ground.

"So." Max barely gave the scene a second glance as he yawned and continued talking. "The accident waiting to happen, aka the bastard on the floor, is Jason. Don't ask him about his black eye, he'll just get pissed." He stood and made his way over to me. "Also, the one causing said accidents, that's Milo. She's my ex–best friend." He whispered in a low voice, "My fiancée gets that title now." He blew the girl in the black dress a kiss. Her response was to swat it out of the air and grab a giant glass of wine, tilting it back until it was gone. Smart woman.

"And this"—Max wrapped his arm around me—"is Colton."

Colton stood and offered his hand. "Milo, the accident causer's other half."

I nodded and shook his hand. "Great to meet you."

"So." Colt crossed his arms. "Fake orgasms? Do I even want to know? And what the hell does Max have hanging over your head that he forced you into our monthly get-together?"

"Oh." I took the drink from Max's hand. "I doubt you'd believe me."

"You'd be shocked what I'd believe where this one's concerned." He nodded to Max. "Also, I'd start with the hard stuff right away. Wine won't work when he's in the room."

"Please." Max sniffed. "I'm standing right here and I make your freaking sun shine, Colt. Just remember, I helped you win your wife. Without me you'd be a lonely bastard with blue balls."

"Let's leave his balls out of it." Milo rounded the corner. "Hey, I'm Milo. Are you Reid's date?"

"Uh." I shifted uncomfortably in my heels. "Kind of."

"She's his roommate," Max added helpfully. "And his publicist."

"Oh." Milo frowned. "Is that normal?"

"She's also his shrew." Max nodded. "He has to tame her for the people. Give them what they want, that's always what I say!"

"Shrew?" Colton took a step back.

What, was that word the universal indicator that I wanted to kick men in their parts, then point and laugh?

"It's a long story." My eyes greedily searched for Reid. Finally, he made his way over to me, his swagger both pissing me off and making me a little bit breathless.

"We're, uh, together." Reid coughed into his hand, then awkwardly put an arm around my waist.

"Oh, dear Lord." Max made a cross motion in front of his body. "All those years at theater camp boil down to this moment and you just coughed while introducing the shrew."

"Am I late?" an elderly, hoarse voice said from the door. When I turned to greet the woman, I nearly lost the wine I'd just tossed down my throat. A small black wig was placed on her head. It was backward. Her lipstick was halfway across her mouth, joker style, and her blouse was three buttons away from being completely open.

Reid made the kind of noise I'd only ever heard on the Discovery Channel and ducked behind me while Max muttered, "You play dirty? I play dirty."

"Grandma!" Max shouted, making his way toward the old woman. "Glad you could make it!"

Grandma tittered, her black wig dipping across her nose. Was she blind? Then again, earlier today people could have easily said the same thing about the rat growing on my head. "Oh, I do love being naked too. Thank you, Max, don't mind if I do."

The woman started unbuttoning what was left of her shirt. She swayed on her feet, clearly intoxicated. Reid gripped my hand and tugged me backward, whispering in my ear, "We're going to make a run for it."

"Really?" I didn't turn around. Another button popped. "And miss the show?"

"Trust me." His lips grazed my ear. "I've seen this show. I had to go to therapy because of it. On the count of three, you faint and I carry you out."

"Wait." The sad elderly lady was fighting a losing battle with that last button. I'd never been so thankful for strong thread in my entire life. "Isn't she your grandma?"

"If she were"—Reid's grip on my wrist tightened—"the things she did to me would have landed me on *Dateline*."

"Fine," I huffed, setting my wineglass down on the table. "I'll faint."

"Thank God."

"Grandma, no, no." Milo ran to the woman's side and jerked the shirt tight across the woman's chest. "This isn't that sort of establishment."

"What's that?" She cupped her ear.

"No nudes!" Max shouted helpfully.

"Prudes!" Grandma scoffed. "I have no time for them." Her eyes scanned the room and landed on me. Or at least I thought they did. Reid went absolutely still behind me. "Lover?"

Without missing a beat, Reid flipped me around and smashed his mouth against mine, digging his hands into my ass so hard I was going to have bruises. One minute I was standing, the next he was slamming me onto the table and silverware went flying, clattering to the floor. A plate was making a permanent indent in my back, but I didn't care.

Because not only was Reid a movie star—he kissed like one.

You know those kisses you see on TV? Where you wonder if the kiss is as good as it looks?

It is. Trust me, it so. Is. My entire body trembled with delight. For a brief second I forgot where we were—or that we had an audience.

His mouth was aggressive while his tongue was smooth and calculated as it invaded my mouth with such finesse that I wanted to eat the poor man alive.

"That's enough," Max hissed from somewhere in the room.

Reid pulled back, face flushed. "Sorry."

"Huh?" Seriously, the building could have caught on fire and I still would have been trying to figure out a way to pull the guy back on top of me and wrap my legs around his body—trapping both of us until we burst into flames.

"Damn." Grandma snapped her fingers. "Didn't know I'd been replaced."

I choked. "Replaced?"

Reid's expression was pained. "If you care about me as a human being, you'll lie. And make it good."

"What will you give me?" I whispered out of the corner of my mouth.

"Really?" He pinched my ass. "I don't know—a place to live so you don't have to roam the streets and live in a cardboard box with Otis while eating people's leftover hotdogs?"

"Grandma!" I yelled and opened my arms wide. "We haven't met! I'm Reid's girlfriend, Jordan." Yeah, that little lie felt way too easy to tell.

The grandma in question glared and flipped me off, then waddled over to the table and started chugging wine.

Max winked. "She'll get over it. She gets very attached to her boy toys, though. She's just sad because poor Reid was so broken after playtime."

"So many things in that sentence that will probably scar me forever," Reid said under his breath. "Thanks, man."

Max nodded. "So shall we order?"

"Damn it!" Grandma slammed her fist onto the table.

Jason poured her another glass of wine. "Here you go, sport."

"He was my favorite," she said, disappearing behind a glassy-eyed stare. "That boy's mouth."

A horrified expression crossed Reid's face while I sent him a judgmental stare. "You're literally every publicist's nightmare. Not only are we lying to the press but now we have a sexually frustrated grandmother we have to please?"

"There is no pleasing her." Reid knocked back a glass of whiskey. "Believe me. At one point I thought trying it would be the only way to escape."

"And?" I crossed my arms.

"I ended up taking her Xanax and threatening to kill myself if she didn't release me from her clutches."

"No way." I fought to hold in my laugh. "So what happened?"

"She called my bluff . . . and her pills weren't labeled correctly. Apparently Grandma likes to get high—a lot. They were . . . happy pills, and for thirty minutes I thought I was a mama eagle training my eaglets to take flight. Oh, and by training I mean I was under the impression I needed to show by example."

Max came up and slapped him on the back. "He tried to jump off the roof."

I gasped.

"Chill with the hero worship." Max shrugged. "It was ten feet. Home skillet would have been just fine."

"Where's the damn waiter?" Grandma shouted. Somehow the wine bottle was empty, and her lips were red. She was the antivampire—the picture you showed children in order to get them to realize vampires weren't cool but terrifying and covered with liver spots.

"So . . ." Max squeezed Reid's shoulder. "Do you concede?"

Reid's nostrils flared, his jaw clenched in a hard line. "Never."

Max lifted a glass into the air. "Then shall we toast?"

Reid slammed his glass against Max's. "May the best man win." At this point I was a bit confused as to what winning entailed. It almost seemed like it was more of a competition between how long Reid could torture Max before he broke. After all, Reid and I were still in a situation where we had to pretend to be in a relationship, so really all Reid had accomplished with his silly taunt was keeping Max from sex for a few extra months.

"He already has," Max offered in a bored tone. "Trust me, a few weeks of trying to tame this one—" He paused and offered an apologetic smile. "No offense, small fry, but when I went through your stuff, I didn't even find red underwear. It wouldn't hurt you to try to look sexy, just sayin'." He shifted his eyes to Reid while I was ready to scratch his eyes out. "And you'll back down, they always do. At least until this whole media storm blows over. You guys will have had some good times, right? Playing house while living in hell." He chuckled.

Reid let out a bitter laugh. "Please, all I have to do is make everyone believe I care about her. How hard can it be?"

Something inside me snapped. It's not like Reid owed me anything. I mean, for the most part I was semi in his debt, but hearing his lack of interest from his lips still made me flinch and my heart skip with disappointment.

Because he was gorgeous.

And even though I was no longer invisible to him.

I'd turned into something else much worse.

A game.

A means to an end.

And I knew it would end. He'd walk away happy as a clam, successful, rich, even more famous. And I'd still be lonely, at home with my dog and my plant. I needed to stop focusing on what I'd be losing and think about what I'd be gaining.

More money.

I knocked back more wine.

A promotion.

Someone filled up my glass again.

An impeccable reputation!

More chugging.

"I like her," Max whispered. "She drinks when she freaks out. Does she know any party tricks?"

I ignored his jab and met Reid's stare. "We've got this."

He reached for my hand and squeezed. "Of course we do."

# CHAPTER TWELVE

## REID

Of course, as life—or the universe—would have it, the minute the words *of course we do* left my mouth, a few cameras went off.

Several screams followed.

And to save time and the embarrassment of retelling the story and suffering through it for a second time, I'll condense.

Grandma's shirt flew off, landing on Jason's head.

Midtoss, the shirt grazed the candle, landing near Jason's hand and causing second-degree burns.

Max, trying to be helpful, threw wine in Jason's general direction.

Jason, before the wine could reach him, stopped, dropped, and rolled. This is where I pause the story and say, kids, Jason made the right choice in this situation, and at any other time we'd be talking about the importance of fire safety.

What Jason didn't know was that Grandma had used the commotion as a way to slink under the table and make her way on all fours in my direction.

Jason landed on her.

Her wig covered her face.

She felt man.

And just went for it.

Let's pause again. An on-fire Jason is being held down by a freakishly strong elderly woman with smeared lipstick and a thirst that can't be quenched.

Oh, and there are cameras.

Somehow, Milo managed to grab Grandma before anything illegal and not very biblical took place.

Colton tried to usher the paparazzi out of the private room.

And everything seemed to be dying down.

Until Max.

You'll hear me say that a lot. *Until Max. Because of Max.* That's my life. I'm used to it by now, or I should be.

But what he did in that moment was so unforgivable he's lucky he's not walking funny.

"Jordan!" he yelled. "How dare you! I'm to be married! Married!" he screeched, then dumped water on her hair. Immediately her hair started fighting against the constraints of whatever flimsy pins she'd put in it to fasten it down.

It popped out of its bun.

Cameras went crazy.

I rushed over to her, tripping over Jason, who was still on the floor rolling and smoking like a sausage.

My hands reached out to grab something to stabilize myself. That something just happened to be Jordan's wrap dress.

I fell.

And took the dress down with me.

Leaving her exposed for the world to see.

"Huh." Max knocked back another glass of wine. "Didn't take her for the corset type of girl, but look at that—black!" He lifted his glass toward me. "Black lingerie for the win, bro!"

"Reid!" Jordan shrieked at the top of her lungs.

I slowly released her dress and winced as I used Jason's head to help myself to my feet. Jordan's cheeks bright red.

"Bravo!" Grandma shouted as she made her way out from under the table. "What a show!"

I groaned as Jordan hurriedly covered herself up and seethed in my direction. Body trembling, she looked like she was ready to burst into tears.

"Jordan, I'm—"

"Don't!" she hissed.

•  •  •

"It's not that bad," I said helpfully as Jordan slammed a newspaper onto the breakfast bar a few days later. Quite honestly I'd thought the worst was over and Jordan had managed to do what she did best and spin the story into something that even I would believe—we were acting out a scene from the movie.

It was the only way to explain the craziness of the situation.

But, as luck would have it—or should I say, Jordan's luck—it was leaked that there was no grandmother in the movie, with the help, I'm sure, of Max's talking to reporters, and, well, suddenly all the pictures surfaced. I coughed into my coffee, the noise distracting me from Jordan's seething. She'd been living with me for four days and already we'd stumbled into a routine. She made coffee, I made breakfast, and no words were spoken until both were consumed. It worked.

She cursed as she turned the paper over.

I winced. "I mean you look great naked, so . . ."

Jordan's nostrils flared. "The headline says 'Trouble in Shrewland'!"

I made a face behind my coffee cup. "Right. Let's focus on the positive. Any publicity is good publicity, right?"

She slammed her hand onto the newspaper and pointed at the rest of the pictures. Grandma's blouse was open, Jason was on fire, wine was taking flight midair along with Jordan's hair, and I was on my knees—like either I was waiting to get knighted or my head was about to get chopped off. Then again, one could also argue that it looked like I was about to sexually please Jordan amid the chaos. That had to be good, right?

I took a sip of coffee. The silence in the kitchen was deafening. I'd woken up to Jordan pacing back and forth in my living room, coffee in hand, arguing with someone I could only assume was her boss on the phone.

The dark circles under her eyes screamed no sleep.

And I had to report to set in about a half hour.

Meaning, she was on her own as far as our publicity was concerned, which was kind of nice, if you asked me. Having Jordan was like having my own personal OnStar button. I pressed her, she dealt with the drama, and I was free to work without stress.

I cracked my neck and went to pour myself another cup of coffee while Jordan continued silently fuming, her fingernails making an irritating tap, tap noise against the granite.

She stopped tapping.

And for some reason, the hair on the back of my arms stood at full attention. "Jordan?" I asked without turning around. "Don't do anything crazy, okay?"

"Reid . . ." Her voice was syrupy sweet. I'd always hated sweet things—candy, ice cream—and holy shit, this was why: because after you eat something sweet you always feel sick. My stomach rolled.

"Yes?" I said hoarsely.

"Your brother was on a reality show . . . yes?"

Dread pumped through my system. "Uh-huh."

"And you were one of the producers, right? On *Love Island*?"

I backed away slowly. "Sure, but that doesn't mean anything, right? Hey, Jordan, I need to go—"

"Stop!" she yelled in a low voice. "Right there."

I did.

"Turn."

Hanging my head, I slowly turned around. "Whatever you're thinking, it's not going to work! I'm a professional, I still have two more weeks of filming and—"

Her toothy grin was captivating albeit terrifying.

"How do you seduce a woman?"

"Huh?" My jaw snapped shut, then opened. "Not what I was expecting, but okay . . . you give her compliments, buy her drinks, tell her she's—" I stopped talking as fear trickled down my spine, leaving me a little shaky. I crossed my arms as her eyebrows shot higher and higher at my explanations. "What? What's wrong?"

"They want a story." Jordan bit down on her bottom lip. "So we're going to be the ones to tell it."

"I'm confused."

"Two weeks of complete access . . ." Jordan clapped her hands. "It's perfect! We'll air little snippets of your"—she snorted—"advice on taming."

I nodded. "That could work."

"You have a YouTube channel?"

"No."

"Oh, then we'll just put it up on Twitter."

I frowned.

"Facebook?"

"I'm never on."

"Do you have the Internet?" she said slowly, her mouth enunciating each word like I was three years old and still couldn't sound out *cat*.

I rolled my eyes. "Of course I have Internet."

"Right, but do you use it?"

I shifted on my feet. "I'm busy, I don't have time to tweet or get online and share pictures on the instogram!"

Her eyes widened in what I could only assume was horror as she covered her face. "Instagram, Reid, it's Instagram!"

"Why does this matter?"

"Because!" She slammed her fist onto the table. "I refuse to let you take me down! I'm the best damn publicist in the business and you WILL be successful even if I have to hold your hand and kick you in the ass the entire time!"

"Violent," Max yelled through the wall. "I can dig."

She started pacing in front of me. "This is all my fault! Normally on the first day I grab all the passwords to your social media sites and start scheduling posts about whatever project you're working on to get you to connect with your audience, but I've been so stressed with this shrew business and . . ." She placed her hands on her hips and huffed out a breath.

I set my coffee on the counter and leaned against it. "Jordan, it's going to be fine. So, you hook me up with social media, and we—what?"

Jordan grinned, took a sip of coffee, and winked. It was a hell of a turn-on, that smoky look she was giving me, but I knew, in my gut, it meant bad things for me and all my male parts.

"Why, Reid," she said in a low voice. "We give the people what they want." She stalked toward me, then trailed her fingertips down my chest.

I shuddered out a strained breath as my eyes took in her button-down shirt. One more button and I could see her breasts. Two more and I could grab—

Jordan snapped her fingers. "Eyes up here, focus."

"Huh?"

A soft finger tilted my chin, like I was getting inspected. "You gush about how you're trying to seduce me, how you're treating me, how all men should treat the women in their lives, even the difficult ones. We do a few videos for YouTube, post to Facebook, hell, we'll even do a few exclusive interviews. We hit it hard for the next two weeks, and by the time I'm finished with you, every woman in America is going to want to have your love child."

"Oh, good." I gulped. "Because that's what every little boy dreams of when they're little. Forget being a firefighter, Mom. I want to be a whore!"

"Shh." Jordan released my chin and slapped my chest. "How hard can it be? With eyes like that, you're a natural. Just do what you normally do to get chicks: throw some poetry in the mix, some chocolate, and some personal advice from yours truly and we're going to have the world eating out of your hand. Reid Emory." She nodded slowly. "America's newest heartthrob. So sweet it hurts."

My balls were tingling, like they're prone to do when the male body senses danger. I took another step toward the door. "Okay, but . . . you can't freak out when it works."

"Works?" She frowned.

I grabbed my keys and smirked. "When you want me so desperately you can't think of anything else except finding ways to rip my pants off and crawl into my bed."

"Oh, please!" She snorted. "If you're done dreaming"—she pointed to a nonexistent watch on her left hand—"you should get to set. I'll meet you there after I send out the press release."

I froze. "You'll meet me? Why?"

She grinned. "Because I'm your shrew . . . and you're seducing me, taming me, showing me how big bad boy actors get shit done. It may be fake, but it's a love story and people want to believe in love. Look at *The Bachelor*! Almost every single couple breaks up, yet this last season was the highest rated in history. People want to believe it's real even if they know the facts point in an entirely different direction. Your movie is a love story, but if they think it's not just a movie but your life, we can drum up some incredible PR. Now, you better knock my socks off during your first break today. Because it's going to be the first thing America sees. Welcome to day one, soldier."

"I don't remember signing up for the army. Or boot camp, for that matter."

Jordan gave me a knowing grin. "Welcome to Hollywood."

# CHAPTER THIRTEEN

## JORDAN

It was the perfect plan. The type of plan that would solidify the promotion. I'd been so terrified of being in the public eye that I'd forgotten what it could actually do to help Reid. If I controlled what the media saw and was able to time everything myself, then I wouldn't be as stressed. It was so perfect that I was irritated with myself that I hadn't come up with it sooner. Give the people what they want, just like Max said. And what did they want?

What I told them they wanted, that's what!

Women want an actor they can identify with. They want the next Channing Tatum, the next Ryan Reynolds. The hot guy who loves his wife or significant other, has gorgeous babies, smiles all the time, and is both sexual and sexy. Never over-the-top, always willing to party with Jimmy Fallon, and so thankful they're in blockbuster movies that they feel the need to blurt said thankfulness on social media on a daily basis. They're kind, selfless, buy groceries, and never party on the weekend.

I was creating the perfect actor.

I had no idea if Reid was any of those things. Was he nice? Yes, he saved me from homelessness.

Did he love his family? Of course! One could even say he loves others' families too! Grandma, anyone? Ha!

Was he dedicated to his career? How could he not be? Since he took in his poor shrewlike publicist and was teaching her the art of seduction?

My fingers flew across the keyboard as I put together his press release, including all the information about how breakout star Reid Emory was going above and beyond the role of a lifetime and truly dedicating both his mind and heart to his craft. He wasn't just taming the shrew—he was going to be taking her, or me, with him to all public events.

I threw in a few key details about the movie as well as some of the reviews his show had gotten on Broadway. It was about piquing people's interest, making them want to interview him. What makes Reid Emory tick? And why was it imperative the public not only see him for who he really was, but adore him?

I was brilliant.

And the best part? I wasn't asking him to be anything he wasn't already! Did I feel slightly guilty that he'd be forced to act like someone he wasn't in some situations? No. That would be like feeling guilty for putting on makeup every day. I have eyes, you just can't see them very well without eyeliner. Does that mean that my eyes don't exist? No, it just means they exist better with my black Nars pencil!

I giggled out loud and took another sip of coffee.

"I recognize that laugh well!" Max yelled from the other apartment. "Don't you work?"

He coughed twice. "Doctor's appointment?"

"Right, and I'm naked."

He was quiet. And then: "Does Reid know?"

I took a soothing deep breath and licked my lips. "Look, if you have something to say, just come over and say it rather than yelling through these paper-thin walls."

He didn't answer.

Which led me to assume he was done bothering me.

I learned very quickly one should never assume where Max was concerned. The door to the apartment opened and Max waltzed through holding two Starbucks cups.

It was like he knew my thoughts.

My eyes narrowed. "How'd you know?"

He handed me a cup and shrugged his muscled shoulders. The man wore a suit well, and I was pretty sure he was aware of it. "I'm Max."

"Right." I took the cup and sniffed. "Caramel macchiato?"

He gave a firm nod and sat next to me. "Typical default Starbucks drink, because who doesn't like them? Also, a test. If you hate them, we can't be friends anymore."

"I wasn't aware we were friends to begin with."

"I've always made friends easily." He leaned back on the couch, his eyes gazing out the window. "It's Reid I worry about. Like a mother hen."

"Mm-kay." I stood. "Well, your concern is noted. So if there's nothing else, why don't you just . . ." I made a scoot motion with my hands.

"You're pretty." Max licked his full lips. "I'll give you that much. At least when you have a rope tying that hair together, or a metal clamp."

"Also known as a rubber band."

"Ah, made of steel, is it?" He took a long gulp of coffee. "I know what's going to happen here. I've read the book a billion times, mainly because I wrote it."

"You wrote a book?"

"It's for sale on my website, MaximusHightower4Prez.com."

I burst out laughing.

He didn't.

Taking another drink, I finally sat back down and waited. I figured it was best to let him get whatever he needed off his chest and just go with it.

"So what's going to happen, Max?"

"You'll slowly fall for each other. Something will rip you apart, maybe a misunderstanding, a possible blast from the past from an ex-lover? Who knows? You'll argue in the elevator. Share a heated kiss. Slam doors. But wait!" He thrust his hand into the air. "You live together and you could just swear," he said, shaking his head, "that each time he breathes, nay, each time he moves in his bed, it's because he misses you beside him. So you pop out from underneath your covers, because of course you're curious . . ." He set his cup on the coffee table and leaned forward. "He opens his eyes the minute you walk in. The air is thick with tension."

I gulped as my erratic pulse picked up.

"He checks you out like you're the only woman in the world, and you return the favor, eyeing his sexy six-pack, his built chest, and then your eyes home in on his lips, those perfect, full lips." Max leaned forward, his cologne floating off him, hitting me square in the face. "You want him. Badly. And you know he wants you too. You don't know who moves first. You? Him? Does it matter?"

I shivered.

"Mouth hot and urgent, desperate to take you to places you've never been. He moans, you deepen the kiss as his fingers dig into your hips, the primal need he has for you awakens. And. You. Just. Can't"—his voice was a hoarse whisper—"stop."

My palms flinched with the sudden need to touch Reid.

Max's grin was shameless. "Oh, I know the story, Jordan. The sex won't just be average. It will blow every fantasy you've ever had out of the water. And then . . ." He sighed. "Just when things are getting good. It breaks. Good things always break, and it's always up to the two people in a relationship to fix it, to make it work, but you'll have nothing to fall back on. No friendship, nothing. So when it breaks for you two, it shatters. You'll fight. Say things you don't mean. And then you'll leave in tears. He'll be lonely. Famous, but lonely. And you'll swear to yourself never to trust a man again." He finished his coffee and clasped his hands together. "Now. What are you going to do about it?"

"Huh?" I felt dazed. Owned. And somehow manipulated, like I was at a fair and Max was the hypnotist telling me I was a chicken.

"Aw." He patted my hand. "Good talk. I just wanted to make sure you understood how this would end. I feel it's my job to emotionally prepare you for the road ahead. Fall you will." He shrugged. "How could you not? Swear your hair's probably already picking wedding colors."

I slapped his hand away as he tried to grab a bit of my curly mess. "I'm his publicist. Not his girlfriend. And this isn't a romance novel, which by the way is pretty much what you just described. This is real life. Things like that don't happen in real life. Believe me, I know."

"What will I get?"

"Max, would it kill you to ask direct questions?"

He tapped his chin. "Yes."

I growled.

"When I'm right." He picked up his empty cup and stood. "When you come over to my apartment sobbing like a Taylor Swift concert attendee. I'll tell you what—I won't get anything for being right, but I will let you sleep on the couch. When it all goes south."

I snorted. "You're just trying to convince me to back off so that you can have sex with your fiancée again. I won't fall for it."

"Okay." Max pulled me in for a jerky hug. "But remember our chat. Oh, and you spilled coffee on your white shirt. That one of your things?"

"Crap!" I stomped my heel.

He held up his hands. "Cold water, not hot."

"Go home!"

"Pfft." Max winked. "I have work this afternoon; this world doesn't run itself."

Just let it run Max-less. Amen.

"Toodles." He waved and slammed the door behind him while I was left feeling a bit turned on by the thought of me and Reid kissing in his bedroom. Ugh!

"Max!" I seethed. He was just trying to get into my head. That's what people like him did. For crying out loud, he set his own brother up to be a laughingstock!

This was my job.

I worked with attractive actors on a daily basis.

Working with another one?

Not going to be a problem.

I used cold water on the stain, threw on a white blazer, and shoved my black sunglasses on my face. Making sure I had the apartment key and my red purse, I confidently pressed the elevator button and waited.

And I'm happy to announce I didn't once think about the elevator fight.

Or the kiss.

Or the moment in the bedroom.

Or the way Reid's hands would feel on my hips.

Nope. Not once.

But twice.

"Damn, Max," I cursed, walking out into the New York sun.

I quickly sent a text to Reid.

```
Me: Your brother is certifiably insane.
Has he been locked up before?

Reid: Arkham Asylum wouldn't take him.

Me: This saddens me.
```

Reid: Just don't ask him anything related to the Joker. You'll get a hell of a long answer.

Me: I'm stopping by in a few minutes. Be ready to wow me, lover boy, this shit's going public.

Reid: I like it when you say shit and lover boy in the same sentence. Do it again.

Me: Shitty lover boy.

Reid: I stepped into that one HA ^^^ See what I did there? Genius.

I fought a smile and rolled my eyes.

Me: Just do what you normally do when seducing the poor soulless women of Manhattan and we'll be just fine. Also, I'm scheduling a date for us tonight. There will be cameras. So make sure the charm is on.

Reid: It's never off.

Me: Arrogance part of your charm?

Reid: Yes. GTG, break over.

Me: Later, lover.

Reid: Later, Sebastian.

I burst out laughing as I collided with someone else.

"Watch out!" the man yelled.

I held up my phone and mouthed *sorry* before making my way down the street. Reid and Max didn't just live in one of the most expensive parts of Manhattan—they lived in THE most expensive part, where it wouldn't be weird to see a Hollywood celebrity walking a small dog.

I would hate them both if I wasn't so thankful that I actually had a roof over my head that wasn't made up of neon lights and smelled like Chinese takeout.

The day felt like a fresh start. I was stain-free thanks to Max. My white-on-white top with leather leggings was chic and very early fall thanks to my shopping addiction.

And I was about to make Reid Emory the most sought-after actor on the planet.

What could possibly go wrong?

# CHAPTER FOURTEEN

## REID

"That kiss was so not convincing," Mona whispered. "Seriously, what's wrong with you?"

My apartment.

With a hot frizzy-haired sexually repressed homeless person. Right, say that out loud and see if it doesn't land you in the psych ward.

"Sorry," I grumbled. "I'm tired."

"Well, grab a Red Bull and make that kiss feel real!" Mona was Indian and had the most gorgeous mocha skin and thick brown hair. She'd taken Bollywood by storm and was on her third blockbuster hit in the United States. "Bud will know something's wrong."

Bud, our very anal director, had been on a tirade all morning because it looked like it might rain and he wanted to shoot another kissing scene in the park.

I yawned behind my hand.

Mona elbowed me.

"Take fifteen." The PA slated the scene again and walked off while I gazed longingly into Mona's eyes.

"I love you," I whispered. "I didn't mean it. What I said."

Mona's thick eyelashes fluttered before she leaned up on her tiptoes. "Prove it."

Our mouths met.

It was nice.

That's it. I was kissing an A-list star and all I could think of was "nice." You know, like when you get dressed up in nice clothes for dinner. Nice. Nice as in, *oh, that purple tulip sure is nice!*

Shit!

"Cut!"

I rubbed my face with my hands.

"Reid!" Bud yelled. "Where the hell is your head?"

If I said, "In my ass," would that get me fired?

"Sorry, Bud." I faked a yawn so he'd think I was tired. "I'll do better."

"Hey, Bud." The AD ran over. "The lighting's really good by the bridge. We should move if we want to get that shot."

"Thirty minutes!" Bud yelled. "Reid, get your shit together and be ready for the kissing scene in thirty minutes."

I nodded, hanging my head. I'd never had issues getting into character. Nor had I ever had a problem kissing an attractive woman. I was a guy. They had a name for male actors who had issues kissing women with passion. The word is *fired*.

But I seriously was not feeling that scene, or Mona.

"Practice?" she offered with a helpful shrug.

"Nah." I exhaled. "I'm going to go take a power nap, do a few pushups, bang my chest, take a shot of whiskey, hell, I don't know. I'll figure it out. Thanks, though."

Mona cracked a smile. "Maybe just the nap, Reid. We all know you're a man. No need to get drunk or bang your chest to prove yourself."

"Good advice. Quite sound," I teased.

"I'm mom to three boys," she whispered in a low voice. "I know things."

"Mona!" John yelled. "Your nanny called. Something about one of the young terrorists flushing the goldfish down the toilet? Alive?"

"Aw, hell." Mona moved away. "Speak of the devil."

I laughed and watched her get on the cell the PA held out to her and start talking in a mom tone about flushing things down the toilet. I had to admit that tone had inflicted terror in my heart as a child.

Smiling, I turned on my heel and went back to my trailer.

The door was slightly ajar.

When I pulled it all the way open, I found Jordan. Typing furiously on a laptop, black-rimmed glasses askew, and hair pulled back into a high ponytail that made her look so damn cute I couldn't stop smiling.

"Taking over the world, I see?" I stepped into the trailer and shut the door.

Jordan glanced up and grinned over the computer screen. "Yeah, well, I thought it would piss Max off, so . . . here I am. Give me his social and I'll do some real damage."

"Ha. Sell my brother out? Where do I sign up?" My eyes zeroed in on the still steaming Starbucks cup next to her. "Please tell me that's mine."

Jordan smirked. "You gotta play harder to get, champ."

"I'm easy. Shh, don't say it out loud, Grandma may hear." I shuddered outwardly. Saying her name always left me traumatized.

"Speaking of Grandma. I found her a home!"

I nearly spit out my coffee. "What? Why? Not that I mind, just tell me it's in Siberia and we're getting married right here, right now and naming our firstborn Maxine to spite my evil brother."

"Er . . ." Jordan winced, her cute lips forming a little pout. "Close. Jersey, okay?"

"Are we talking ten-minutes-away Jersey or—"

"We're talking a few hours' drive Jersey in a nice little town where people still get stuck behind cows on their way to work and honk their horns to say hello."

I took a long sip of coffee; it burned down my throat. "Hmm, can she escape? They have fences? GPS trackers? Guards? Alcatraz." I sniffed. "That's a damn pipe dream and you know it."

"I said a home, not prison, Reid. She'll have to commit a crime to go to Alcatraz and even then it's sadly no longer an option for us. Sorry, I can't work miracles. I have to admit, after meeting her I figured it would be smart to send her away for a few months while you film so close to her hometown, and she was more than thrilled to go when I showed her the picture of the activities director, who's in his late twenties, sandy brown hair. She sighed and asked if he did private lessons."

Someone knocked loudly on my trailer. "Fifteen minutes, Mr. Emory."

I let out a long sigh and set my coffee down.

"What?" Jordan shut her laptop and crossed her arms. "You have actor eyes."

"What?" I jerked my gaze to hers. "Is that a thing?"

"It's a thing."

"You sure?"

"Look, I'm a publicist, I'm saying it's a thing. Now, why the *Oh, no, they're going to fire me and I'm going to have to give back the doughnuts I stole this morning on set* look?"

"I don't steal doughnuts. I eat them. All of them," I pointed out. "And what is your fixation with food?" I stretched out on the couch and put my hands behind my head. "And I lost the sizzle."

"Ah, the sizzle blues." She leaned back against the couch and set her leather-clad legs up on the coffee table. "I know them well."

"Oh, yeah?"

"Last year." Jordan held up a manicured hand—it was pretty, and distracting, and did I mention pretty? How were hands so fascinating?

Her long slender fingers waved in the air before she thrust one in my direction. "He had the sizzle blues, couldn't heat things up with his latest costar, and was terrified it would show on camera—which it always does, I don't care how good of an actor you are."

"Wow, not helping. Not at all. You suck at this."

Jordan slapped my chest with that perfect hand. "Not finished."

I rubbed my chest where she hit.

"So this actor, let's call him . . . Max."

"Really, his name is interchangeable in so many situations," I grumbled. "Son of a Max!"

Jordan nodded. "I like it." She wiggled her heeled feet. "Anyway, the problem was that he wasn't in a relationship, hadn't been on a date in weeks, and had lost his . . . touch." Her eyebrows rose in that knowing way that had me ready to kiss her just to prove her wrong.

I squirmed uncomfortably as Max's prophetic words hit me square in the chest. Holy shit, was the universe really working against me? Was that a thing?

"So." I tugged at my shirt. "What did he do to fix this problem?"

"He went to the Victoria's Secret fashion show, hit on one of the models, kissed her, and married her two days later."

"Huh, scrappy little thing." I checked my watch. "But since I'm on a time crunch?"

Her eyes narrowed behind her thick glasses. "What's that?"

"What's what?"

"That look? And that smile, stop smiling!"

I smiled wider.

"Reid!"

"Hey, you're my shrew, you do what I say."

"That's not how this works!" Jordan wailed. "And here I was feeling sorry for you!"

"I'll make it fast."

"Oh, good." Jordan threw her hands into the air. "You'll make it fast? What girl wants to hear that? Especially when a sexy guy—" She covered her mouth with her hands.

My chest puffed up. "You think I'm sexy?"

"No." She shook her head twice, three, four times. "I meant—" Her eyebrows furrowed.

"Wow, well, while you give yourself a stroke from thinking too hard, I'm going to use you as practice. I need help and you're going to help me."

Jordan glanced at the door.

"Seriously? Now you're worried about cameras? Aren't I supposed to seduce you tonight at dinner anyway? Give pointers out on my Twitter feed?"

"That you don't have," she said through clenched teeth.

"Please?" I held my hands out in front of me. "I'll beg. I'm not above begging. I'm not one of those guys with pride for days. I will honest-to-God get on my hands and knees in desperation. I love my job. I need this job. And I need to sell that damn kiss."

Jordan made a choking sound, then jerked her glasses off her face, nearly taking a few stray pieces of frizzy dark hair with her. "Fine. But if this is going to work, I'm going to correct you on where you're going wrong and what you need to do more, all right?"

"Fine."

"Good."

I stared.

She stared back.

"Uh." Jordan's face flushed red. "Are you going to do it, or do I need to suddenly grow a pair since yours are MIA?"

I glowered and leaned in, bracing my hands on either side of her body, my chest nearly touching hers as my lips brushed her mouth.

Jordan pulled back. "Weak."

"Not done," I said through clenched teeth, then gripped her shoulders. "Just getting started."

"Wha—"

Our lips fused. She tasted like rich coffee and sugar. Swear it was more about her taste than the way her mouth felt—and it felt hot, soft. Shit, I was going to start panting. My hands moved to her face as I tried a different angle, a different dip with my tongue. Damn, she was tasting better and better.

When I pulled back, Jordan's face was white as a sheet.

"That bad?" Panic made my voice hoarse.

"Um, I'm not sure I—" Jordan gripped my shirt and launched herself against me, her mouth attacking mine with a ferocity that would have been a little frightening had it not felt so damn good I was ready to sell Max and his firstborn in order to keep experiencing it.

We broke apart. Both out of breath.

"You lied," Jordan huffed. "You don't have the sizzle blues, your sizzle is off the charts."

"Really?" I smiled. "I'm not horrible?"

"In a world full of fives, you're at least a nine."

"My shrew just loves her compliments." I kissed her mouth again— it was instinct. But to be fair, she kissed me back.

And suddenly we were making out like teenagers.

Rocking my damn trailer for the world to see.

I was just about ready to rip that blazer from her curvy body when the door opened.

"Mr. Emory, you're needed on set."

Jordan and I broke apart.

Her lipstick had completely disappeared. I'd most likely devoured all traces of it.

"Go get 'em." She winked, her voice heavy with lust.

I was worried someone was going to have to physically restrain me from jumping on her when a throat cleared. "Mr. Emory. Now."

I almost gave the PA the finger but knew my publicist, aka the best kisser in the universe, would be pissed.

Besides, what the hell was I doing?

She wasn't my girlfriend.

Or a real shrew.

Or anything.

She shrugged and picked up her computer like we hadn't just been ready to rip each other's clothes off.

Right. I was her job.

I needed to remember that.

A job.

A means to an end.

"Let's do it." I slapped the PA on the back and made my way to set.

It took us one take to get the kiss.

"Cut!"

"Damn," Mona whispered under her breath. "That must have been some girl you were thinking about to get you that hot and bothered."

"Ha-ha." I laughed. I had to. Because I wasn't thinking about just anyone. No, I was thinking about my very off-limits publicist with the crazy hair and an inability to keep it contained.

I was thinking about her coffee stains.

About her tight leather pants.

Her high heels.

And again her hair, it was big enough to need at least two thoughts.

Her lips.

Her soft moans.

"Shit," I muttered.

"What?" Mona winked. "Problem?"

"Nope!" I lied.

Hell, yes, there was a problem. I was falling for someone who was very much off-limits, someone I needed to NOT screw. My career really did depend on her ability to do a good job.

I gulped.

It would be fine. As long as I remembered it wasn't real. It was fake. Everything I did with her was fake.

Fake.

Fake.

Fake.

"Huh?" Mona asked.

Shit, I'd said that out loud. "Take." I licked my lips. "Let's do another take."

# CHAPTER FIFTEEN
## JORDAN

Our kiss had lasted twelve minutes.

It had taken place more than six hours ago.

And my hands were still shaking.

It had taken every ounce of willpower I had not to give his snotty little PA the finger and lock the door to the trailer. It was a bit terrifying how much his kiss affected me, and not in a healthy way.

Not at all.

His kiss made me want to smother him.

In an *I love this so much I may end up killing the person who brings me pleasure* kind of way.

Terrifying, to say the least.

I was the mama who accidentally sat on her young and smothered them. Yup, that's me. His kiss made me that desperate, which just proved the point that when this was all over with, I needed to find a nice young man and go on a date.

Reid was supposed to meet me at the restaurant bar. But before that, I needed to give Ren all the details of my publicity plan.

After a two-hour meeting where, after the fact, I had to change out of my shirt because I was sweating so much, Ren decided that I was brilliant.

My strategy was simple—plaster Reid and our relationship everywhere. Make people believe he was a dedicated actor who was truly trying to seduce the socks off me while making me approachable for other men, and well, what could go wrong? Nothing. Again, I controlled the narrative, not the other way around. Besides, it could have been a nightmare, because who knew what kind of crazy broad Reid could have ended up with? And even though I'd dug my heels into the ground and nearly strangled him to death when he said my name, the ball was going to always be in my court, so I had nothing to worry about.

I even had a staged breakup planned after a few weeks that I'd be able to spin in Reid's favor. Reid gave me confidence, he made my heart soar, it's just meant to soar in another direction. Blah, blah, blah.

Brilliant.

"Damn," a voice whispered in my ear, lips grazing the edges, making my body shiver with excitement. "You look killer in black. And don't even get me started on those heels. Your legs would look so good . . ." He stopped talking and flipped me around to face him. "Sorry, finishing that sentence would have been borderline inappropriate due to our publicist-client relationship." Reid winked.

While I nearly choked on my spit and begged him to finish what he was going to say.

I didn't realize my mouth was open until he nudged it closed with his thumb and winked.

"Er." Oh, good, lots of brilliance coming from my end. "How was work?"

Shoot me now.

Reid gave me a curious stare, then waved the bartender over. "Well, you'll be happy to know the kiss was awesome, thanks to your tutelage."

"Mama's so proud," I teased.

"Yeah, poorer words have never been chosen." Reid nodded. "Seriously, you kissed me, you didn't make my lunch, Jordan."

I winced. Did I really just compare myself to his mother? After visually assaulting his body with my eyes?

"What can I get you?" the bartender asked.

"Rum and Coke for this one." He pointed to me. "Make it a double, and I'll have a gin and tonic with two limes."

I purposefully ignored the fact that he remembered my drink and crossed my arms. "Two limes. Go wild. That's what I always say."

"I almost said three but didn't want to freak you out." Reid casually leaned against the bar and gazed out at the patrons. "This place is pretentious and filled with trust fund babies, you know this, right?"

"All part of the plan." I eyed all the twentysomethings and their inability to put down their phones. "Trust."

Our drinks arrived.

"Shall we?" Reid held out his arm. "I mean, I take it we are eating, right?"

"Dinner and a show." I nodded. "It's what we promised."

"We?"

"Me."

"To?"

"Does it matter?" I fired back, enjoying our little exchange. "That is the mission, if you choose to accept it."

"Somebody's been watching too much *Mission: Impossible*, but I'll bite." He turned his aqua eyes in my direction.

I stopped walking and took a slow sip of my drink. Top-shelf. Did I mention he remembered my order? Yes?

"Just do what you normally do during a date. The mission is to get you trending on Twitter. The only way to do that? Be THAT date."

"That?"

"Yup."

"I don't understand whatever language you're speaking. You're cute as hell when you get that *I want to take over the world* look on your face. But I'm completely lost."

"Grand gestures," I explained. "Doing something out of the ordinary. Making girls swoon and guys want to punch you in the throat."

"Guys always want to punch me in the throat." Reid shrugged.

"Have I mentioned how much I love your humility?"

"Fine." Reid ignored me and looked around the restaurant as we made our way to the hostess stand. "Big gestures, like roses?"

I frowned. "Reid, roses? Roses are for pubescent preteens who have acne and headgear! I'm talking flash mob, breaking out into song, getting down on one knee, reciting a freaking poem!"

The more I talked, the more Reid paled.

"You have done things that like before, right? To get the girl?"

Reid tugged at his collar while my hand clenched tighter around my glass. "Reid?"

"Hmm?" he croaked, then downed the rest of his drink as his shifty eyes glanced at the door. If he made a run for it, I was going to throw my shoe at his head; that would at least get something going on social media.

"Reid."

He motioned me to step closer. I did.

He motioned more.

Rolling my eyes, I leaned up on my tiptoes while he whispered in my ear. "I'm slightly . . . shy."

"What?" I roared, jerking back so fast I nearly became one with the potted tree behind me.

"Shh," Reid snapped as he tried to stabilize my drunken movements. "Keep your voice down!"

"How are you shy?" I smacked him in the arm. "You're Reid Emory!"

"Shout my name a little louder. I don't think the grandpa sitting outside on the park bench heard you!"

People were already starting to stare, not enough to take pictures and give us a few choice hashtags like #pottedplantsforthewin, but enough that if Reid didn't do something awesome within the next few minutes I was going to resort to flashing someone.

I took the two straws from my drink in between my teeth and chomped. "Reid, you're an actor. Being in the public eye is part of the job."

"I get that," Reid hissed. "I just don't do public displays of affection . . ."

"Well." I slammed my hand against his chest. "You're going to have to learn, and fast. I promised media fireworks, so find your groove, Stella."

"What exactly did you promise them?" His eyes narrowed into tiny accusing slits while I greedily searched for a napkin to pat down my suddenly clammy hands.

"Romance." I shrugged a shoulder and twisted the straws with my fingers. "Fairy tale romance."

"Shit."

"Ah, there's a good start. Real great, Reid. *Shit* does not scream love!"

"Reservation?" the hostess asked. She was wearing all black, her hair was pulled back into a tight low ponytail, and I could have sworn she actually hissed the word *reservation* before taking in both my and Reid's outfits.

"Litwright," I said through clenched teeth while she continued to check Reid out longer than necessary. Animal possessiveness washed over me before I managed to gain control of my emotions and put one foot in front of the other instead of cheerfully up her ass.

"Right this way."

"Creepy smile alert," Reid said under his breath. "Good job wearing your emotions on your sleeve, Joker. I can almost feel your need to bitch slap the poor thing."

I waved him off, dropping the smile and returning to business mode.

Reid put his hand on my lower back as we walked toward the middle of the restaurant, a prime location for him to do something epic. Though his epic and my epic were two very different things. For the love of cheese. *Roses?*

Reid held out my chair while the hostess placed a napkin on my lap.

"Chew that straw any harder and you're going to get plastic on your teeth," Reid joked, taking his seat.

"Your dining companion will be with you shortly," the hostess said in a seductive voice, aimed directly at Reid.

"Companion?" he asked, his eyebrows shooting up.

"Sorry." Sorry, my ass, she sounded anything but sorry. "What lower-end restaurants call a waiter."

"Oh." Reid pressed his lips together while I tried not to bark out a laugh. "How . . . lucky for us."

She nodded and walked off.

Reid shook his head over the menu. "We get a companion tonight. Wonder if they charge extra for a happy ending? Dessert?"

"No," a cultured British accent announced. "We do, however, charge for food, so if you can't afford to eat here, I suggest you take your drinks to the bar and enjoy some peanuts."

"Allergic," Reid coughed into his hand, hiding his laugh. He eyed the short man up and down before turning his attention to me. "Is rudeness part of the experience?"

The man huffed.

I nodded. "I think the accents are extra as well."

Our waiter—or companion—started turning red.

Reid grinned. "A bottle of your house wine. Wouldn't want to go broke in such a fancy place, shucks." So apparently Reid was now from Texas. "I just wish Grandpop could see all the fancy folk. It's a treat, a real treat!"

I had to look at my menu to keep from bursting out laughing.

"If that will be all for now?" Our companion snorted. I glanced at his name tag.

"Fred." I nodded. "Thanks, Fred, we'll also start with the calamari."

"Gah!" Reid hit his hand on his jeans. "Don't suppose you got some crawfish to wet my whistle too?"

"Crawfish," Fred repeated. "Yes, I'll go check with the cook. Perhaps he fetched some out of the gutter."

"You're a real gem." Reid winked. Then, honest to God, he slapped the waiter's ass as he walked off.

I reached for my drink. Empty.

"I think it's an Emory thing." I shook my head. "Needing alcohol to numb the experience."

"Aw, you really wanna numb this, sugar?" Reid winked and tilted back the rest of his drink, then slammed it onto the table. "Didn't you want a scene?"

"Romantic scene!" I threw my hands into the air. "Not a cameo on *Nashville*!"

Reid's eyes lit up.

"I was kidding."

Reid stood.

"Reid, sit down."

Reid didn't sit.

"You said you were shy!" I hissed.

"But I'm acting . . ." Reid grinned. "And right now . . ." He leaned over the table, pressing his hands on either side of me and kissed the top of my head. "I'm auditioning for the role of a lifetime, right? So, big gestures." He stood straight. "Watch. Me."

Panic turned into full-blown fear as Reid made his way around the table, pulled out one of the chairs, and then tugged me to my feet only to pull me into his lap.

My knee hit the table, knocking over a wineglass. Thank the wine gods it was empty.

Not that it mattered.

People were already staring.

This was NOT going the way it was supposed to.

Romance by way of a crawfish-eating southerner would not charm the pants off the ladies, though it might earn some points with the dudes.

"Darlin'," Reid said loudly, "you want romance." His lips tickled the edge of my neck as he reached around my body for my shoes.

In that moment, when his hand touched the bare skin of my arch, I realized something.

I'd completely underestimated Reid Emory.

In every way that mattered.

He held my heel by the tip of his finger, then started to sing, "Take off those heels, lie on my bed, whisper dirty secrets while I'm pulling on your hair."

Talking around us all but stopped. He was singing Chase Rice's cover of "Ride" . . . and he was owning it. And I officially stopped breathing altogether as he dropped the shoe to the ground, removed the next one, and then ran his hands up my legs, his forehead touching mine as he continued singing.

"I'm gonna ride, I'm gonna ride, I'm gonna ride, I'm gonna ride . . . on you, baby, on you, lady, all night, all night. I'm gonna take care of your body . . . I'll be gentle, don't you scream . . ."

His voice was rough, masculine, and so sexy that I wanted to hold on to the way it sounded and keep it all to myself. My chest rose and fell like I was about ready to pass out—but it was him, all him. Reid was doing that to me, making me feel weak in my knees even though I wasn't even standing.

"Yeah, girl, we can go slow." His lips teased mine between words. He smiled and taunted me with his mouth and then kept singing.

It couldn't get better—or any hotter.

And then he started moving very slowly beneath me. In. The. Chair.

I nearly hyperventilated as he mimicked parts of the song as he massaged my arms, his hands pulling down each strap of my dress to kiss my bare skin. I arched under his touch, because really, I'd have to be dead not to respond in that way.

He kept singing against my skin, his tongue tasting every inch he could until the words vibrated against me.

I shivered.

The restaurant was dead silent.

"Oh, oh, oh." He finished the song and then whispered against my lips, "How's that for a grand gesture?"

Cross-eyed and weary, as if I'd just been made love to, I managed a wobbly, "That works."

I looked up.

Cell phones everywhere.

Mine started buzzing on the table.

And then the crowd erupted with applause.

Our companion returned, his face flushed. I'm sure he was about to say we were in a restaurant, not a brothel, when our hostess returned and held out a napkin.

"I knew I recognized you! You're Reid Emory!"

"I am." His grin was tantalizing, addicting. Where the hell was that wine? I was going to have to guzzle the entire bottle to forget what just took place. My body buzzed while he signed a few autographs.

Our waiter was substantially nicer for the next hour.

By the rate my phone was buzzing I knew Reid had been a hit. His Google alert was going to kill my phone battery.

My hands shook as I scrolled through the notifications. Feminine laughter caused me to glance up.

Two women were hovering over Reid. Both of them had tight dresses on, boobs on display, with perfect complexions. Nobody would ever accuse them of being invisible. I tried not to let the fact that Reid chose to make a scene with me not because he wanted to but because he had no other choice bother me.

One of the girls ran her hand through her long brown hair while she thrust her chest out.

Reid stared.

Then again, he was a guy, not a monk—not in any sense of the word, considering the way the guy kissed.

I cleared my throat.

Both girls shot me a glare at the same time.

I raised my eyebrows. Hey, I was playing the shrew. I didn't need to play nice. I just wanted them to leave so Reid and I could finish dinner and go home. I needed sleep, with the crazy week we had ahead of us.

"Ah, I should probably finish eating. Thanks for stopping by." Reid casually dismissed the women, then turned his attention to me. "Did you growl?"

"No." I rolled my eyes and reached for my empty wineglass. "I'm just tired, and they were lingering."

"Damn, I hate lingerers," he joked.

"They're the worst," I agreed with a wink. "Refuse to read social cues."

"And always in your personal space." He shook his head. "Thank God I have you, Jordan. What would I do without you in my life?"

My eyes narrowed. "Laying it on thick."

"Dessert." He tapped his hands against the table and motioned for our companion. Fred scurried over to our table like he was in a race and losing.

"Yes? Sir? Ma'am?"

"Wow, I'm a ma'am now," I said under my breath.

"Chocolate." Reid nodded. "We need something with chocolate and a dessert wine to go with. Think you can handle that, Fred?"

"Yes, sir, right away sir."

I watched Fred retreat. "Did he bow?"

"Fred has a bald spot on the top of his head, who knew?" Reid poured some wine into my glass. "Now, what's the plan for this week? I only have a few more scenes in the city, then I have a week break before filming ends."

I chewed my lower lip. "Tomorrow we're going to do an impromptu video blog in which we'll give out relationship advice."

Reid coughed out an uncomfortable laugh. "You mean like bring roses on a date? That type of advice?"

"For the love!" I threw up my hands. "What is it with you and roses? Is that all your father taught you?"

"Hey!" Reid pointed an accusing finger in my direction. "I'll have you know my parents have been married for over thirty years!"

"Then I'm guessing roses are your mother's favorite?"

He frowned. "Yeah, but—"

"Reid." I checked my phone and turned the screen to him. "You have exactly sixteen hours to find your inner Romeo."

He nodded, then crooked his finger. I leaned in. "So I can't use the roses thing? Like at all?"

Did I really have to do everything? "Roses are dead to you," I hissed. "Shit would be better than roses. You are above roses, and I swear if you say roses one more time I'm going to run you over with a golf cart."

"You have a golf cart?"

"I was being sarcastic." I folded my hands on the table to regain control of the situation. "Just Google your ass off, and you'll be fine. But you have to be convincing—we need this to go viral. You giving normal guys advice on how to pick up a girl and . . . put your hand down, Reid, I'm not finished." He put his hand down. "Proper advice does not include bringing roses, nor does it include flashing them with their eyes, because let's be honest, that only works with you. If some dude with a lazy eye stares too hard at his crush, she's going to call the cops and he's going to end up in prison and you may be sued." I took another deep breath. "Now . . . tell me one morsel of wisdom you can give to the average Joe. Make me believe it."

Our dessert arrived at that moment.

The wine was poured.

And if Reid squinted any harder he was going to give himself an aneurysm.

"One thing, Reid. I'm not asking you to perform brain surgery on Fred or anything."

I attacked the chocolate soufflé with my spoon while Reid thought.

"Okay." He licked his lips. "To the average Joe, I'd say . . ." He folded his hands. "Bring a gift."

"Bringing a gift means you've already solidified the date." I shook my head. "Next."

"Say she's pretty."

I rolled my eyes. "This tablecloth is pretty. You gonna date the tablecloth, Reid?"

"No?"

"Is that a question?" I snapped.

"Okay, fine." He smacked my spoon with his, then dug into the chocolate. I tried not to appear as angry as I felt that he had freaking pushed my spoon away from sugar. My death grip on the spoon tightened. "Just be straight up. Will you go out with me?"

I dropped the spoon.

"That good?" He grinned.

"The last time I heard that line I was in eighth grade. Mind you, it wasn't directed at me, but it still counts. I can't believe I'm saying this, but . . . you either need to Google or go talk to Max."

"The hell I will!"

"He was a bachelor on *Love Island*. If anyone knows how to hit on a girl without getting castrated, it's him."

"I won't do it."

"You will."

"I won't!" He jerked the dessert away from the table just as I reached for it, causing my spoon to fly back at my face and chocolate to land on my dress and my cheek.

I glared.

"See . . ." He smiled and reached across the table, dipping his finger in the soufflé. "Getting stuff on your clothes is totally your thing."

Just as he was bringing his finger back, I latched on to it and then sucked the chocolate off, twirling my tongue around it, sucking in and out. Reid let out a hoarse moan and gripped the table with his free hand. "You'll talk to Max."

I licked again. Just to be sure the chocolate was gone.

"I'll talk to Max," he said, breathless. "Well played."

I dabbed the corners of my mouth. "Why, thank you."

# CHAPTER SIXTEEN

## REID

If Jason and Milo's grandma taught me anything—you know, besides the fact that you can't always outrun the elderly—it was that panicking did nothing to help the situation. So when Jordan told me I needed to hash out some romance advice, yeah, sure, I got a little nervous, but I didn't think it would be that hard.

By the time I went to bed that night, I decided that I'd think back on all my past relationships and figure out how they started.

The problem arose almost immediately when I realized: I'd never legitimately asked a woman out.

Ever.

Not even in first grade, when Sara Murf offered to share her carrot sticks and pronounced us married once I jammed one in my mouth.

It took me six months of bringing the woman ranch dip for her carrot sticks to get back into her good graces after I told her I didn't want to be her boyfriend because girls had germs.

There was also that time in high school when the vice principal trapped me in a janitor's closet and said, "Nobody has to know."

I thought she meant that nobody had to know she showed me the janitor's closet. That thought was extremely short-lived when she grabbed my hand and placed it on her ass. To be fair, she was just out of college, so it wasn't as creepy as it sounded.

And I was eighteen.

But still.

I shivered at the memory.

At least she didn't have a mustache, like Grandma. I shivered in bed and pounded my pillow with my fist.

There had to be one moment, at least one, in my short life when I actually asked a woman out and dated her.

My brain hurt.

And after another half hour of tossing and turning, the panic set in. It was slow, almost like jumping into a hot tub and midair yelling, "Oh, shit!" into the night, knowing that the heat was coming, knowing I was about as screwed as a lobster in Maine.

The worst part, if I can be completely honest, was that I'd always been extremely secure in my ability to get women, only to finally realize at age twenty-eight that I never actually pursued them in the first place.

I needed Max.

Loath as I was to admit it.

I just needed to do it in a way that he wouldn't hold over my head for an eternity.

•  •  •

There are ways to ask for favors and there are ways to ask for favors. Max was the type to whom you never actually admitted out loud that you needed help. Rather you tricked him into talking so much about a certain topic that he inevitably bragged about himself and his experiences, and then suddenly started spouting off what he considered wisdom. Really, his advice was just a lot of bullshit that he managed to make creatively smell like roses, but somehow it ended up being spot-on at least 90 percent of the time.

Damn it! There I go with the roses again.

What's the saying? Gird your loins? Yeah, I was going to do a hell of a lot of that in the next few minutes. I told Max to meet me for lunch at Shake Shack. I hoped that the sheer volume of people would deter him from either making a scene or stripping in public or landing us in jail—take your pick. Nothing was out of the question where my brother was concerned.

"Well, well, well." Max peeled off his aviator sunglasses and shook his head slowly. "The prodigal returns."

"Never left."

"And by the looks of it, he needs my help."

"No, I don't." Oh, and by the way, of all the people to gift with mind reading, God gifted Max. It's a real thing, just ask anyone who's ever met him.

"Yes, you do." Max ran a hand through his wavy dark-brown hair and grinned. A few teens standing next to us started whispering. I half expected him to turn around and pose for a picture, not that I blamed him. It was an Emory thing, females being drawn to us. Women stared, and Max had always been more than happy to let them look their fill, all the while signing their bra straps like he was a rock star. I hated that I needed Max, but if anyone could help, it was him. How the hell was I supposed to romance? Did I even know the definition of the word? "You're stalling."

"Huh?" I blinked against the sun, shielding my face with my hand.

Max motioned me toward the long lunch line. "Spit it out, we don't have all day, and by the looks of your shaky disposition the longer you keep that shit in the more susceptible you are to the elderly."

I rolled my eyes. "Please."

"Grandma loved it when you played the victim."

"You know what? Thanks for meeting me for lunch, but—" I stepped away, but Max jerked me back by my white T-shirt, nearly hanging me in the process, and shoved me toward the cash register.

"What can I get you two?" the chipper adolescent squeaked, braces flashing, black-rimmed glasses falling down her nose.

"Two burgers." Max wrapped a muscled arm around my shoulder and squeezed hard enough for my spine to pop. "A large fry to share with my lover."

"Oh, dear God." I looked heavenward, although I wasn't sure why, considering all these years God's been ignoring my plea to strike Max where he stood.

"And a strawberry milkshake . . ." He winked. "Brings all the boys to my yard, feel me?"

The girl blushed and typed in our order, then called it via the microphone. "Will that be all?"

"For now . . ." Max said, almost like a threat, though the girl seemed excited about it.

"And we're walking . . ." I shoved him toward the tables.

Our order came a few minutes later.

I stared at the fries.

And my burger.

"Spill." Max made a slurping noise through the straw, his expression bored. "I don't have all day and I need to get back to the office to make sure my new desk gets delivered to the right floor."

"New desk?"

He nodded. "The other broke."

"How?"

He grinned. "He asks how . . ." With a bout of laughter he made a spanking motion with his hand. "Taking my work home, feel me? Or maybe it's taking my home to work? Becca liked the idea of possibly getting caught, though thanks to you the only thing people may catch is a flash of boob and some heavy kissing—maybe some blue balls if they're lucky. BTW, have I told you how much I loathe you and this little stunt you pulled? No?" He sneered. "Lean forward."

"I'm not letting you slap me."

"Damn it, and I was so sly about it."

"Your slapping hand was midair."

Max looked up, then brought his twitchy hand back to the table. "That it was." He placed the milkshake back down and shrugged. "Now, tell Max your problems."

"It's not a problem . . . per se."

He nodded emphatically. "I see, and when did you first realize you had ED?"

"WHAT?" I roared.

"It happens!" he held his hands in the air. "Just ask Jason."

"I'm not asking Jason about his ED."

"Good call." Max tapped his chin. "Because last time I mentioned it, he tried to kick me in the balls . . . probably because I asked it over the intercom at McDonald's, but whatev."

"They let you in McDonald's?"

"Please," he huffed. "Ronald McDonald had no basis for his claims!"

"Well, last I checked, we were both still blacklisted on account of the fact that we share the same last name."

He popped his knuckles. "Jason may have snuck me in. I had a craving for a nugget."

I groaned into my hands.

"Fine, fine, so if it's not ED, is it the shrew?"

I didn't answer.

"Ah, young grasshopper, is there trouble on set?"

I frowned.

"And by set, I mean is there trouble"—he leaned forward and cupped his mouth with his hand—"in the bedroom?"

I rolled my eyes. "Kinda defeats the purpose of you cupping your mouth if you aren't going to whisper."

"That was my whisper."

With a sigh I dipped a fry into some of the sauce and shrugged. "Well, we aren't exactly in the bedroom, considering we aren't really together, therefore no sex."

Max froze, fry midair.

I waved my hand in front of his face.

"Uh, Max?"

He shook his head, then pounded his chest as if he'd been holding his breath the whole time, then tossed a fry to the waiting pigeons. "Honest, Reid, I think I stopped breathing. What do you mean, you aren't in bed together? What the hell are those noises I keep hearing at night?"

"First . . ." I held up my hand. "I'm ignoring the fact that you cup your ear to the door late at night. Second." I gulped. "It's the TV. She likes to watch Starz at night and then forgets to turn it off, so my guess would be you were hearing the latest porno."

Max exhaled a sigh of relief. "Good God, I thought you were an animal! Honestly, I was starting to feel a bit insecure. Good to know the balance has been restored. Also, I may have been concerned when I started hearing barking. Never had that happen—not that I'm opposed to it, you understand."

"Max." I checked my watch. "This has been fun, but I'm just going to come out and say it. I need help, all right, and right now, you're my only option."

"Interesting . . ."

I clenched my teeth and crooked my finger. He leaned forward. "If you had to give someone dating advice . . . or relationship advice, what would you say?"

Max's blue eyes narrowed into tiny slits. "So you're asking for you or . . . a friend?"

"Friend," I lied. "A friend I have to help."

"Hmm, and this friend's name?"

"Jason." Sorry in advance to my accident-prone friend, but I was desperate not to be Max's target. If he knew it was me, he'd probably send a singing hooker to set or sign me up for self-help classes, get me a prescription for ED pills. Hell, the possibilities were endless.

Note to self: send Jason a Christmas goose.

"Well." Max rubbed his hands together. Oh, good, the evil genius was warming up. "First of all, I'd say that relationships take work. A lot of work—"

"Wow, Max." I frowned. "That's actually really—"

"—in the bedroom," he finished. I sighed—he'd started off so good. "But in order to get there, you need to actually ask the girl out, make her realize you're datable." He shrugged. "Let's be honest, if you aren't an Emory man, you don't really have a lot going for you."

Yeah, like I was going to say that out loud and have men everywhere hate me. Pretty sure that was the opposite of what Jordan was trying to accomplish.

"Jason doesn't have the eyes like you do, and let's be honest, if he and I were running for president, his signs would say, 'Vote for Boring,' while mine would say 'Join Team Awesome—Win a Free Puppy.'"

I hated when he actually made sense.

"So, for simple folk, like our friend"—he hooked his fingers and made air quotes—"'Jason'"—he put his hands down—"the advice is this." He closed his eyes very briefly before opening them again. His jaw had a slight tic. Either he was thinking too hard or the milkshake was making a comeback. "Start with a compliment, something innocent, nothing creepy. You can't just walk up to a chick and say, 'Nice ass,' or, 'Wow, you're beautiful.' The first gets you slapped, the second gets you ignored."

"Okay . . ."

"So, pre-Becca, I used pickup lines, but only ones I knew would get the girl to laugh. Stupid pickup lines coming from a dead sexy guy equal immediate laughter and witty banter."

"Should I be writing this down?"

Max frowned.

"For Jason," I blurted. "You know, since he can read."

"Can he? I've always wondered." Max shrugged. "Sure, whatever, or I can just tell him myself. Why didn't he just join our lunch date?"

"Not a date, and he's helping his grandma with her groceries."

"That woman has the strength of ten men and you know it. The last thing she needs is help carrying a banana." He smirked. "Get it? A banana? Because she held your bana—"

"Focus!" I snapped my fingers to regain his attention. "I have to be back on set and you need to get back to work." Right, let's call it work, so everyone feels better that he earns millions a year by staring out a damn window.

Sure helps me sleep at night.

"Fine." Max cleared his throat. "Once you've secured said laughter or the date by using your crazy eyes . . ."

"Thanks."

"Welcome." He examined a french fry, his eyebrows narrowing as if he was counting the salt crystals. "You need to actually secure that date, which is harder than you think. I mean, have you seen the type of crays that walk the streets out there?" Why, yes, I have. I'm looking at one and for some reason taking his advice. But I digress. "How can this feminine creature trust you if she doesn't know you? I've always learned it helps to call home."

"Call . . . home?"

"I call Mom."

"What?" I yelled, startling the pigeons as they swarmed away from our table. "You call our mother?"

Max grinned shamelessly. "She vouches for my awesomeness."

"Is she drunk every time you call?"

Frowning, Max checked his phone, then answered. "I may send Dad a text just to make sure she's had her nightly wine. I find she's much more agreeable when she's liquored up."

I chose to ignore the fact that he used my alcohol-induced mother to get girls. "Fine, so you call Mom and she says what?"

"Well, sometimes she goes off script—"

"There's a freaking script?"

"Dude, let me finish."

I held up my hands in defense.

"'My Max is the sweetest gentleman.'" Max spoke in a high-pitched, feminine voice that had pigeons sweeping in and landing near our table. "'Why, he saved four little ducklings when they were just hatched! He's a beautiful soul. Did you know he's wanted to be president since he was four?'"

I rolled my eyes.

"And usually this gets the girl to engage more . . ." His voice returned to normal.

"Really? Why?"

"'Well.'" Oh, good, the voice was back. Pigeons continued gathering, and I kicked them away. "'I'll never forget the moment he watched the news and said, "Mom, I want to change the world someday. Who makes those changes?" I said the president, and the very next day he wrote "President Max" on his door.'"

"You weren't even potty trained until five!" I yelled.

"Details." Max waved me off. "At any rate, the advice I'm giving is this: third-party references seal the deal at least ninety-nine percent of the time. It's marketing genius. Think of dating as a lesson in business marketing. Don't take my word for it, but this guy over here? The one with the kind smile and 'I Love Kitties' T-shirt? He just LOVES me—you should too! Oh, what? What was that? You need someone trustworthy? Shucks, I just helped him save an old lady from a tree! And that police officer over there accepting an award? My cousin. I shit you not!"

Mouth open, I simply nodded. "So, they trust you by association."

Max rolled his eyes. "It's all on my website. Have you seriously never read my book?"

"I thought you were joking."

"It was a *New York Times* bestseller."

"Now I know you're joking."

"*Publishers Weekly* called me a literary genius."

"Were they high?"

"Please, like I'd drug my own reviewers." His lips curled into a smile that I chose to ignore, for obvious reasons. "Okay, so once you have the date, it's important to spend more time listening than talking."

"Right."

"You're not listening!" Max slammed his fist against the picnic table, tears filling his eyes. "Are all men this dense?"

"Uh." What the hell? Why was I panicking? It was Max! Not some crazy girl!

"Boo." Two giant thumbs pointed downward. "Wrong. The first date is crucial, you are never right on the first date, you are never smarter than her, better looking, or funnier. You are simply honored to be sitting at the same table as her. When you pick her up, you get down on one knee and bow your head in humble adoration. Whatever the hell it takes to get her to get in the car without having to hit her over the head and drag her, caveman style."

"Because if that doesn't land you in prison . . ."

"Look!" Max stood. "I'm just trying to help our friend Jason. On second thought, I'll just call him. It's so hard explaining romance to simpleminded fellas."

I think I was the fella to which he was referring. "Jason changed his number."

"Did he?" Max's eyes narrowed. "Without telling his best friend?"

"Colt's his best friend."

Max pulled out his cell.

"Wait!" I grabbed Max. "It wasn't for Jason, it was for me."

"And now you're covering for him!" Max shouted.

"No." Oh, shit, Jason was going to kill me. "You know what? I should go, and remember, you have that desk delivery don't want to miss, right?"

Max's eyes clouded. "It's made of steel. Do you even know what I can do to that desk?"

"You mean on the desk. Please tell me you mean on the desk."

He rolled his eyes. "Duh, I mean the other way around would be . . . well, there has to be a word for that. Sex with inanimate objects? Probably lands you in the cray-cray bin, am I right?"

"Go to work, Max."

He saluted me and started walking off, then turned. "Hey, Reid?"

"Hmm?"

"You do realize that this won't end well."

"What won't?"

"You and Jezebel."

"Jordan?"

"That's what I said."

"Stay out of it, Max . . ."

He held up his hands. "Just don't get too attached. She isn't the type to stay around. She scares easy. Trust me."

"What the hell does that mean?"

"Just trust." He pounded his chest and walked off.

I checked my phone. In less than two hours I had to meet with Jordan and give her my relationship advice.

And all I had to go on was "Call my mom."

I was screwed.

# CHAPTER SEVENTEEN

## JORDAN

He was late.

I promised Ren that we'd have the video up by six that night, and still no Reid. I tapped my phone, willing it to notify me with a text, a call—anything! It was nearing five thirty and I knew it would take a miracle to get everything done in under half an hour.

Finally, the door to the apartment burst open and a very crazed-looking Reid made his way over the threshold.

At least five books were stacked in his hands and his normally bright blue eyes looked tired.

"Study date go late?" I asked sweetly.

"Bite me. I was at the library."

I blinked in confusion.

"Where there are books," he said slowly.

"Right, but why were you there?"

He shoved the books onto the counter. One fell to the ground. I tilted my head to read the upside-down title—*Men Are from Mars, Women Are from Venus.*

"Shh!" Reid launched himself across the living room and covered my mouth with his hand. "He'll hear you!"

"God?" I spoke against his fingers.

"Max," he hissed. "The last thing he needs to know is that I went to the library and borrowed books, books on dating, books on dating advice, books that are supposed to help me get smarter."

"Word of advice." I pushed his hand away from my face. "You gotta open them and read."

"Oh, really?" Reid's expression was one of complete dumbfounded awe. "Open book, then read book? Man don't know how to do such things." He pounded his chest and then winked one of his flashy eyes at me. Down, girl. Down. "You know, this is all your fault."

"You keep saying that, but I'm not the one with Max as a brother."

"Like I can control those things!"

I shrugged and opened my laptop. "Okay, let's get down to business. We'll record for around ten minutes. I'll give three dating and relationship tips, you give three. We'll discuss them as we go, and yeah, should be a piece of cake!"

"Great!" Reid jumped onto the couch and rubbed his hands together. "Oh, and by the way, I got all my dating advice from Max and library books, so . . ."

"So it should be good." I patted his hand. "Great. Ready?"

"No." Reid jogged over to the freezer, pulled out a bottle of vodka, grabbed two shot glasses, then returned, setting them on the table. "First we take a good luck shot."

"Why?" I eyed the shots warily. Mixing alcohol and a video for the masses wasn't smart—at all.

He didn't answer, just filled both shot glasses to the rim and handed me one. "Don't be a shrew, Sebastian, drink up!"

"Call me Sebastian one more time . . ."

"Someone's a crab."

"Ooh, funny." I narrowed my eyes and took the shot. It went down hot. You know that feeling where the alcohol burns an actual hole through your esophagus because the last thing you ate just so happened to be a spicy taco at noon? Yeah, it felt like that.

Reid poured two more shots.

"What are you doing? We're supposed to be working."

"And you"—he handed me the shot—"are supposed to be letting me tame you. Let me do my job."

"I'm not a job."

"So drink."

"Fine." I threw it back, my tongue going completely numb, and then slammed the shot glass onto the table. "If I didn't know any better, I'd think you were nervous about this whole thing."

"Me?" Reid snorted. "I don't get nervous. Ever." He licked his lips and poured another shot. "For luck," he said, then tossed it back. Three shots? Maybe we should have done a list of don'ts for our video, starting with: don't take three shots before your first date—chances are you'll puke down her dress before you actually make it to the bar.

"Ready?" I asked.

"Yup." Reid tilted his head, then licked his palm and patted the top of my hair. I let out a little growl.

"What? I'm trying to tame it, and we both know that the best kind of discipline is habitual. If I continually tell your hair to calm down, eventually it will."

"Or it could just reject said discipline and take over the world."

"That too."

"Reid—"

"Fine." He rubbed his hands together. "No stalling. Go."

I forced a smile and hit the "Record" button on my MacBook Pro. My voice was all business. "Dating advice from one of Hollywood's hottest stars—you girls ready? You guys have pens?"

"Jordan." Reid shook his head. "Don't use the fake voice. The fake voice sounds fake."

"Fine." I deleted and tried again, clearing my throat. "Hey, guys and gals, welcome to—"

Reid hit "Stop." "What the hell was that?"

"What?" I pushed his hand away from the mouse pad. "I'm a business professional, not a cruise director! What do you want from me?"

"Smile!" He pointed at his own smile. "And don't look so upset to be sitting next to me."

I tucked my hair behind my ears and straightened in my seat.

Reid looked down. "Why the hell are you still wearing work clothes?"

"Because this"—I pointed to the computer—"this is work. This is my job. You're my job."

"Funny." He leaned in, his lips inches from mine. "I thought I was the tamer . . ." His lips hovered as he reached around me and hit the "Record" button. Chest heaving, I waited for him to move away; instead he pressed his body against mine. "Boys, pay attention." He didn't look at the camera. "This, this right here is what you want. You want to be in a position where you're stalking your prey."

"Ha." I snorted. "Girls, write this down—if a man calls you prey, run, very fast."

"Do it." Reid laughed, his lips tickling my neck. "Isn't that right, men? What's the fun in chasing if the antelope doesn't even run?"

"So now we're antelope?"

"I could have said you were a warthog."

"Aw, so sweet." I ignored the way Reid pinned himself over my body and glanced at the computer screen. "So apparently we're doing a segment on what not to do on a date. Name calling? Probably a bad idea unless you want to get punched in the face."

"You mean you don't like it when I call you Muffin Butt?" Reid feigned a hurt expression. "You know the only reason I call you that is because you fed me muffins in bed after the first time we had sex."

WHAT? I let out a self-conscious laugh. "We've never had sex." I shook my head vigorously at the computer.

"You were there." Reid nodded innocently. "I mean, I know I take you to places you've never been before, but like, not literally." He winked.

"I'm going to kill you!" I shoved at his chest. "Take this seriously! I knew we shouldn't have done shots!"

He quickly grabbed my hands and pinned me onto the couch. "Men, pay attention. This is my favorite part. Foreplay."

"Touch me with any part of your body and I'm cutting it off!"

He ignored me. "Women are timid, like birds, and a lot of times they don't mean what they say. Take, for example, the heavy breathing coming from my lady friend."

"Not breathing heavy!" I lied and tried to hold my breath.

"Witty banter." He shrugged. "A bit of violence." He dipped his mouth to my neck. "And, oh, look, there it is."

"What? Where's what?"

"Your tell."

"I have no tell. Get. Off!"

Reid's cursed aqua eyes were like homing beacons. When this was over with, I was going to make him wear sunglasses over those laser beams. "You do."

"Do not." I bucked beneath him.

He cupped my chin, and my very treacherous body moved.

"There it is again."

"I'm not doing anything!" I squeezed my eyes shut.

"The arch," he said, then ran his hand down my side, his fingers moving to my back. "She arches . . . because no matter what insanity may be coming from that sexy little mouth of hers—her body still responds."

He kissed my cheek.

I told my body not to react.

Arch.

"Stop it!"

He kissed me again.

And another arch. Freaking men! "Reid . . . this is . . . assault."

He jumped off me and hit "Stop" on the camera. "So, I think that went well."

"No," I huffed. "Not well. We're doing it again and sticking to the script I wrote out for both of us!"

"Script? That's for movies—this is life."

"The hell it is! This is my job!"

"Mine too!" His voice rose an octave. "And people will like this a hell of a lot better than the shit you write out." He grabbed my notepad. "Tell him he looks nice."

"Give me that!"

He held it high above his head. "Compliment his shoes?"

"It works!" I argued, still trying to grab the notepad away.

"If you're gay!"

"Lots of straight men respond to that compliment!"

"Because they think if they say thank you they can get in your pants! Damn, are you really this dense?"

I finally wrenched my notepad free and slapped him with it. "Are you really this childish?"

"I'm not the one doing the hitting."

I hit him again. Because I could. "My relationship advice was to compliment the person you want to go out with. Not lick their hand, pat their hair down, call them names, then crush them with two hundred and twenty-five pounds of muscle until they nearly break in half!"

"Two ten," he corrected.

I opened my mouth, then snapped it shut, slamming my notepad onto the table. "We're doing it again. My way."

Reid yawned.

"Oh, please." I snorted, jerking my computer from the table. "You just don't want to do it my way because you don't know how to get a girl. Admit it!"

"Oh, yeah?"

"Yes!"

"Want to know what my research taught me today?"

"How to read?"

His eyes narrowed as he tugged my computer away from me. "No. It taught me this. Be real. Be honest. And at least if you don't secure a date you know it wasn't you—but them."

"Well." I licked my lips and looked down. "As far as advice goes, that isn't horrible."

He handed me back my computer.

"And you didn't even hit 'Stop' on the screen."

"Yeah, I did."

"No." I tried sliding my finger over the mouse pad. "You didn't, and somehow I just froze my computer."

Reid frowned. "Let me see."

"Fine." Done arguing, I handed it over while he tapped a few keys, then tried to double-click the mouse.

"Stop clicking all over the screen, you're just going to make it worse!"

"Stop looking over my shoulder like I'm looking at PORN so I can concentrate!"

I sat back and crossed my arms.

Reid's eyebrows furrowed. "What the hell—"

"What?"

He paled.

"Reid?"

"Uh . . ."

"Reid. What. Did. You. Do?"

"You know the difference between a live feed and just recording a video, right?"

I clenched my hands into tiny balls, my nails digging into my palms. "Please, I know how to use a computer."

"I know, but—"

I grabbed the computer and stared at the screen. It was still frozen. And the little line above the video was green.

As in live.

The video was live.

For the world to see.

"No." I shook my head and pounded the mouse pad with my thumb. "No. No. No. No."

"Everything okay in there?" Max called.

"YES!" Reid shouted while I went into a catatonic state, my eyes glued to the screen—the screen I no longer had control over.

Reid very slowly peeled the computer from my death grip and set it on the coffee table. "It could be worse."

"That's our catchphrase—it could be worse." I started chewing my nail.

Reid batted my thumb away. "Bad habit."

"My parents are going to see you seducing the crap out of me. Oh, crap, the arching! I was arching!"

"Now she admits it."

"And the world is going to think I'm a hussy! Damn it, Reid, let me chew!"

He sighed and ran his hands through his glossy dark hair. "Look, is it really that bad? Jordan, life isn't scripted. And honestly, if that's what you're looking for, then I think I'm out."

"Out?" I seethed. "You can't be out! It will ruin you! Think of Max."

"Woman has a point," Max yelled.

"NOT NOW!" I shouted back, my voice vibrating off the high ceiling.

"Come on." Reid grinned. "Don't you ever just . . . let your hair down?"

A snicker came through the wall.

I gave the wall—and the man behind it—my middle finger.

"Last time I let my hair down, I had people calling me Mufasa."

Reid choked back a laugh.

"A Rafiki sticker decorated my locker for two weeks." Sadly, I hadn't cared, because it was the one time in high school people actually paid attention to me.

"*Nants ingonyama!*" Reid sang.

My hair chose that inopportune moment to stand erect, Alfalfa style. Always good to know *The Lion King* did it for my hair—no shame in that sad fact. None at all.

"Sorry." He licked his lips. "Tell you what . . . I spent the better part of my day learning how to date from my brother, which, as much as I'd like to say was pointless, actually has me questioning my entire childhood, since I discovered my mother used to lie in order for Max to get chicks."

I perked up. "Seriously?"

"He uses her as a third-party witness."

"That's . . . brilliant."

"Shh." Reid covered my mouth with his hand. "He'll hear."

I nodded.

Reid didn't move his hand. My lips liked it way too much. "We're living together. We kind of skipped the dating part, since you rejected me and thought I was gay." I smiled against his fingertips. "But why don't we practice what we preach, hmm? I'll make some popcorn, liquor you up, and we can have a date night in."

My heart pounded.

"Nod your head if that scary look in your eyes means yes. I'm guessing if it's a no you'll just bite my hand." Or I could do both just to see what he tasted like. I nodded my head.

"Good." He rubbed his hands together. "First things first, no checking the Internet, phones, Facebook—nothing! We're on a date. Deal?" He held out his hand.

I stared at it, reached out, then paused. "Fine, but this isn't a real date."

"It isn't?" He winked, then walked off, leaving me confused and breathless, again. My body arched even then. Oh, who was I kidding? Dating Reid Emory in real life was the equivalent of winning the lottery for a girl like me.

A girl who, by all accounts, he shouldn't even see.

But did.

Possibly more clearly than anyone in my entire life ever had.

# CHAPTER EIGHTEEN

## REID

I wasn't nervous. Please. The nervous guy was always played by a dude who had no fashion sense, had never kissed a girl, and thought that foreplay was an actual play—in baseball.

I had killer fashion.

Had kissed tons of girls—even secured my first by the age of four from a six-year-old riding the bus to school.

And foreplay was my specialty. I like to think that some men are just gifted in that area—not to boast, but I'm one of them.

Oh, and I was a hell of a baseball player.

So that weird, shaky feeling currently residing in my stomach, slithering its way up my chest? Heartburn.

I popped two Tums.

"Hey, you okay?" Jordan asked. Her big brown eyes were makeup free—making them look even prettier—more natural. She'd given up on her hair so it was wildly cascading in every direction known to mankind, giving her a sex kitten look I wasn't at all comfortable her sporting outside my apartment.

"Yeah." I coughed. "Heartburn."

"Weird. I wonder why you have heartburn after all those shots, five slices of pizza, and three glasses of red wine?"

I grinned. "Beats me."

She rolled her eyes and grabbed the remote from my hand.

"What are you doing?" I asked calmly, trying to keep my voice from shaking.

"Changing the channel?" she answered without looking at me. "The movie ended an hour ago and you usually go to bed at eleven, so . . ."

"But this is date night."

"Uh-huh, and now date night is over. I'll tell you what." She turned and tucked her legs beneath her. "Since you're new at this whole dating thing, I'll give you a free pass and let you in on a little secret."

"I'm listening." Okay, so I was trying to listen while my eyes zeroed in on her low-cut blouse and fringes of the black lacy bra that was peeking from beneath. Focus. Focus. Focus. Did she have pizza sauce on her breast?

"When girls come home from a date, they don't take a hot shower and run their hands all over their body moaning and groaning and replaying every touch, every caress, every kiss."

Can't. Look. Away. I leaned forward. Yup, definitely pizza sauce. "Well, that's disappointing."

"Usually, they pour themselves a glass of wine, toss off their tall heels, turn on the TV, put on their sweats, and read while *New Girl* plays in the background."

How was it possible she wasn't aware she had food on her chest?

"Reid, are you listening?"

"Of course I am!" I nodded. "Wine, heels, TV, books, *New Girl*." I know, neat trick, right? Just pull the details out of what they said and repeat them. Works nine times out of ten. Unless you're Max. If you're Max, you usually just get punched, because he tends to brag about the fact he remembered in the first place.

"What?" Jordan looked down. "What are you staring at?"

"Sauce."

"Huh?"

"Sauce." I pointed. "Right there."

Jordan rolled her eyes. "I'm not falling for that trick where you point and I look down and you hit me in the face. How old are you, ten?"

"No, seriously." I moved forward. "You have pizza sauce right here." I swiped it with my thumb and then licked it off.

"That should be gross," she breathed.

"I know."

"But it was kind of sexy."

"I know."

"Stop saying 'I know.'"

I smirked. "Sorry . . . oh, look, you have something right here too." This time she did look down. And my ten-year-old self cheered as I knocked her in the chin and said, "Gotcha."

Defeated, her shoulders slumped forward. "I deserved that."

"I couldn't help myself." I watched in a hypnotic trance as her tongue sneaked out and teased her lower lip. It was the perfect moment for a kiss, but the line had been . . . skewed. I wasn't sure if it was okay, in the privacy of my apartment, to actually kiss her. I mean, I'd kissed her, but this felt different, more intimate.

"This is the part"—Jordan leaned forward and gripped my shirt with both hands—"where you either kiss me or cough awkwardly, make an excuse, scratch your balls, and cower back in your bedroom."

"Wow, so many choices," I mused, meeting her halfway. "Eenie, meenie, minie—" Our mouths met in a frenzy. She tasted like wine and pizza.

Holy shit, it was hotter than it should have been.

My hands moved to her hips as I tried to pull her onto my lap. But her skirt was too tight.

"Damn it." I tugged harder and heard a split.

Jordan reared back. "Did you just rip my skirt?"

"Small tear."

"Rip."

"No." I gripped the fabric until it gave with a scratchy tearing sound. "That's a rip." With a grin I tossed the discarded remains onto the ground.

Jordan stared at the skirt for a few seconds before wrapping her legs around my torso and fusing her mouth with mine. "You owe me a skirt."

"Can I rip you out of that one too?"

She laughed against my mouth. I stood, lifting her with me, and walked her backward toward my bedroom.

We looked good. She was half-naked, sexy, I was carrying her around like a badass, and then things went . . . south.

And not a good south.

"Watch out for my shoes—"

I tripped over two spiked heels, sending Jordan flying into the wall. She slid down said wall and landed on the plant—yes, THE plant, the one she'd kept alive for all those years.

"My plant!" she yelled. I burst out laughing as remnants of dirt and plant sifted through her hands. "YOU KILLED IT!"

"Whoa!" I held up my hands and backed up, tripping over the damn shoes again and stumbling to the floor.

I shit you not, Jordan giddyup crawled toward me, faster than lightning, straddled me, and started fighting.

"We'll get you a new plant!" I yelled as she smacked my chest. I gripped her wrists and flipped her onto her back. "Don't you think—"

She bucked beneath me.

"—it was probably time to let the plant go? You know, cut the apron strings!"

"It's not my child!" she wheezed, tuckering herself out.

"Exactly." I nodded, then released her hand and patted her cheek. Her eyes went wild.

"Shh . . ." I braced myself over her. "This is my favorite part."

"Me killing you?" she heaved.

"No." I licked the seam of her lips even though she fought me every way. "Foreplay."

"Sorry, plant killing wasn't in the *Kama Sutra*, Reid!"

"Yeah it was, right next to spanking. Trust me, I bookmarked the page," I joked.

She tried to get me off her again.

"Won't work." I fake yawned then kissed her neck. "Besides, I have you right where I want you. Forget the bedroom. I do my best work in the hallway anyway."

"So now I'm work?" she challenged.

"No, baby . . . this is all play." With that, I tugged her lower lip with my teeth, released her hands, and ripped open her shirt. Buttons went flying, joining the plant, the shoes, the skirt.

Her body was all lush skin and curves. I'd never been with anyone who looked as perfect as her—wasn't sure if I ever wanted to go back to skinny malnourished models when I had a real woman beneath me, one who had breasts that filled my hands, an ass that I could grip, a lip I could bite.

I moaned.

Jordan's body responded to my every single touch and caress.

"Now I know why you've never had to ask a girl on a date." She hooked her legs around me and wrapped her arms around my neck, her tongue intertwining with mine, sucking, so. Damn. Hard that I couldn't help but keep moaning. The things that woman could do with her mouth.

I deepened the kiss, my hands reaching for the clasp of her bra. I flicked it off. Jordan immediately froze. Her hands quickly covered her breasts.

"What are you doing?" I tried prying her hands free.

"Too fast." She nodded, her cheeks staining with color. "You know for our, uh, date night."

"Move your hands."

"No."

"Jordan."

"Reid." She laughed nervously.

"Fine." I nodded. "I didn't want to have to do this."

Jordan frowned.

I raised my hand.

She frowned harder.

I flipped her onto her stomach and slapped her ass. Hard.

"WHAT are you doing?" she yelled.

"Why, sweetheart . . ." I kissed her ear. "I'm taming."

"The hell you are!"

"You like it." Another swat. "And I'm barely spanking you, but a man's gotta do what a man's gotta do. Cover them up again and I won't be responsible for my actions."

"But—"

I flipped her back around. "But what?" I honestly wanted to know why a girl that gorgeous would cover up.

"It's just that—" Jordan chewed her lower lip. "I'm the lights-off girl."

"Lights off?"

"Yeah." She shrugged a shoulder as more color stained her cheeks. "You know, the girl you don't really notice right away until you've had one too many, then you take her home and have your way with her—in the dark."

Horrified, I could only stare in shock. "Please tell me that hasn't actually happened."

"Reid." She shoved me away and started to get to her feet. "Look, I'm not stupid, okay? And I'm not even that insecure anymore. I know how guys think, all right?"

"Oh, yeah?" I stood, pulled her flush against my very hard body. "What am I thinking about right now?"

"ESPN?"

"Damn."

Her shoulders deflated. "See?"

I burst out laughing. "Honey, we have a pretty big problem if ESPN gets me this excited, don't you think?"

"Hey, sometimes baseball just does it for people." She gave me a sexy-as-hell smile. "It's not your fault you like balls."

"I can't believe you just challenged my manhood when it's saluting you like that. Damn, woman, I'm basically giving you the equivalent of a high five and a home run all in one and you're making jokes?"

"It's what I do best. Joke when I'm uncomfortable."

"I think out of the two of us," I said, grabbing her hands and placing them on my shirt, "I'm the one who's uncomfortable. Wanna know why?"

Her face fell.

"Because I'm still dressed and you're gloriously"—I kissed her mouth, teasing my tongue against its entrance—"naked."

"I still have panties on."

I gripped the black boy shorts in my hand and gave a hard tug. "A horrible oversight on my part."

She gasped.

"Don't look so shocked." I backed her up against the wall. "Now, you have two choices."

"I'm listening."

I caressed the side of her face with the back of my hand. "You either go pour your wine . . . put on your sweats, turn on *New Girl*, and read."

I cleared my throat. "Or, you let me take you into my bedroom. Lay you down on my bed. And let me show you what I do best."

"Sleep?" She winked.

"I'll sleep when I'm dead. So as long as I'm living . . . I better make good use of what I've been given, right?" I flicked her mouth with my tongue and pressed a series of soft kisses, alternating between teasing her lips and running my mouth up and down her neck. "Say yes."

"Yes."

# CHAPTER NINETEEN

## JORDAN

I should have said no.

But his hands.

That body.

Those eyes.

And even more than that? No man had ever made me feel wanted. I'd spent my life fixing other people's problems, living in the background, blending in. And for the first time, I didn't want to blend.

I wanted color.

God help me. I wanted Reid Emory.

It was a horrible idea. For one thing, we were working together. It wasn't like I could do the walk of shame a few feet back to my room and drown my sorrows in a pint of ice cream. I still hadn't found an apartment and I really would be homeless if Reid kicked me out.

My job was to make him look good.

Keep him in the limelight.

And here I was, getting distracted by a six-pack and a movie-star smile. He was an actor. How hard would it be for him to act like he wanted me when he really didn't? Maybe he was just being horny.

And I was available.

My shoulders slumped more as Reid hurried me into his bedroom. "I can't." I swallowed, once more covering myself up while he came up behind me and kissed my neck. "I can't do this."

"Okay."

Seriously? Now he didn't want me at all? "That's it? Just okay?"

He flipped me around and tilted my chin toward him. "I'm not going to force you into having sex with me if that's what you're thinking. I'm not that guy. Just like you're not the lights-off girl." Reid wrapped his arms around my body. "When was the last time you let a man look at you . . . in the light?"

"Never."

"So . . . I'll tell you what." Reid's smile was so gorgeous I had to look away. So tender it made my heart clench. "Even though I'm paying you, you're still doing me a favor by being my publicist, making sure that my career doesn't tank on account of my brother being certifiably insane, and you've cheerfully gone along with this whole charade."

Ugh, my stomach sank. Again, he kissed me because I was available.

"I'm going to teach you how to love yourself."

I rolled my eyes. "I'm not insecure. I'm a realist."

"Turn around."

"No. Reid. We've had a lot to drink, I'm just going to shuffle off to bed and—"

Reid gripped my arm and dragged me into the bathroom. Flipping on the lights, he turned me toward the mirror. "What do you see?"

"Boobs."

"You aren't a horny thirteen-year-old boy. What do you really see?"

Honestly? I saw a lot of what I didn't want to see. I saw flaws. So many of them, even with his killer lighting. My shame got worse as I realized my hips were wider than his. I mean, I'm a girl. I get that big hips equal childbirth, but still, it made me want to disappear into the floor. I was all curves.

I saw a scar on my stomach from when I got my appendix out.

A bit of cellulite on my thighs.

Breasts that were too big for my taste.

And a stomach that was only flat because I was sucking it in.

"Reid, this night stopped being fun about five seconds ago."

He ignored me. "Soft . . . perfect . . . supple skin." He ran his fingers down my ribs. "Breasts that render a man incapable of focusing on anything else." He shook his head, his breathing heavier as his mouth landed near my ear. "And hips that my hands itch to grip, to thrust into . . . A lights-off girl? Hell, no. You're a spotlight girl. You just need to stop looking through your eyes and use mine."

I choked back the emotion in my throat. Things went from playful to real in that moment, and I wasn't sure I could handle it if he didn't really mean it. If it was fake.

"I think I like what you see better," I whispered.

"Yeah?" He kissed the top of my head. "Well, I played a plastic surgeon once and I wouldn't change a thing about you."

"Well, that basically makes you an expert."

"Right?" he teased. "And I'm sorry . . . if I overstepped my bounds . . . you know, trying to have sex with you, forcing you to stare at yourself naked while I lusted even more after your body. But I'm a firm believer in truth and I couldn't for one more second let you believe a lie."

Insert swoon here.

They actually happen in real life.

I'd read about them in novels. Made fun of the girls whose knees buckled when their men puked out such romantic words that they had no choice but to collapse into their arms.

My knees knocked together. "T-thank you."

"Bed." Reid nodded to the door. "Like I said, I won't pressure you. Go sleep, read your damn book, and . . . sorry things got . . . crazy. It won't happen again. I know we're supposed to have boundaries, so—"

In my mind my next movements weren't jerky or uncertain, they were fluid, sexy, hot, and unstoppable as I launched myself at his body, pushing us both into the general direction of the bedroom.

With a heave, Reid caught my flying ass, midair. We fell back against his mattress. A hard book caught his fall while throw pillows went careening by my face.

"Oof," Reid huffed. "That was . . . unexpected."

"You okay?" I winced.

"Sure thing." He nodded. "The book broke my spleen, but I think I can still perform if I try not to breathe."

I covered my mouth with my hands to keep from bursting out laughing. "I'm so sorry! I just . . . reacted."

"I'm glad." He winced. "Really. I'm a huge fan of the sneak-up-and-pounce attack. I just didn't take into account hard surfaces on my bed."

More laughter escaped from my lips.

"You won't be laughing when you have to take me to the hospital because you landed on me wrong."

I stopped laughing as a visual of having to take Reid to the hospital and explain how he got his injuries crossed my mind.

"Yeah, explain that to the doctor. Believe me, they aren't very understanding downtown. Last time I visited a hospital, it was—"

He stopped talking.

"Do continue," I urged, still hovering over him in attack mode.

"Nope." He shook his head. "I do have a question, though."

"What?"

"Since I've seen you naked, does that mean I get to shower with you and cop a feel whenever I want?"

"How cute, you really are a pubescent teen with headgear. Quick, give me a rose!"

Reid gasped. "Take it back!"

"Never!"

He reached around and started tickling my sides while I threw a pillow at his face and tried to escape. He tugged me back against his body while an angry Max shouted, "Sleeping here!"

"Jealous?" Reid called back.

"Where is his fiancée?"

"She has late class on Friday nights."

I turned. "You know her schedule."

"Every other night I have to wear earplugs. Damn right I know her schedule."

"Every other night, huh?"

Reid grinned.

I burst out laughing. "You thinking what I'm thinking?"

"Yes." He nodded, then threw me a pair of sweats and a T-shirt that were folded on his chair. "I better get more wine."

"Okay."

"Oh." Reid stopped and snapped his fingers. "Also, giving you clothes when I want you to live every day naked—not easy."

"Go!" I laughed.

When Reid returned with more wine, I knew I made the right choice. Maybe we were better just . . . being us and not ruining things by having sex.

After all, when this was all over with.

He'd be famous.

And I'd be back to blending in with the wallpaper.

# CHAPTER TWENTY

## REID

I held the door open for Jordan as we walked out into the hall and waited for the elevator.

My hand flew to my face as I covered up a huge yawn and took a sip of coffee. It had been a long night.

We'd nearly burned down the building with the hot sex we weren't actually having.

After seeing her naked, I was surprised I was actually able to say no to real sex and yes to fake sex, but the moment was off. Well, that, and there was the whole she's technically a coworker/boss/has my career by the balls. Then again, it would be worth it. She would be worth it. Visions of her body still hammered through my skull like a hangover from hell.

It went like this.

Ass, hips, breasts, repeat.

Over and over and over again until I almost blurted it out and tossed her against the wall and had my way with her.

Max's yelling from the other room ended up killing that idea anyway, and Jordan had a much better idea. Drive him insane, just like he was driving us insane. Give the evil genius a taste of his own medicine. Hell, yeah.

"Was it good for you?" Jordan joked, her eyes were wide with amusement, long black eyelashes blinking up at me. Damn, she was pretty.

"Best fake sex I've ever had." I struggled not to stumble over the word *sex* considering my body was still ready to explode. We're all lucky she didn't have to take cover.

Ha, that's just what I needed to be known as, exploding penis man. Awesome.

She stole my coffee and took a big gulp—she'd finished hers an hour ago. "I think the moose sounds and banging coconuts really upped our game toward the end there."

"Huh." I jerked my coffee back, careful not to touch her fingers since wanting to explode from the sheer need to be inside her was making my blood pump in all the wrong places. "I was thinking that the real sweet spot was when you started yodeling."

Jordan blew across her nails and sighed. "Gosh, I just love a good yodel."

The door to Max's apartment flew open, then slammed as he shuffled toward us. He reached into his pocket, his hand flailing until he finally gripped his sunglasses and managed to get them on his nose after three more attempts.

All was quiet and then Jordan asked, "Tired?"

Slowly, Max slid his sunglasses down his nose, his eyes bloodshot red. "Yodeling, really?"

"Hey, when a man like Reid sticks it to you, what other choice do you have?"

I choked on my coffee and started coughing wildly while Jordan pounded my back. Shit, it was going to be a long day. She said *stick*. My anatomy liked that phrase way more than it should.

Max cursed under his breath. "Oh, I don't know, how about anything but yodeling and purring. And screaming, 'Reid Emory is a god' probably wasn't necessary either, nor was the incessant wall banging. Pop-pop's picture fell from its spot on the mantel and shattered into a million pieces." He shook his head violently. "He'd be so ashamed."

I rolled my eyes. "Pop-pop grew up in the Vegas. Highly doubt he'd be all that surprised."

"Seventeen times," Max hissed under his breath. "Seventeen times that jezebel"—he yelled it, peering around me and thrusting his finger into the air—"shouted your name at the top of her lungs. Have you no shame?" He pulled some breath spray from his pocket and squirted it in his mouth. "I half expected you to go hoarse."

"Not hoarse yet, though the day's still young." Jordan winked. I kept calm on the outside, while internally my horny self threw a freaking parade.

"People work." Max sniffed. "And luckily my fiancée will be back tonight, so we'll see who keeps up who."

"Whom," she corrected.

Max lunged for her, but I stepped between them.

She shot Max a confident smile. "It's a good thing Reid's so accommodating, letting me stay with him until who knows how long?" Insert fake laugh. "Maybe invest in some earplugs, Max, since our sexuality clearly offends you."

"Now see here!" Max huffed. "It's not the sexuality that offends . . . I have all the sex, all the time, or I used to, until you showed up with your offensive hair and killer shoes." He stared at her heels. "Damn, I may despise you, but your taste in shoes is incredible." Max's eyes went clear with respect, then clouded with anger all over again. "What was I saying? The heel distracted me. Hell, I love it when Becca wears heels." He got a starry look in his eyes, then cursed. "No sex just may kill me. Reid," he said, turning to me. "Promise me you'll take care of the goat."

"You have a goat?" Jordan crossed her arms. "Is his name Billy?"

Max rolled his eyes. "Like I would ever be that unoriginal."

"So?" she asked. "What's his name?"

"I see what you're doing here." Max's eyes narrowed. "No, we will not be friends. Ever! Never, ever! Not even by way of my goat!"

"Chill, I'm not kidnapping your goat." She laughed. "Get it, kid-napping?"

"Ha-ha, you're hilarious!" Max shouted. "Now go be funny away from my brother so I can continue engaging in all sexual activity."

"Nah, think I'll stay . . . maybe forever."

Max's eye started to twitch behind his glasses.

"Eyelash in your eye, brother? Or is Jordan's condition wearing off?"

He shoved his glasses up his nose. "No. Just a bit of dirty slut."

"What was that?"

"Dirt and *mud*," he said slowly. "And I know what you two are doing. I won't stand for it. Two can play this game."

"Yeah, but only two will win." Jordan nodded. "And by the sounds coming from our apartment and the silence coming from yours, well . . ."

Max scowled. "I had no partner!"

"Still lost." Jordan shrugged. "You do know that only winners get prizes, right?"

"You." Max pointed his finger in her direction just as the elevator doors opened. "I may have underestimated you."

"That's a compliment," I mused.

"It's all you're getting!" Max yelled. "Also, thought you guys might want to check this out." He tossed his cell in the air. I caught it and looked at the screen: REID EMORY TAMES PUBLICIST #THEARCH.

"What's that?" Jordan looked over my shoulder.

I shoved the phone in my pocket. "Nothing."

"Dude, not your phone." Max held out his hand.

Panicking, I wasn't sure what to do.

Max decided for me when he shoved his hand in my pocket, missing my balls by only a centimeter, and snatched his phone back, then read aloud what I'd just read silently as to not piss Jordan off and send her and her hair on a witch hunt through the city in which she tried to confiscate all forms of technology.

"I'm a hashtag," she said in a monotone voice.

"Cheer up." Max grinned. "It could be worse."

I opened my mouth, but Jordan smacked me in the chest. "Don't. Just don't."

The elevator hit the bottom floor. Max waved. "Toodles. Have fun at work today, kids. Try to play nice. Oh." He snapped his fingers and turned. "Also, Jordan you may have flashed some boob in that video, but don't worry, I highly doubt anyone will notice."

Jordan lunged.

I jerked her back by her purse.

"Let me at him," she seethed.

"That's what he wants . . . you to chase him so he can record it and put it on YouTube with the hashtag #hairchasesmandownstreet."

Jordan touched her hair. "Hey, it's in a bun today."

"Putting your hair in a bun is like wearing tight pants on Thanksgiving. Eventually the stuffing's gonna pop right on out."

"Wow, should have saved that romance for the video."

"Unfair! You're just pissed because I was right and because you did arch, you little archer!"

"I was sitting at a weird angle!"

"So you arched ten times beneath my touch? Because of the angle of your ass?"

Jordan's eyes went crazy as a stray hair spiked up out of her bun. "I'm so glad I didn't have sex with you last night, because I'd so be regretting it this morning."

My body tensed while both my heads screamed, "Abort, abort!" Arguing with her meant no sex, no naked time, no Jordan, but words just kept pouring out of my mouth. It was an out-of-body experience. Like watching myself dig the hole I was going to be buried in. I wanted to stop, but jump I did. "Honey, the only thing you'd be regretting is that I wouldn't be giving you a repeat performance!"

"Like you could even perform without injuring yourself!"

The dirt piled over my head, I could barely see the sky, yet I continued digging the hole because my manhood was at stake even though I wanted her—desperately. She attacked my sexual prowess—nobody does that to an Emory, least of all me. "You're just mad because you didn't get an orgasm!"

Yeah, may have said that a bit loud.

At least ten phones were thrust in our direction, smiles on people's faces. Great, glad I made their Saturday morning!

Jordan swallowed, then looked shyly around while I cursed and searched for my sunglasses.

"Ten bucks *orgasm*'s the new hashtag by noon," Jordan said under her breath, grabbing me by the arm and jerking me into the outside air.

"Twenty." I coughed uncomfortably and looked up and down the street, anywhere but directly at her face.

"Reid." Jordan snapped her fingers in front of me, like you would do to a dog when you were trying to teach it a new trick. I'd be insulted if I wasn't still so sexually frustrated that my eyes lingered a bit too long on the hot dog stand. It was like a gentle reminder that my hot dog should be doing no standing, none at all. "We're adults. We can get through this. I only have a few more things scheduled for us over the next few days and then I think we'll be past the worst of it. This little . . . thing will be done."

For some reason that made that stupid heartburn come back full force. I cleared my throat and clenched my jaw. "Fine."

"Fine."

"So, maybe you should actually find an apartment, since there will no longer be any need for us to be working such crazy hours together." What the hell was I saying? If she moved out, what would happen? I'd no longer be able to hear her toss and turn at night, or face her in the morning and share a pot of coffee. I froze. Wait. What the hell. Was I in a relationship? My body started to shake a bit. Would I miss her? Was that the issue?

Her face fell as she chewed the lipstick off her lower lip. Swear, it was physically impossible for the woman to keep anything on that pout of hers, not that I minded. Damn it, and now I was staring at her lips. "I'm working on it."

"Work harder," I said hoarsely, just needing her to get the hell away from me so I could think without her perfume making me want to take her into my arms and kiss the crap out of her.

She rolled her eyes. "You're an ass."

"Not what you said last night."

"I was inebriated!"

"You were naked!" My voice raised. So. Naked.

Ass, hips, breasts. Damn those breasts.

Another phone in the air.

"We really need to get this under control," Jordan muttered as more people took pictures of us. "Look, you have an interview this evening for Sirius radio. I'll text you the address. Don't show up drunk, and make sure your shirt's tucked in."

"Oh, good, I'll do that. Just make sure you don't have any stains on your breasts so I don't get distracted."

"I'll be sure to eat with a napkin tucked into my shirt." She grinned wide.

"You know, they do hand out those bibs with little crabs on them over at the Crab Shack. Meet me there for dinner," I blurted.

She fidgeted with the strap of her purse, her eyes downcast as if the idea of dinner made her uncomfortable. "Why?"

"Because," I said, rocking back on my heels, "we both need to eat."

"Oh." Her eyebrows scrunched together while her shoulders noticeably slumped.

"Look." I ran my hands through my hair. "We're both exhausted after keeping Max up all night with our fake sex. We need food and hydration, and everything will look better once all that happens. Let's have dinner after my interview, on me."

Jordan sighed and checked her watch. "Okay, that's fine. I'm going to go meet with another client, then I'll—"

"Whoa, whoa, whoa!" I held up my hands. "Other client?"

"Reid." She rolled her eyes. "I don't have time for this. Of course I have other clients."

"Who is he?" I didn't mean to yell. Not really. But yell I did.

She smirked. "Why? Jealous?"

"No." Yes.

"And what makes you think it's a he?"

"Is it?" Say no. Just. Say. No.

"It's Casey Carter." She pulled out her cell while my entire line of vision went hazy with red.

"Casey Carter?" I repeated. "Casey 'Can't Keep It in His Pants' Carter?"

"He keeps it in his pants just fine."

"No."

"Excuse me?" Her hip jutted out. I knew that look; I knew that stance. It would behoove men everywhere to memorize it so they recognized when it was time to stop talking and take cover.

"Just . . ." I took a few steps back. "Be careful with him. He's British."

"And that means what, exactly?"

"They, um, don't . . . have the same . . . moral code."

Jordan nodded mockingly. "You're so right. I mean, those damn accents can only mean one thing. Sexual deviants. How could I be so blind? Tell you what, you can do this with your moral code talk." She flipped me off, Italian style.

If I didn't already like her, that would have sealed the deal.

It meant she didn't give a shit.

Just another thing that made me like her more than I should. Wait, what? My arms started nervously itching. I did not do relationships—ever. The sooner she moved out of my apartment the sooner I could get back to being . . .

Lonely.

Shit.

I was screwed.

"Oh!" Jordan ran back toward me. "I forgot about Otis!"

"Otis is just fine."

"Otis will pee all over your fancy apartment if you don't take him out!" Her lower lip pouted. "Please?"

"What will you give me if I do?" Yes, I just went there.

"You know what—" She gripped her purse harder. "Fine, I'll just be late. Forget about it."

"Wait." I held up my hand. "Fine, I'll do it, but this isn't a thing. I mean, we aren't a thing."

"What?"

"This . . ." My hands flailed in the air between us. "This can't be a thing where we get all cozy and I take your dog for a crap in the park."

Jordan looked heavenward. "It's just a potty break, not an engagement announcement. I promise I'll be out of your hair soon, all right?"

She stomped off.

And I was left feeling like a total ass. She was probably confused. Hell, I was confused. Things were getting muddled where our relationship was concerned. On one hand, I employed her. Yet I was living with her and fake seducing her, though at some point it had turned more and more real. I made a face and clenched my fists as her curvy ass made its way down the street. One minute I wanted to kiss her senseless, the next, kick her to the curb and lock my door. I needed to stop blurring the lines, both professionally and emotionally, or else things were about to get a lot worse.

# CHAPTER TWENTY-ONE

## JORDAN

Casey's bright white smile was so blinding I had no choice but to wear my sunglasses indoors. Our waitress nearly dropped her drinks after looking directly at him. Poor thing was probably going to have to wear a patch on the eye closest to him.

"So." He cracked his knuckles. If his smile didn't irritate me to death, it was going to be his cracking habit. "What's going on, Jo-Jo?" Or the nickname. Crack, crack, crack. I inhaled slowly and counted to three before answering.

"You tell me." I placed my phone on the table, screen up, and pointed to the picture of him kissing one stripper while another girl, stripper number two, was grabbing his man junk from behind. Empty champagne bottles were littered everywhere, along with drug paraphernalia, and the caption read, CARTER GOES OVER DEEP END AFTER BREAKUP WITH SUPERMODEL GIRLFRIEND.

Casey glanced at the screen, his green eyes narrowing before he rubbed the back of his neck and smirked. "Make love, not war, that's what I always say."

The grin was back full force.

I was immune to it.

Unfortunately for him.

It hadn't always been like this. Casey was my very first client. Both of us had been trying to make names for ourselves. I poured everything I had into him. I'm pretty sure I didn't sleep for an entire year. After his breakout role in a superhero franchise, he needed constant supervision. He wasn't the type of celebrity that handled fame well, and the minute his name exploded he went from a friend who brought over Chinese takeout and texted me when I was having a rough day to jet-setting to the South of France and dating supermodels. He was one of the good ones—he'd made me adore my job—but the minute the money started pouring in, he changed right along with his bank account.

At the time, the changing friendship hurt, but I knew it was for the best. Our lives were going in completely different directions.

Besides, we'd still celebrated birthdays together and met once a week for a coffee break.

His movie roles became more demanding and suddenly he wanted to be taken more seriously. As his publicist I told him it wouldn't be a good idea to alienate all of his avid female fans by taking a year off to do an indie flick none of them would even see. He saw Academy Award, I saw flop. I was right, and things had only unraveled since then.

"Aw, come on, Jo-Jo." He reached for my hand, smile tight. "I was lonely."

"Buy a dog."

He laughed. "Guys like me don't get dogs."

The arrogance I could really do without. What happened to the guy who used to pull out a woman's chair and open doors?

"No, guys like you are dogs. I'm saying get one to keep yourself from turning into one."

"You're funny." He grinned and cracked his knuckles again. My right eye twitched. Oh, hell. "Hey, tell you what, why don't we share a bottle of wine like we used to and forget this ever happened?" Was he really trying to use our past emotional connection to manipulate me? My throat ached with the swell of emotion as it continued to mount. I was ashamed that it had worked before. That a year ago I would have made it all better while he promised to be a better friend and client.

Clearly, I wasn't the same person anymore. Was I that insecure? That attention from a good-looking man was enough to make me forgive a multitude of sins?

Casey reached for my hand again.

"No." I jerked my phone back and tossed it into my purse. "This is the sixth time you've been out partying this month. A new stripper each time, and the paparazzi are having a field day. You wanna get taken seriously? Stop hitting on women half your age and buy a dog."

"What's with you and this dog thing?" He raised his voice. "I'm not getting a damn dog."

"It's like this," I said slowly. "I'm trying to teach you how to be a responsible adult rather than a man so obsessed with his own penis he had a mold made of it to put in the middle of his apartment!"

Casey shrugged. "I've never gotten complaints about my art."

"It's not art."

"It's art." He nodded. "Ask the ladies."

"Look." I held out my hands. "Parents buy their kids dogs to teach them how to take care of something other than themselves. Maybe it would be cruel to the dog. Maybe I'll grab you a goldfish, because at least if it goes belly-up I won't feel like a puppy killer."

"Huh?" He snapped to attention. "You want me to kill a puppy?"

"Lower your voice," I hissed.

He blinked, his eyes a little too wide.

I sighed. "Are you high?"

He paused and then chuckled. "Maybe."

"Forget the goldfish—you couldn't even take care of a Tamagotchi!"

"A what?"

"Never mind." I waved him off and gripped my purse tightly with both hands. "I won't keep doing this with you, Casey, I can't. I've been with you five years. You were my first client, and I don't want to quit, but you've left me no choice."

"No!" Casey shot to his feet. "Jo-Jo, damn it, just sit! All right? Look, I'm sorry, I'm just . . . it's been a bad month." A bad month? Try a bad year!

"So stay sober, stop getting high, and make better choices. People will never respect you if you don't respect yourself."

He shrugged. "It's just a little fun."

"Is it fun when you're no longer drunk or high?"

He stared at the tablecloth.

"Right." I nodded. "Look, I'm going to go. I have a meeting with another client. Shape up. This is your last warning. If you can't do it, I'm dropping you."

"You don't drop me!" he sneered. "I made you!"

And there it was. What was left of our friendship shattered in front of my eyes.

"What was that?" I said in a lethal tone. "You made me?"

Casey paled. "Jo-Jo, I didn't mean that, I'm just—"

"Save it."

"Wait!"

"'Bye, Casey."

"You're just pissed because I didn't sleep with you!"

I froze while the restaurant fell silent. This from the man who used to tell me to wait for the right guy, the man who kissed my tears away when my college boyfriend dumped me like yesterday's news. Casey and I never went past friendship. He'd tried kissing me once, but I told him I didn't want to ruin our friendship. Pain filled my chest as I tried to breathe evenly and think professionally.

"That's it." I licked my lips and tried to keep my shaking to a minimum. "We're done." Forget that I was going to lose a crap load of money. Sadly, I was also losing a friend. Then again—I took another look at him—he'd stopped being my friend a long time ago. I'd just chosen to ignore the fact that on the road to fame, he'd given up his soul and sold it to the devil.

I should have seen the warning signs, but I was making money too and I was proud of him.

So proud.

And now he was nothing but a high stranger, so obsessed with himself I half expected him to check his reflection in the damn spoon.

"I'll send the terminated contract to your manager by fax." I whispered under my breath, "'Bye, Casey."

His eyes shuddered as he stood and flipped his chair over onto the ground. "You bitch!"

I walked away.

And when I heard dishes shatter against the floor, I began to run.

He wasn't my problem anymore.

By the time I reached the corner, I was full-on sobbing. Hating myself for taking it so personally.

It was my fault that I'd gotten too attached.

And now . . . I was in danger of doing it again.

I looked up. As luck would have it, Reid's face was plastered across the nearest billboard—THE TAMING OF THE SHREW: RELEASING SPRING 2016.

A vision of Casey's first movie billboard popped into my head. Already, Reid felt more like a friend than a client. What was worse? Both of us had crossed those lines, and now it just felt like history was repeating itself, and it would, because it was Reid. What girl wouldn't get obsessed? What director wouldn't notice his obvious talent? Not again. I couldn't go through it again. I wouldn't. Why the hell didn't I tell Ren no and save myself the heartache of watching someone else I cared about succumb to fame and fortune while I did what I did best and stayed in the background, invisible?

I swallowed the lump in my throat and wiped the tears from beneath my eyes.

Head held high, I hailed a taxi, more determined than ever to make sure Reid was a success. Maybe I needed to prove it to myself more than anyone else, that I could handle it, handle him. I needed to keep my personal feelings on lockdown, even if it meant I had to completely sacrifice my heart in the process.

# CHAPTER TWENTY-TWO
## REID

Something was wrong with Jordan. For one, her hair was pulled back so tight it looked like her eyebrows hurt. Two, her eyes were puffy. And three, well, her smile was off and seemed forced. Pathetic that I knew which of her smiles were real and which were fake, but there it was.

She'd bulldozed herself into my life three days ago, and now I was concerned for her welfare, all because she looked like she'd just watched the latest Nicholas Sparks and was pissed because he killed someone off—again.

"So." Jordan cleared her throat. "The segment is on love and sex. They'll ask you questions about the movie and then some personal questions about relationships. Make sure you sell the whole 'I'm taming a real-life shrew' thing, and lucky for you I'm in a hell of a mood so it won't be a hard sell to the host. Got it?"

I frowned. "Are you sick?"

"What?" She jerked back. "No, why?"

Her hair looked like it hurt. It wasn't soft or tame—hell, I would have even taken the wild sex hair over the bun she was currently sporting. It also irritated me because it made her look too professional. My eyes greedily searched for some stains on her shirt.

Nothing.

Pristine.

"Did you have a bad day?"

Her shoulders tensed.

"Holy shit, did Casey hit on you? Swear I'll kill him. Where is he? Give me his number, I'll break his leg in half!" I started pacing in the elevator.

"Whoa, there." Jordan braced my shoulders just as we reached the fifth floor. "He's no longer my client, no breaking necessary."

"If he touched you—"

"Nope." Another forced smile. "Creative differences. Let's get this over with, shall we?"

She swept past me and greeted the host, made introductions, then shooed me into the small room.

"Today on *Sirius Sex and Love*, we have Reid Emory. You may know him from his long stint on Broadway as the Phantom. His debut film releases next spring, *The Taming of the Shrew*." Mikey M had a deep voice that I'm sure many a woman listened to on a daily basis. He laughed. "Early reviews are saying this is going to be a breakout role for the young actor, and I gotta say, the buzz surrounding you these last two weeks has been out of this world. So, if you don't mind, Reid, let's jump right into it, shall we?"

I took a seat in front of the microphone. "Sure."

"Now, your real-life *Taming of the Shrew* with your publicist has been all over the media. Hell, the little video you two shot last night already has over a million hits on BuzzFeed." Really? Did Jordan not think I should know that little tidbit before going on live radio? "The arch is officially the second-highest trending topic on Twitter, and I just have to ask . . . this thing between you two, is it real?"

"Y-yes." Oh, great. Stuttering was super helpful. "I'm—" I stopped talking and glanced at Jordan. She wasn't even paying attention! Her face was ducked and she was typing furiously on her phone. I smirked. Fine, two could play that game. She was embarrassed by me? Trying to ignore the fact that she had responded to me sexually? "Can I shoot straight, Mikey?"

"Sure thing!" He chuckled.

"It's going horrible."

I heard Jordan suck in a breath while Mikey leaned forward. "I'm sure our listeners are curious to know why."

"It's work. I mean . . . I try to kiss her and she pulls away. The video last night isn't even the half of it. After we shot it, I took a shower and she got pissed because I forgot to put my clothes in the hamper."

"So you're living together?"

"Yeah, and let me tell you, it's not a cakewalk. The woman basically beats me in my sleep."

Jordan jumped to her feet and marched over to the microphone while I ducked and covered my head with my hands.

"Whoa." Mikey shook his head. "Um, listeners, you can't see this, but it looks like the shrew has a violent streak."

"I have the bruises to prove it." I nodded.

"Domestic violence isn't something to joke about," he said soberly.

My lower lip quivered. "Sometimes, I make her a sack lunch. I mean, that's romantic, right? Making my girl lunch. And if I don't cut off the crust . . ." I shivered.

Mikey held out his hand. "Do you think she takes out her aggression on you because there are issues in the bedroom?"

"Ha." Jordan kicked my shin, then pulled a seat out and spoke into the microphone. "He jokes . . . it's what Reid does, right, Reid? You're joking?"

I smiled shamelessly. "Mikey, I think you hit the nail on the head . . . the bedroom is . . . well, it's where we should be connecting on both a physical and emotional level. Instead, she wants to take control . . . which frankly just takes all the pleasure out of it for me."

Jordan blushed furiously.

"Oh, wow." Mikey laughed. "Our phone lines are lighting up right now. We'll take a few questions in a minute. Let's talk a little bit about the sex life between you two. Now, Jordan, why do you think you need to control everything? Have you always struggled with that?"

I leaned back and crossed my arms. "Yeah, Jordan, why so controlling?"

She gave me an *I'm going to kill you* look and then spoke sweetly into the microphone. "I wouldn't have to if he knew how to use his equipment."

"What the hell!" I roared.

Mikey laughed again. "And when you say equipment . . ."

"It's like . . ." Jordan tapped her chin. "He has the hammer, and he sees the nails, but doesn't quite know where to hit 'em in."

*Oh, shit. She just took it too far.*

I kicked her under the table. "Now who's joking?" I laughed awkwardly. "I'll have you know, I am fully aware of where to hammer, though it needs to be said that a man's very sensitive about his hammer, protective, even. How do I know she's going to allow me to do my job if she's constantly yelling the instructions at me!"

"Please!" Jordan rolled her eyes. "Like men ever read instructions. Maybe if they did they'd be able to actually complete a project with some satisfaction!"

"Are you saying he doesn't satisfy you, Jordan?" This from Mikey.

"I'm sure he has the equipment to." Jordan eyed me up and down. "The question is . . . does he have the ability?"

"Want me to prove how much ability I really have?" I whispered. "Because I have nothing against public displays of affection."

Her cheeks reddened.

"Let's, ah . . ." Mikey coughed. "Take a few calls. You're on the air with Mikey M and Reid Emory."

"So . . ." The voice was familiar. Oh, shit. "Our mother favored me over him when he was a child, and I think it left him feeling . . . small. If you get my meaning."

"Small? Who is this?"

"Max Emory . . ." Max coughed. "And let's further discuss Reid's smallness. It's a tiny, well-known fact that when one feels . . . insignificant and . . . petite, they shy away from dominance in the bedroom."

"Dude," I yelled into the microphone. "He's kidding."

"Small fry," Max wailed. "They called him small fry during gym class."

Holy mother of chickens. I was going to throw Max into a furnace and light it on fire.

"Small fry?" Mikey looked as uncomfortable as I felt. "Well, then, thank you for that . . . er . . . very interesting piece of information."

"Every LITTLE BIT helps," Max said cheerfully.

Jordan coughed out a laugh.

"You're on with Mikey M and Reid Emory."

"Hey." The voice sounded like it came from an eighteen-year-old girl. "I don't buy it. They have no chemistry. Boo. Publicity stunt." The caller hung up.

Mikey shifted in his chair. "One more call. You're on with Mikey M and Reid Emory."

"She's his publicist . . . I highly doubt he's sleeping with her. I agree with the other caller. The video was funny as hell, but I'm not convinced. Give me something real."

Hang up.

Shit, shit, shit, shit. Jordan grew paler by the minute.

I did the only thing I could think of doing, hoping that Mikey M would at least vouch for us. I grabbed her by the back of the neck and kissed her right in front of Mikey M, then spoke softly into the microphone. "I guess we'll just have to prove to everyone once and for all that this is it for us."

Jordan nodded.

"Baby," I crooned. "I know it's only been a few days, but I feel like I've known you all my life."

Her eyes widened.

"Would you—"

She shook her head violently.

"—do me the honor of marrying me?"

The gum dropped out of Mikey M's mouth.

"You're it for me." I got down on both knees. "We both knew it was heading this way. I loved you the first minute you spoke my name." Never mind that she called me a gay handsome stranger. "And when we held hands the first time." Or when she elbowed me in the ribs. "I felt whole for the first time in probably my entire existence."

Jordan's hands shook in mine.

"The movie is . . . well, it's my job. But baby, you and Otis, you're my life!"

"Who's Otis?" Mikey asked.

I waved him off. "Say yes."

Dead silence.

"Yes," Jordan said, voice hoarse. "Yes!"

I jumped to my feet and twirled her around while Mikey scratched his head and then said into the microphone, "Well, folks, I guess our doubts have all been settled. Reid Emory has taken *The Taming of the Shrew* from the silver screen and actually lived it! Thanks for being on the show, guys, and congrats."

• • •

Jordan was silent as we made our way down the elevator. And when we got into the waiting sedan, she was still quiet.

It wasn't until we pulled out onto the street that she smacked me in the head with her purse. "What the hell were you thinking?"

"I was thinking that people weren't buying it!" I yelled. "And I fixed it!"

"By proposing marriage?" she wailed. "Marriage is forever! You can't just propose marriage on a national platform, then two days later say it won't work out! It will RUIN you. It ruins any credibility you have."

I opened my mouth, then shut it. "It's good publicity. You're just mad you didn't think of it."

"Right." She smacked me twice more. What the hell did she have in there? Bricks? A Taser? Probably both. "Because that's what I want after a crappy day where my very first client all but verbally assaults me, then accuses me of wanting to sleep with him. A husband!"

"Wait, what?" I held up my hands as she kept smacking me. "He hit on you?"

"No. Yes." She stopped swinging the purse. "Does it matter?"

"Hell, yes, it does! I'm your husband!"

"Um, no, no you're not. As of right now you're barely my friend, and I'm even rethinking that little lapse in judgment. You've managed to make a mess of our entire PR plan all within three days! I can't fix this type of crazy!"

"Well, you can't quit!"

"I know that!"

"Stop yelling." I crossed my arms. "You're being unreasonable and I hate your hair."

"What?" She tugged at her tight low ponytail. "It's tamed!"

"I prefer it wild." *Like you.* But I didn't say that. I felt stupid, stupid that I'd panicked and proposed, and stupid that I was offended she wasn't elated at the idea. But then again, what the hell type of woman would be?

An insane one.

"Crab Shack," she muttered. "Let's eat and then I'll try to fix this mess."

"I already did." I reached behind her head and tugged the rubber band away, letting her brown hair bounce loose around her shoulders. "Let's think about this logically."

She rolled her eyes. "Oh, now you want to be logical."

I pressed my finger to her lips. "Logically, does it work? Movie star falls in love and marries his pet project while filming in New York. Most interesting couple allows media to view parts of their relationship while he finishes up filming. Oh, look, a picture of the couple by the lake. Oh, what? There they are kissing by the hot dog stand."

"Nobody kisses by the hot dog stand."

"Wasn't finished." I shushed her. "Riding bikes down the trail! A picnic at sunset!"

"We aren't in *Anne of Green Gables*. There will be no picnics."

"Just . . ." I braced her shoulders. "Does the marriage angle work?"

Her eyes fluttered closed and then opened. A sliver of hope raced through me at her defeated look. "It can work."

"Yes!"

"But—" She held up her hand. "But the story won't be about taming anymore. You've made it bigger than that—"

"So what's it going to be about?"

"Love and seduction," she whispered. "Seduce me, and you seduce them."

"Them?"

"The audience." Jordan frowned. "You'll be seducing me and making me believe you want something permanent, but they'll be experiencing it with me, living it with me, which means that in the end . . ."

"What?" What end? Things were ending? A choking panic seized my lungs as I tried to digest what she'd just said.

"In the end," she repeated, "I'll have to be the bad guy. It will have to be me that ends things with you. So I guess we come full circle. You'll seduce the shrew, and the shrew will decide in the end that she doesn't want to change. That's how the story ends. That's how this ends."

"You're depressing the shit out of me, Jordan, you know that, right?" Talking about ending things when it seemed like something was just starting between us was making my mood worse.

She shrugged.

"Hell, he must have done a number on you."

"What?" She flinched and tucked her wild hair behind her ear. "What are you talking about?"

"Casey. You guys date?"

"No."

"Then I don't understand."

"You wouldn't." The car pulled to a stop in front of the restaurant. She reached for the handle, but I put my hand over hers and stopped her.

"Try me."

I inhaled her perfume as I waited for her response. Her breathing picked up as she glanced down at our joined hands and closed her eyes.

"Casey and I were best friends. He was one of my first clients."

"So when you quit today—"

"I lost my friend, but to be fair, I lost him years ago. I lost him to the money, the fame . . ."

"I'm sorry."

"Me too."

"That won't happen," I felt the need to add. "To me, to us."

Jordan shrugged. "We have to be best friends in order for that to happen, and I'm pretty sure Max staked that claim on you long ago."

I rolled my eyes. "Max thinks he's everyone's best friend."

Her frown turned into a small smile. "I wonder why?"

"Never wonder where he's concerned. Should we eat?"

"Yeah." She nodded. "Good idea."

The conversation was forced throughout dinner, so forced that I had our waiter box up our food. Maybe Jordan needed to go back to the apartment and think. She'd had a day from hell and I'd made it even worse.

Gold star for Reid.

As distressed as she was, I knew I couldn't help her. I never said I was good at comforting women. I almost offered to get her drunk when we got back to the apartment, but I knew that wasn't going to work.

Because Max was sitting on our couch, arms crossed, a scowl marring his features. Becca sat on the other couch, pity etched on hers.

"Oh, hell," I muttered.

He smiled.

I hated that smile. Because damn it to hell, I'd just played into his greedy little hands. Get married first? Me? Yeah, I'd said that. He'd officially won, and I'd been too ass hurt to realize it.

On second thought, the girl who called sounded familiar too.

He wouldn't.

Becca looked at her hands guiltily.

He would.

"You bastard!" I charged toward him, fist flying.

# CHAPTER TWENTY-THREE

## JORDAN

Max jumped onto the couch and held up his hands. "Before you do this, remember, our mother has a Jesus sticker on her car. What would she say?"

"Must you bring her into EVERYTHING?" Reid roared, stopping in front of the couch, chest heaving.

Max shrugged. "It's not my fault I'm her favorite son."

"Says who?"

"Mom. This morning."

"Was this before or after you added vodka to her coffee and slipped her a pill?"

Max gasped.

Becca made her way around the brothers and motioned for me to walk with her toward the kitchen. No words were spoken. She simply popped the cork from the wine bottle and poured what looked like three servings into a glass and slid it toward me. "Believe me, it helps."

I took the glass and sipped while she drank straight from the bottle. "Does he ever . . . stop being . . . Max?" I asked. "Curious minds want to know."

Max jumped off the couch, and naturally he made his own swish sound effect before landing on his feet, thrusting his hands into the air, and turning toward Reid. "I've been her favorite ever since I won at gymnastics."

"You don't win at gymnastics," Reid said through clenched teeth. "You get scored."

"Perfect ten." Max winked back at us, then covered his mouth and said, "Zero," while pointing to Reid.

"We were six!" Reid argued.

"Dude!" Max held up his hands. "I'm just saying, it's not your fault you're not the favorite. Let it go, man, just like Rose let go of Jack."

"Who's Jack?" I whispered.

Becca choked on her wine. "Oh, well, uh, last year Reid had a momentary breakdown because of Max peer pressuring me to shoot Reid in the ass with a tranq gun . . . he spent an hour singing 'My Heart Will Go On.'" I winced. "Off-key."

"Damn you!" Reid turned on his heel and thrust his finger in our direction. "What did I ever do to you!" I think he was talking to Becca. "I hit on you once, one time—"

"—thrice." Max coughed.

"And the only reason was so that I could get back at this one." He jerked his hand back to Max, nearly hitting him in the face. "Because he told Grandma the lock on my door was broken. I was taken advantage of!"

"Well, it was!" Max rolled his eyes.

"Because you took a sledgehammer to it, you bastard!"

Max grinned. "Guilty."

Honestly, I wasn't sure what they were talking about. So I did what any sane girl would do. I drank.

And when my glass was nearly empty, Becca very kindly refilled it while Reid and Max continued pacing around the living room.

"You think if we chant *fight*, they'll take their shirts off?" Becca asked.

I eyed Reid's near perfect physique. "One can only hope."

"Dirty girls," Max shouted. "Both of you! Jezebel! I won't have you poisoning her mind!"

"Oh, please." I rolled my eyes. "And stop calling me a whore!"

"Term of endearment when Max says it." Becca patted my hand. "Next time just say thank you. It's easier that way."

I glanced back at the guys just in time to see Reid launch himself at Max, hands wrapped tightly around his neck, holding him against the couch while Max screamed. "Help, help!"

"We should probably intervene." Becca took a long sip of wine and set her glass down on the table, then yawned.

"Yeah." Max started turning purple. "We probably should. What do you normally do? Take off your top? Blow a whistle? Call the cops?"

"Cops refuse to come when Emorys call—believe me, it's like the whole McDonald's thing. Public service refuses to help them now."

"Makes sense."

Max made a choking noise while he tried to kick Reid in the shin.

"Oh, well." Becca walked slowly toward the guys. I followed. I expected her to gently ask them to stop fighting and separate them.

Instead, she punched Reid in the face and then separated them.

He stumbled back.

I caught him and fell backward against the other couch while he rubbed his face and whispered, "My hero."

"My lungs broke your fall," I wheezed.

Max gasped for air. "You know my biggest fear is not breathing!"

"Not breathing?" I had to ask, I just had to.

Reid chuckled. "For six years Max was convinced every food was going to cause him to go into anaphylactic shock because Oprah did a segment where some chick nearly died after eating a kiwi!"

"A kiwi!" Max repeated hoarsely. "Who dies from kiwi? That chick." He shook his head vigorously. "I refuse to go down eating."

Reid moved off me and sat back on the couch. "He took Benadryl every time he ate fruit."

Max narrowed his eyes. "Make fun now, but we both know that watermelon gave me hives! My throat closed, you bastard!"

"Maybe if you took smaller bites . . ." Reid said helpfully.

Max lunged again.

Becca grabbed him by the shirt and tugged him back onto his own couch. "No more fighting, we have engagement pictures tomorrow."

"Oh, good." Max glared at Reid. "Now the photographer's going to think that I like my bride to choke me during sex because I have man-size fingerprints around my neck." He tugged at his shirt. "Damn it!"

"You mean you don't like that, baby?" Becca winked at me.

I burst out laughing while Max pointed between the two of us. "No, not happening, I'm sorry, you can't be friends."

"Why?" I asked. "I could always use more friends. After all, Reid did kill my plant, so . . ."

"Plant?" Max's eyebrows narrowed in on Reid. "You sick, sick man. Why the hell would you kill a plant? Don't you know what those stand for?"

Reid frowned. "Uh—"

"Love!" Max shouted. "Life! Completion! What the hell is wrong with you? You may as well run over a mama duck and her little lings!"

"Lings?" I whispered.

"Ducklings!" Max shouted. "Damn it, Reid. Mom raised you better."

"Oh, really?" Reid snorted. "We're going there, huh? How about you setting me up on national radio! You KNEW if you pushed hard enough I'd propose marriage."

Max cackled. "You were always easy to break. Always."

"I will seriously punch you in the throat."

Max grabbed Becca and placed her on his lap, then grinned behind her.

"Human shield." Becca sighed and looked horribly guilty. "Can't say I'm surprised, nor disappointed by this sudden change of events—after all, my loving fiancé made me call in as well."

"Why help the evil genius?" I said.

"She called me a genius." Max puffed out his chest.

"Note that she said *evil* first." Reid lowered his voice. "Just saying."

"Well." Becca shrugged. "He's been impossible to live with this past week. Every time I come home from class, he has his ear pressed to the door like some lovesick teenager playing Girl Talk."

"Oh, my gosh, I loved that game!" I gushed.

Becca laughed. "Me too! I can't believe I actually called my crushes and—"

Max snapped his fingers. "Becca, this is Max time; you two can play later."

"Punch him." I glared at Max while Becca reached between her legs and flicked her fingers.

"Damn it!" Max yelped. "Low blow. Literally."

"So." I cleared my throat, ignoring Max's sobbing. "What were you saying? About helping him?"

Becca shrugged. "I thought making him promise we wouldn't have sex until we got married . . . was a good idea at the time—a few months isn't long to wait and I thought it would bring some excitement into the wedding night!"

I nodded.

Max gave me the finger while Reid wrapped a protective arm around me.

"Anyway." Becca shrugged. "I figure either I live with Max while Reid slowly drives him insane one fake orgasm at a time." I blushed. "Or I help him and finally get some sleep without having to drug my own fiancé!"

"I knew that milk tasted funny!" Max roared.

Becca smirked. "Slept like a baby last night."

Amazing, it was like watching a sitcom, only in real life. Max started to gag. "You know I'm allergic to pills, ALL PILLS!"

Becca wouldn't let him up.

Otis, sensing unrest within the home, came barreling down the hall and jumped onto the couch nearest Max.

Max froze. "Holy shit, aliens really do exist! Hey, E.T.!"

"OTIS!" I corrected. "He looks nothing like E.T."

"Damn, you look smaller in real life, wanna go on a bike ride?" Otis's tail started wagging. "You do? You do want to go on a bike ride? Quick, phone home!" Bark, bark, bark.

"What is he? The dog whisperer?" I elbowed a silent Reid.

"The one and only day he went to Boy Scouts was when they went to a petting zoo . . . he got a badge for taking care of the animals. That damn badge has been a thorn in my side for years. Years, I tell you."

"Reid's jealous." Max patted Otis's head. "The only badge he got was for selling cookies—then again we all know what really happened. Don't you know drug dealers aren't supposed to take their own product?"

"Huh?" I blinked at Reid. "Drug dealers?"

"Girl Scout cookies," Reid explained. "Legal crack."

"Ah." I nodded. "Got it."

"So." Reid stood. "This is what's going to happen. Jordan and I are going to try to fix what you guys ruined—thanks for that, by the way—and Max, I don't want to hear or see you until all this is through."

Max looked guiltily down at the ground.

"Max?" Reid repeated. "Max, what did you do?"

Max yawned. "It's getting late. We should probably—"

"—Max."

Max rolled his eyes. "Oh, fine. Under the slight possibility that calling in didn't work, I may have sort of . . ." More coughing. "Booked us all flights to Vegas this next weekend. The plan was to get you drunk."

"Good plan." I nodded in approval while Max winked in my direction. "But we aren't going."

Max pouted.

Reid touched my arm. "Maybe it wouldn't be a bad idea. I mean . . . we have to go through with this, or at least pretend to, right?"

Crap. Crap. Crap. He was right, but . . . the last thing I needed was to be on a plane with Max, of all people.

Or sit next to Reid.

Or pretend to marry him in what's actually one of my favorite places in the world. It just seemed unfair.

"Jordan." Reid turned me toward him. "Come on, you had a shit day; it's been a hell of a week. Let Max pay for a weekend getaway. We'll go to a few choice clubs. You can call ahead of time, right? And let them know we're making appearances?"

I nodded and bit on my lower lip, almost drawing blood. "But you still have a few scenes to shoot."

"I'll finish up this week, and if they need me for anything else, I'll stay, but we've gotten a lot done. We're ahead of schedule."

Why couldn't they be behind?

Max stood and crossed his arms. "What say you, Shrew?"

I say Max should have to fly on the outside of the plane, strapped to the wing with a cape, so it gets caught.

"Fine," I huffed. "Let's do it."

"Vegas!" Max yelled.

# CHAPTER TWENTY-FOUR

## REID

The week went by painfully slowly. Probably because I was looking forward to getting away from the media. It had gotten worse since Jordan's and my announcement. And when I say worse, I mean we'd gone from trending for a day on Twitter to being followed by cameras everywhere we went. It was impossible to get a damn cup of coffee without someone snapping a picture or asking why we weren't together.

The attention I could get used to—I was an actor, it was part of the game. But the negativity toward Jordan seriously pissed me off. I was painted as some sort of hero for dating a girl who didn't meet the entertainment industry's standards for pretty.

Apparently people thought it was romantic that I'd fallen in love with the ugly girl. The Wonderwall on MSN was filled with unflattering pictures of Jordan with spilled coffee on her shirt and lipstick askew, among other things, while all of my pictures looked flawless. If they only knew her, they'd realize she was just accident-prone, not ugly—not by a long shot.

One entertainment blog went as far to call me a saint for dating an average girl with big, childbearing hips.

I almost cussed them out on live TV when the interviewer brought it up, but Jordan, bless her heart, managed to kick me with one of her sharp heels before I made an ass out of myself. Fat? Who the hell would call her fat? She had curves, gorgeous, luscious, spellbinding curves that had me losing sleep every damn night because my stupid hands refused to forget what it felt like to cup her perfect ass.

Thankfully almost all of my on-camera interviews included Jordan, meaning she was always right there, pinching me before I said something stupid, and ever since news of our engagement broke loose, I was more than likely to say something that would be offensive, probably because of all the stress and lies.

"Dude." Colton cleared his throat. "Am I interrupting a moment between you and your Starbucks? Because I'm not gonna lie, I feel really uncomfortable with the way your gaze is lingering on that mermaid."

I rolled my eyes. "Sorry, just thinking."

"Good." He exhaled. "Because for a minute there I thought were going to have to have a serious talk about your Starbucks addiction."

I sighed and took a seat. "When's the flight leave again?"

"Five o'clock on the dot from JFK." He toyed with his coffee straw and then started fidgeting with a napkin.

"What's wrong?"

"Huh?" He glanced up. "What do you mean?"

I rolled my eyes. "Colt, you're shit at hiding things. What's wrong?"

He cleared his throat. "Do you, uh, think this is a good idea?"

I let out a long sigh through my lips. "Well, it's not a bad one, I can tell you that. Jordan lined up three separate appearances for Vegas, the buzz is huge for the movie, and according to *Entertainment Weekly*, I'm the next Jeremy Renner. So, yeah, I'm thinking it's a better idea than staying here and holing up in my apartment just because the lie got a little bit bigger than we all expected."

"Bigger." Colt's eyebrows shot up. "*People* named you the hottest couple of the year. Bigger is an understatement."

I waved him off, even though my chest started clenching with what I'd assumed was panic. "I trust Jordan. She's the best. If she says it's going to be okay, then it's going to be okay."

"And that's another thing." Colt leaned forward, his voice barely above a whisper. "How do you know she's not really falling for you? I mean, are you sure things aren't progressing past a simple PR trick?"

"Because she's a professional," I said quickly, even though my heart started hammering against my chest so hard I was afraid Colt was going to see right through the bullshit. Forget Jordan, I was the one I was worried about. Was that selfish? Yeah, a bit, but I liked her, really liked her.

She was beautiful.

Hilarious.

Held her own with Max.

Focused.

Goal oriented.

Had the sexiest mouth I'd ever seen.

Oh, right, and she held her own with Max. That demanded to be said at least twice, possibly three times.

Hell, what wasn't to like?

"You're staring at the mermaid again," Colton deadpanned. "And sorry to break it to you, but your cup isn't a magic lamp, and no matter how many times you rub the Starbucks logo, the topless mermaid won't pop out of the cup and offer you three wishes."

One. I really only needed one.

A do-over with Jordan.

A way to make her see me as more than just her client. It was a bad idea. A horrible idea.

Try and really seduce her.

Because for the first time in . . . hell, I didn't even know how long—she made me want more than just a first date.

Or even a third.

"So should I go now?" Colt stood.

"Sit." I pushed the cup away. "Sorry, lost in my thoughts."

"Do that shit on your own time." Colt put a napkin over the mermaid and folded his hands on the table. "Look, I just don't want to see anyone get hurt, and girls . . . they're emotional. Believe me, I'm married to one."

"Damn it, I knew there was something different about Milo!" I snapped my fingers and pounded the table.

"Hilarious." Colt rolled his eyes. "Just be careful." A camera flashed outside the window. "Now that you can't piss without having your picture taken, if things go south . . ."

South. I smirked. Please let them go south. I could do a lot of damage with south.

"Dude, look at me that way again and I'm going to punch you in the nuts."

"You sounded like Max just then." I laughed.

Colt didn't.

"Not a compliment, was it?"

Colt shook his head very slowly.

"Sorry." I stood. "I'm going to pack and I'll see you guys later at the airport . . . Jason's coming, right?"

"Yeah." Colton threw our cups in the trash as we walked out. "But his parents made him swear to bring a helmet."

"He's twenty-four, why the hell would he need a helmet?"

"Because Milo will be there, and the last time they traveled together Jason suffered three blunt head wounds and a black eye. Guy wore a patch for a full week. We still call him Sparrow."

I nodded. "Think if we get him drunk enough in Vegas we can convince him to get an actual Sparrow tramp stamp on his lower back?"

Colt chuckled and rubbed his hands together. "We can always blame Max once Jason wakes up from his drunken stupor."

"Really, we'd be doing him a favor."

"Yeah, we'll just have to make sure we tell him that when he wakes up with ink above his low-rise jeans."

I checked my watch. "All kidding aside, I really need to get back to the apartment." I kept my head down, making sure my hat and sunglasses were in place. "I'll see you at the airport."

Colton put on his black Ray-Bans and nodded. "Think they'll have enough alcohol on that plane to sedate us? I'm worried that we'll all be traveling with Max in such confined space."

"Welcome to my hell." I turned around and waved. "See ya soon."

Colt returned my wave and hailed a taxi while I made my way down the street.

While waiting for the walk signal, I pulled out my phone and texted Jordan, who I'd programmed into my phone as Sebastian.

Me: You packed?

Sebastian: NOTHING FITS!

Me: Why the all caps?

Sebastian: You cook too well and my swimsuit from last year looks like . . . hell, it looks horrible. I can't wear it. I can't.

Me: Naked suits you. I thought we discussed this?

Sebastian: Prison, however, does not, so if you want me to stay out, I need to go shopping, but I don't have time and Otis cried when I dropped him off at doggie day care.

Me: Dogs don't cry.

Sebastian: Full-on sobs!

Me: He's fine.

Sebastian: I left him a toy, do you think he thinks I abandoned him?

Me: Yes.

Sebastian: I CAN'T GO TO VEGAS!

Okay, damage control was seriously not working. With a flick of my wrist, I looked at the time. I had a few hours left—I could pack like a champ. I was going to officially fix one problem.

Me: You're going to Vegas. What's your size . . . I'll stop by Saks.

Sebastian: Never ask a woman what size she is!

Me: If you don't tell me I'll just buy every size and return the rest.

Sebastian: . . .

Me: Spit it out. Didn't hear you!

Sebastian: Eight.

Me: And what a beautiful eight . . . I'll pick out a few suits. And before you freak out, I have amazing fashion sense. Also, Otis is fine, he's just spoiled and wants to go with. It's the weekend, not a month. He'll make friends and probably fall in love with a Chihuahua named Milo, they'll hump like rabbits and have miniature E.T. aliens and all will be right in the world. Now get your ass packed.

Sebastian: A Chihuahua? Really?

Me: PACK!

Sebastian: DON'T YELL!

Me: Pack, please.

Sebastian: Fine, and I like black.

Me: Great, because you're getting red!

Sebastian: I said black.

Me: Sorry, losing cell service.

Sebastian: Texting service?

`Me: A:DGJDG:HDGJSDLKJGF`

`Sebastian: REID!`

`Me: JORDAN!`

I shoved my phone back in my pocket though it continued to buzz, I'm sure with expletives and other choice language. I couldn't remember the last time a girl getting irritated with me actually made my day.

Whistling, I crossed the street and went into Saks.

In the past, spending money on a woman seemed pointless. Why buy them something when it wasn't going to last? But for some reason, after picking out the suit and a few other items, and sliding my card across the counter, the relationship felt . . . real.

And I liked it.

Maybe too much.

# CHAPTER TWENTY-FIVE

## JORDAN

I had a hard time swallowing the fact that I was traveling to Vegas with relative strangers, one of them a known terrorist—okay, maybe that was an exaggeration on my part. But I don't care what Max claims about his so-called innocence. There was no way a guy like that had never been zip-tied to an air marshal. No way in hell. And when I asked him if he'd ever been arrested on a plane, his answer was to start singing, "I've got friends in low places."

Pretty sure by the end of the trip one or all of us would wish we'd brought sedatives or at least some masking tape to cover his mouth. Already I'd been tempted to physically harm the guy after an incident where he unzipped my carry-on and started riffling through my crap.

"What are you doing?" I asked, trying to keep my voice calm while my nails dug into my palms so I wouldn't deck him.

Max continued riffling, then paused. "Oh, sorry, I thought it was my bag."

"Mine's pink."

"Right." He nodded. "And mine's green, but I'm color-blind."

"Highly doubt it." I jerked my bag away from him, but not before his pinkie finger shot into the air with my new red leopard bathing suit hanging from it. "Kitty gonna play?"

I swiped the suit and shoved it back into the suitcase and growled. "Kitty's gonna play with your dead body if you search through my stuff again."

"Please, like it was on purpose." He grinned.

"Everything"—I sighed—"and I do mean everything, is on purpose when it comes to you."

"Aw." He winked.

Three days. I could do anything for three days, right?

I couldn't back out now, though, especially since Ren thought going to Vegas was akin to Reid and me getting married and having a love child.

"Publicity for this kid has been off the charts!" He beamed. "Good job, Jordan, this is your best yet!"

How could I say no to that? Especially since my promotion was all but set in stone if I could keep myself from killing Reid's next of kin.

As if on cue, Max made a loud joke about how Jason smoked all his pot before he got to the airport so he wouldn't have to lie about having a medical prescription.

It was that moment that solidified that every airport employee hates their job, possibly their existence, as a TSA employee glared in Jason's direction, then narrowed her eyes and started talking into her radio.

Jason glared at Max but wasn't stopped—then again, they wouldn't stop him for something like that, not unless they actually found illegal drugs on him while going through security.

I cracked my neck and clenched my bag tighter. It wasn't my first time in Vegas; I loved it there. I should be excited. Instead, eyes on Max, all I could think was that I should have said no.

Maybe I'd look back on this very moment and say, "This is where things went awry." Yes, awry. And all because of Max Emory and his evil, self-serving plans.

My eyes narrowed in on him as I stepped through security.

And it beeped.

Like twenty times.

I was the last to go through, so the rest of the crew were already waiting on the other side, staring at me.

"Ma'am." One of the TSA people stepped forward. His eyebrow was one giant line across the top of his forehead, and his eyes were rimmed with red. Out of all the employees to be strip-searching me, I was stuck with Bert, not Ernie, who was currently giving a sticker to a little kid along with a high five. "Please step aside."

He pulled out a wand and started moving it slowly over my body. "Spread your arms and legs, please."

Max held up his phone and snapped a picture. I rolled my eyes and got in position as the stick made its way down the front of my jeans. It beeped.

"It's probably the button," I said helpfully.

Bert stood. "Ma'am, let me do my job. You do yours and stand there."

"O-okay."

He ran the wand around me again. If I closed my eyes I could almost imagine he was my fairy godmother and in a few seconds I'd be two sizes smaller with long, glossy hair and boobs that got me through security based on the fact that they were so awesome the metal detector ceased working in their presence.

"Well . . ." Bert brought the wand back. "I think it's just the button."

No crap.

With clenched teeth, I nodded and started walking toward my waiting bag.

"Ma'am?" An attractive twentysomething man with a kind smile pointed to my carry-on. "This yours?"

"Yes." Seriously? Out of everyone going on this trip, I was the one getting stopped? There was no way Max wasn't on some sort of watch list, damn it!

"Hmm." The guy unzipped my bag. "It just seems you have some liquids in here, so let me just—" He froze, his cheeks blushing crimson. "Um."

"What?" Was my swimsuit that daring? Damn you, Reid! I said black!

"Uh." The guy swallowed and looked away, then very slowly pulled out a bottle of KY, and note that I said *bottle*. It wasn't one of those tiny things you could easily keep hidden in your back jeans pocket. No, no, it was huge, as in bigger than my water bottle. It was like someone went to the Costco of sex stores and decided, hey, just in case we run out . . .

"That's not mine!" I blurted.

"It was in your bag," he countered. "Are you saying this isn't your bag?"

I sighed. "It's my bag, but—"

"Because if this isn't your bag, then you need to tell me now. Did someone tell you to carry this bag through security?" He reached for his walkie-talkie.

"It's mine," I blurted.

He nodded, then looked down. "All of it?"

"Yup."

Max waltzed toward us along with the rest of the gang. "Problem?"

"Nope." I clenched my teeth. "It just seems bringing twenty-four ounces of KY through security is frowned upon."

"Twenty-four, huh?" Reid chuckled.

I glared.

He stopped laughing.

"Ma'am, this is going to have to go too." The guy picked up a giant bottle of Her Pleasure massage oil.

I felt myself turn bright red. But I couldn't say *it's not mine* again! He'd confiscate my bag and I really would be walking around Vegas nude like Reid joked!

"And this." A black whip dangled from his hand. "This is technically a weapon."

"I'm sure she's well aware of how hazardous a weighted whip can be." Max nodded solemnly. "Hell, that handle could be a club."

The agent sighed.

I groaned.

All in all, two sets of handcuffs were pulled out.

Pink zip ties.

A bottle of flavored nipple cream.

"Well." The agent stuffed everything back in. "It looks like I'll only have to confiscate the whip and the liquids."

"Swell," I croaked.

"Have fun in . . ." He tilted his head.

"Vegas," Max said helpfully. "Gotta pay the bills somehow." He laughed.

The agent joined in.

And I was left wondering just how much of a weapon that whip could really be, especially if I wrapped it around Max's neck and waited for a popping sound.

I grabbed my bag and walked slowly toward Reid.

He winced with my every stomp.

"Max," I hissed. "Not funny."

Milo and Becca crossed their arms with me and took a stance on either side, while Max, Jason, Colt, and Reid stood opposite us. Already we were divided, guys against girls, yet all of us were against Max as he stood helplessly in the middle.

"Don't start a war you can't finish, Emory." I jabbed my finger in his direction. "I know you're behind the sex toys."

"Aw." Max chuckled. "How cute. If you think those are sex toys, no wonder I've never heard Reid yell your name."

"Let me at him!" Becca held me back.

"Not the face." Max covered up. "It's my best feature." He laughed at his own joke, then sobered. "Actually, it's one of many, feel me?"

"Okay!" Reid stepped between us. "Max, no more practical jokes. All right? This trip is supposed to be relaxing, and we can't do that if Jordan kills you, then asks us to help bury the body."

Max held up his hand. "I hereby solemnly swear to stop putting toys in your girl's bag."

I tried to keep my heart from fluttering at the words *your girl*. It felt good to belong to him.

"Good," Reid huffed, then wrapped an arm around me. "Now, let's find our damn gate so Jordan can drink those images away."

"Hear, hear," I grumbled.

•   •   •

"So." Max turned around in his seat, whiskey in hand. "What's the story, Jordan?"

The airplane dipped, almost sending me careening into Reid's arm, not that it would have been a bad thing. Touching his arm. It had been distracting me since takeoff. All bronzed and muscled sitting innocently within inches of mine.

I was even fascinated with his light-colored arm hair. Like a total freak.

"Uh." I sipped my white wine and cleared my throat. "Story?" I shared a glance with a confused Reid. "I don't think I understand the question."

Max nodded. "Everyone has a story . . . a few choice words that describe their past woes." He took two long sips of his drink and then said, "Take Jason, for example."

"Oh, hell." Jason's expression went from relaxed to straight-up hostile.

"Home skillet can't make it through a twenty-four-hour period without a Little Mermaid Band-Aid." Max shook his head. "Also, he almost got married last year to a total bitch named Jayne, who I'm not entirely convinced wasn't an actual vampire, because when I put garlic under her mattress she made a really loud screeching sound."

"Because you scared the shit out of her," Milo added. "Not because she bites."

"Oh, she bit." Jason shuddered. "Hard."

"Can story time be over now?" Colt asked.

"Colton and Milo are best friends to lovers. It's romantic, really." Max said wistfully. "She's wanted his man package since she knew what it was, though to be fair I'm not entirely sure she knew what it was until about a year ago, when he showed her."

Milo groaned and covered her face with her hands.

"Becca's and my story was freaking televised. No need to rehash that round of awesome, though here's a few hashtags just in case you didn't TiVo every episode: #zombies, #hades, #beccakissesmaxhard, #sevend-warves, #bachelorislandwhereeveryonegoestodie." Max smacked a loud kiss on Becca's cheek and turned. "And Reid." Max chuckled. "I think we all know his story . . . it involves dear old sweet Grandma, dentures, Bengay, and what I'm hoping was a very thorough bout of therapy."

"Don't forget the drugs," Colton piped up. "And climbing the roof."

"Or jumping out of that tree." Milo nodded.

"And the ChapStick," Max said in a hollow voice.

"Okay!" Reid held up his hands. "Maybe we should all rest before we land, yeah?"

Max eyed Reid suspiciously. "You don't know, do you?"

"Know?" Reid repeated. "Know what?"

"Her story!"

Reid gaped. "Of course I do!"

Max sat back and held out his hand. "Then be my guest."

"Er . . ." Reid rubbed his lips together. "Jordan likes chocolate."

"Colt's allergic, and you can find that shit out on Facebook." Max yawned. "Next."

"She's . . . driven." Reid nodded. "And rarely lets her hair down."

"And I think I speak for everyone when I say thank you for keeping that mess contained." Max pointed at my head while I self-consciously patted down my mane. Thankfully, it was still in place and hadn't yet chosen to pop out of its constraints or give the nice old man behind us a surprise heart attack, at which point I'm sure Max would say something like, "Don't worry, I've got this, I'm a doctor."

"Thanks," I mumbled, taking a long, long, very long sip of my wine.

Max eyed Reid. "Still waiting."

"She's a . . . shrew."

I rolled my eyes. "Good one, Reid."

"See!" Max's ice nearly launched itself in Jason's face as he thrust his cup into the air. "You don't know her story . . ." All eyes turned to me while Max said in a quiet voice, "Start at the beginning."

"I was born," I said dryly.

"Wrong beginning." Max cracked a smile. "We all know you're the girl who gets food on everything, no shame in that . . . just means my dear brother gets to lick it off."

"Thanks, man." Reid covered his face with his hands and let out a groan.

"Got your back, son!" Max nodded seriously. "So Jordan . . . story? You keep a plant alive for how many years? And why? You live alone? Why? Fear of commitment? Snakes? Sharks? Holy shit, you like women!"

"Stop." I held up my empty glass. "Fine, I'm . . . invisible."

"Neat trick." Max grinned. "Explain."

I shrugged tightly, irritated he was pulling the information out of me so easily—then again, it could be the alcohol. "Well, in my class picture it actually says, 'Jordan Litwright. Not pictured.'"

"That's what they do," Max said slowly, "when you miss picture day."

"Right." I nodded. "But I was there."

"Oh," they all said in unison.

"In a red shirt."

Max patted my hand. "This happen on multiple occasions?"

"Every. Year."

Max pressed the call button. Once the attendant arrived, he ordered a whiskey on the rocks for everyone. Double for me.

I opened my mouth to continue talking, but Max held up his hand. "We need whiskey for sad stories."

We waited ten more minutes in tense silence. I prayed Max would get bored and forget. But he refused to turn around.

Though Becca tried, bless her heart. I'm pretty sure she was thinking about flashing him.

Then our drinks came.

"You may continue," Max said.

"Fine." I gripped my plastic cup, the condensation making my hand a little sweaty. "I went to prom with my cousin . . ."

"Aw, that's sweet!" Becca gushed.

"He was twenty-seven and had two kids."

Drinking commenced.

"Even though I had tickets and a student ID card, the girl at the door, the same one who had gone to school with me basically my whole life, asked me my name, and when I told her, she said, and I quote, 'She doesn't go here anymore. She died.'"

More drinking.

My cup was empty.

Max gave me Reid's.

"So yeah." I exhaled. "Invisible. That's me. But it makes me good at my job. I can be in the background while the stars get all the attention."

"Bullshit," Reid spat.

"What?" I jerked around to look at him. "What do you mean?"

"That's bullshit. You're lying."

"Reid." Max's tone was warning, almost like he was being protective of me.

"No!" Reid shook his head. "I don't believe it. You're absolutely stunning. Invisible, my ass! A person would have to be blind or just really, really stupid to not see you. I mean, look at you!"

It's official. Reid was my new hero.

Forget Spider-Man.

I was going to get Reid Emory sheets and sleep in them every night.

My cheeks heated as I ducked a bit under his intense stare.

Those aqua eyes refused to let me look down. Instead, he tilted my chin toward him and didn't look away. "You. Are. Stunning."

I could have sworn I heard one of the girls sigh.

Or maybe it was just Max.

"Thanks, but you don't have to make me feel better." I licked my lips. "I'm happy with who I am. Really."

"You should be." Reid nodded. "Damn proud of who you are."

He was doing it again. Casting one of those magic spells with his hypnotic eyes, making me think that a girl like me could really be with a guy like him. Making me believe that the words he'd said to me back at his apartment before he crushed my plant . . . were actually true.

That he wanted me.

Desired me.

Enjoyed touching me, kissing me . . .

"This is your captain speaking," a loud voice interrupted. "I've turned on the 'Fasten Seat Belts' sign, as we've gotten word that there's some rough air up ahead. Sit tight."

# CHAPTER TWENTY-SIX

## REID

The turbulence wasn't *holy shit, we're going down* bad, but it wasn't pleasant either. Max whimpered from the front seat, then begged to hold Becca's hand, only his hand grabbed her breast instead.

The guy was copping a feel all while having everyone believe he was afraid of flying.

He wasn't.

I, however, was.

Maybe it was because when I was in high school as a way to get back at me for being born first—Max's words, not mine—Max told me that whenever a plane hit turbulence it meant that the engine was locking up.

He paid my science teacher to back up his story.

He said this the day before we flew into the Denver airport from New York.

And anyone who's ever flown into Denver just flinches in his seat and winces a little. Turbulence flying in and out of Denver is the stuff of legends.

I cried.

Max got it on camera.

And that, my friends, is how I lost my prom queen girlfriend to an eighth grader with a mind for evil.

I think it's also the first moment I realized Max wasn't like other humans . . .

Or aliens.

Or really any species known to mankind.

"Need a distraction?" Jordan's smile was kind. Her perfect pout formed over pretty white teeth.

"Oh, I don't know." I gripped the armrest. "Care to throw Max out of the plane? That may help my mood."

"He's kinda heavy."

"Muscle." Max coughed ahead of us, then turned around and grinned. "Reid, it was a joke. You know turbulence is normal."

"You classically conditioned me, you bastard!" The plane dipped again. I glanced out the window, just to be sure I didn't see smoke or anything that pointed to the fact that we were going down.

Jordan placed her hand on my arm, her fingernails drawing slight circles around my skin. It felt good. I started breathing in through my nose and out through my mouth while she talked. "I'm guessing Max is the reason behind your fear."

"You'd guess right." I glared at Max. "Turn around before I throat punch you."

Max rolled his eyes. "Adults don't use such language."

My eyebrows shot up as I waited.

"Bitch," he finished, then turned back around.

"There it is," I mumbled.

Jordan patted my arm. "At least you had a brother or someone to hang out with you at school. I would have done anything to have a sibling."

"Only child?" I frowned. "How did I not know that?"

"You gotta ask," Max said from the front seat.

"Could you not?" I smacked him on the head. "Pay attention to your fiancée."

Max glanced back. "She fell asleep."

"Wake. Her. Up."

"Waking up someone while they're in a deep sleep is rude, besides, why would I want to deter her from dreaming of me? Naked? That's just cruel, man. Have you no heart?"

"Earphones," Jordan interjected. "Put them on so your brother and I can have adult time. I'll set my watch for a half hour, and when that's done you can turn around and I'll give you some fruit snacks." Jordan pulled some Teenage Mutant Ninja Turtle fruit snacks from her bag and dangled them in the air. Max's eyes went back and forth, back and forth.

"Those are the best kind." His eyes narrowed. "Damn you for finding my kryptonite!" He gasped. "You read my blog!"

Jordan grinned. "I figured the easiest way to learn the ways of a homicidal maniac was to get inside his head, see how he ticks. I may have browsed it this last week while trying to uncover any of the five hundred skeletons in your closet to make sure you wouldn't be any more of a PR nightmare for Reid."

Max nodded his approval. "We'll keep you."

"Oh, good, I'm going to a good home then. There's that." Jordan snatched the fruit snacks back. "Now, let me and Reid chat, I think *The Lego Movie*'s on."

"Everything . . . really is awesome." Max sighed. "Fine, turning around now, but I want two packs, not one."

"Deal."

"And—" He thrust his finger in the air. "If they're old and not chewy, no deal. Don't go opening the pack just so air gets in. I want them untampered with."

Jordan put a hand over her heart. "Like I would drug you."

"Jezebel," he grumbled. "Don't betray my trust."

"Says the man who put a whip in my bag."

"Turning around." Max shrugged. "Because I want to and because I want the fruit snacks, not because you're forcing me to."

"Right." Jordan smiled.

Max put on his headphones, leaving us in peace.

"You're so good with him." I leaned my head against the headrest and smiled.

"Yeah, well . . ." Jordan shrugged. "I have cousins."

"Aw, how old?"

"Five and seven."

"So about the same age then." I nodded.

"Yup." She let out a low laugh that had me licking my lips and focusing way too hard on her mouth. "Sounds about right."

"So." Why was I suddenly nervous? Max, he was irritating as hell, but he was a damn good buffer, and probably the best person to have on your side if you needed to keep the conversation going, even if it went in really inappropriate directions. "No siblings . . . nobody to sit with you on the bus?"

"Nope." Jordan lifted a shoulder in a haphazard shrug. "It always made me so angry when people would trash-talk their brothers or sisters when I would have killed to have some big brother beat up my first boyfriend for cheating on me."

"Your first boyfriend cheated on you?" I wasn't able to keep the anger from my voice.

"He was seven." Jordan patted my shoulder. "Back down, cowboy. And he only cheated because my mom forgot to pack me a MoonPie."

"Harsh."

"Yeah, well"—Jordan's eyes narrowed slightly—"I moved on and so did he . . . It seems I wasn't the only one who brought MoonPies to school. He and Kristin dated for three whole days until he moved on to greener pastures."

"More MoonPies?"

"Nah, he went on to the hard stuff, like Snickers and Twix bars. Is it wrong that I laughed when he announced to the class he had three cavities?"

"Bastard deserved five, maybe six at least," I said.

"Karma." She winked.

Shit. It was happening. I was officially unable to control my smile and probably freaking her out. I couldn't stop smiling, the muscles in my cheeks hurt, no matter how badly I wanted to stop—to play it cool.

I had hit *that* point in the relationship, where every man says, "That will never happen to me. Love is for saps. I'm a real man. Look, chest hair."

It's where logic goes straight out the window and your heart suddenly grows way too big to be kept inside your chest so you decide, the hell with it, I'm just going to wear it on my sleeve. And hope she doesn't break it.

A girl like Jordan could break me.

MoonPies be damned!

I wanted more than her MoonPie, though that sounded really good too.

"You okay?" She frowned, her smile faltering. "You looked like you're thinking way too hard about my story."

"Yeah." I fake coughed into my hand, embarrassed that she'd caught me daydreaming, then pounded my chest a bit and did a little shake in my seat. She probably thought I was faking a seizure. "I just, I don't know." I pressed my lips together. "You look really pretty, that's all."

And she did.

Her boyfriend jeans were paired with a plain black T-shirt, and the girl was rocking a blue pair of Nike Free running shoes.

It was then I realized she wasn't wearing a skirt. I mean, in theory I knew she was wearing jeans, but . . . my mind had been elsewhere.

"You're not wearing a dress," I blurted. "Or an oxford or—"

Her eyebrows arched.

"Pants." I nodded. "You're wearing pants."

"Yeah, well." Her hand shook as she reached for her hair, and then, as if realizing it was pulled back into a tight ponytail, dropped it in her lap.

"I like you this way," I whispered.

"Ha, unkempt?" she countered.

"No . . ." I licked my lips while she leaned in closer to me. "Just a bit less . . . constricted."

Her smile was contagious and I found myself catching it again. To anyone watching us we probably looked like we were losing our minds, but I knew what was happening.

I was falling.

And I could only hope she was too.

# CHAPTER TWENTY-SEVEN

## JORDAN

The minute the desert air hit my hair, the tresses calmed down. Maybe the heat was so intense my hair just gave up and died. Great, so I'd be bald by the evening.

And with my luck find myself on a magazine cover with a gorgeous Reid.

"Vegas!" Max shouted, arms wide, sunglasses askew on his face. "Admit it, this was probably one of my better ideas." He turned to face us.

Jason yawned.

Reid checked his watch.

Colt and Milo kissed.

And Becca gave Max a really overexaggerated head nod.

"No fun until you guys admit this was a good idea." Max crossed his arms. "Oh, and P.S. I paid for penthouse suites, so—"

Jason launched himself at Max, probably to hug him? Who knew? But he tripped over the suitcase and would have face planted if not for Max's quick catch.

"Good save," I said.

Jason stood and brushed off his shirt. "Swear you guys put obstacles in my way on purpose."

He rubbed his eyes.

"Jason?"

"Hmm?" He blinked wide, then blinked again. "What's up?"

"Are you . . . can you see?"

"Huh?"

"Do you have vision problems?"

"Yes," Milo answered for him. "But he refuses to get glasses, because according to Jason they're nerdy."

"Glasses are hot," Becca spoke up.

Max glared. "People with glasses get called Four Eyes."

"In elementary school." Becca shoved Max; he flailed, then fell backward over the suitcase onto his ass.

"Classy," Max called from the ground. "It's cool, I like my women aggressive."

"Why would you need glasses?" I was still stuck on Jason's vision issue. "Wear contacts."

"Whoa!" Jason held up his hands. "That's crazy talk."

"What am I missing?" I looked around helplessly.

Max, from the ground, held up his pointer finger and said, "Jason, watch, I'm going to touch my eye."

"Do it, you bastard, and I'll cut your balls off and feed them to my mom's chickens."

Max was silent and then said, "She didn't have chickens last week when she invited me over for tea. I'm calling your bluff . . ." He slowly lowered his finger to his eye while Jason paled.

"Ah." I nodded. "Fear of touching your eye? Isn't that an actual phobia?"

Jason shuddered. "Dude, I'm going to puke, just stop."

Max sighed, then dropped his hand. "Fine, but guys, this weekend is about epic-ness. Let's relax, have fun, and get these two crazy kids fake hitched. And if you need to detour from the itinerary, please let me know ahead of time."

"Itinerary?" I repeated as Max got off the ground, opened his carry-on, and pulled out laminated sheets of paper and started passing them around.

"You'll note that we're already late for check-in, which means that you'll have to refresh a lot faster. We're kicking off this party the right way."

I turned the paper over in my hands. Max was detailed, all right, he even wrote in bathroom breaks. Girls got ten minutes, on account of the fact they have to sit on the toilet, and yes, that was actually written in parentheses. Boys got five minutes, because they stand like badasses, also written in parentheses.

"Is this normal?" I dangled the sheet in front of Reid.

He sighed. "Sadly, yes. Every vacation I've ever taken with the guy has a schedule. I'd like to say it makes life a living hell, but it's actually helpful because you don't have to make any decisions. It's easier to let Max rule."

"Hmm." I tapped the sheet against my leg. "Think thirty years from now, when he runs for president, that will be his tagline—'It's easier to let Max rule'?"

Reid snorted. "Wouldn't surprise me."

"All right." Max clapped. "To the Batmobile."

I followed the rest of the gang toward a waiting stretch limo and was handed a glass of chilled champagne before getting in.

I may have been stressed about this trip.

But already I was relaxed and letting my guard down.

So when Reid sat next to me, then put his hand on my knee and didn't move it, I smiled at him . . . and I felt it. That thing every girl feels when the relationship takes a turn. When it suddenly locks into place. Solidifying that thing between you and the guy that makes you get warm and fuzzy inside every single minute you're together.

Techno music pounded through the stereo system.

"To VEGAS!" Max yelled.

I burst out laughing as we all clicked our glasses together.

I had to hand it to him.

The man partied well.

A point he proved again when we pulled up to Aria.

"Penthouse suites?" My mouth gaped open. "Are you sure Max is okay with paying for—"

"Shh." Reid wrapped his arm around me and kissed my head. "He put enough KY in your bag for you to get through a decade of shit sex. Pretty sure you can just say thank you."

"Shit sex?" I repeated.

Reid winked. "I was assuming it would be without me."

"Oh." My face fell.

"Good." He laughed. "Just checking."

"Huh?"

"Making sure you're still interested, which by the look you just had, you are. Wow, maybe I do have some Max in me after all?"

"Sneaky bastard."

"I could probably be his vice president."

"Dude." Max elbowed Reid. "Becca may be my first lady, but you'll always be my first man."

I frowned.

Max did the same. "I could have said that better."

"You think?"

"Come on!" Jason shouted ahead of us. "We only have ten minutes to get ready for the SkyJump!"

"Whoa, whoa, whoa." I fisted Reid's shirt, my hand coming into contact with a firm pec. "SkyJump?"

He smiled. "Aw, you clawed my shirt like a real crab."

I released his shirt and tried to take in slow, even breaths while my heart thudded like a sledgehammer. "I don't do rides."

Reid stepped forward and pulled me against his chest. He whispered across my lips, "Maybe I can change your mind."

That mouth?

Those eyes?

That body?

I kept the whimper in as my legs squeezed together.

Mind changed.

"Come on." He slapped my ass. "Let's go."

"When you guys said Vegas, I thought you meant drinks, a bit of gambling, magic shows," I grumbled.

"Ha!" Max burst out laughing. "Magic shows." He pointed at me like I was the insane one. "I do tricks in my sleep. No, sweetheart. We'll show you how to do Vegas."

# CHAPTER TWENTY-EIGHT

## JORDAN

"When I was on *Love Island*, I learned a few things," Max said once we were in the elevator going up to the sky deck of the Stratosphere. "One." He crooked his finger in his jeans and faced us. His white shirt was plastered on his body and I'd be lying if I didn't admit that he was beautiful to look at—when he wasn't speaking, that is. "Scary situations create an emotional attachment."

"It's weird when he uses big words," Colton whispered under his breath.

"Heard that." Max crossed his arms. "Now, since these two kids are getting fake hitched and, well, since my brother's entire career depends on good publicity . . ." Max took a deep breath while Reid rolled his eyes and reached for my hand. "I've come up with a solution."

The elevator doors opened.

I clung to the railing and stayed glued to my spot in the middle of the elevator. That was ride enough for me.

"SkyJump!" Max shouted.

I started hyperventilating while Reid pried my hands free of their tight grip. I molded my body against his and shivered.

"See, man?" Max pointed at me. "Already working."

"Yeah, and if she pees her pants, bonus points or what?" Becca rolled her eyes. "Men. And I'll have you know the scariest thing Max did was climb a damn rock."

"Wait." I gulped. "Why isn't Becca in her gear?"

Becca gave me a knowing grin. "I told Max I'd make it worth his while if I could skip out."

"No fair!" I shouted. "It's not like we can give the cruise director sexual favors!"

A few curious people looked at me.

I ignored them.

Max rubbed his hands together and laughed. "You'll be fine. Just make sure they attach you to the thingy before you launch yourself off like a flying pterodactyl, feel me? Nobody wants to see you go splat."

I gulped as my hands started to sweat. Double vision made me unable to even walk in a straight line as I held on to Reid like he was my lifeline.

"You'll be fine," he whispered in my ear. "This is fun."

I looked down. "No, no. Nothing about this is fun. This is suicide!"

Reid grabbed me and pulled my body against his as we watched someone walk out onto the small ledge and jump. "Look, no tears, and you don't even fall that fast."

"But you still fall," I pointed out.

"Hmm . . . I was afraid this would happen."

I stiffened in his arms. "Meaning what?"

He turned me to face him. "The uptight skirt-wearing little crab would make an appearance."

I clenched my teeth. "I'm not uptight."

Reid ran the back of his hand down my face and then grazed my breast with his knuckles. I trembled beneath his touch. "Really? Because I'd love to see what happens when you go wild. I'm sure it's sexy as hell."

I gulped.

"Jezebel, you're up!" Max called.

"So what will it be?" Reid's gaze challenged mine. "Did you bring the skirts with you or the big-girl pants?"

"Damn you Emory men," I muttered, stalking off toward the attendant. He fired off instructions, but really all I heard was, *blah, blah, blah, you could die, blah, blah, blah, try not to puke, blah, blah, blah did you sign the consent form?* Pretty sure I should have written my will before this trip.

"Do you understand?" the attendant asked as I tried not to glance down at the ground. Milo and Colt had already jumped—if they were dead we'd know by now? Right?

"Do you understand?" the attendant repeated.

"Huh?" I blinked, seeing two of him. I'm sure he was a nice man— he had a salt-and-pepper beard and was wearing a beanie. His shirt said "Get High." I would have killed Max—actually thrown him off that building—to be high or drunk enough not to actually remember what was about to happen.

I trembled and gave him a weak nod. "So, I'm all tied in, all secure? I can jump?"

"You're good." He chuckled. "You just walk the plank and . . ." He made a jumping motion with his two fingers. I'm sure he meant it as encouragement, but all I could focus on was the sound effect of *splat* running through my head.

Reid was the only person I could still see, the only person I wanted to see.

In that moment I realized something.

I was in Vegas.

With friends.

And maybe that was pathetic, but . . . I had friends, albeit crazy ones, but we were all together. And I had Reid.

Reid! My client.

Reid . . . who was so much more than that.

*You got this*, he mouthed and gave me a thumbs-up.

I gave him a weak nod and then turned back to the attendant. "You promise I'm all secure?"

"You've been secure for a while now." He patted my back. "Now, keep walking and then do your thing. Remember the instructions. Arms out, legs out, no flips or anything wild like that."

"Ha, I'll try to restrain myself from flipping." I swallowed as hot air hit my face. It was getting louder and louder as I made my way slowly out the side of the building. And then I was at the edge, the toes of my Nikes peeking over the ledge.

I'd never done anything crazy in my life.

Ever.

One time I bought a pencil skirt in lime green.

That was my crazy.

Buying Otis special dog food. My brand of crazy.

Three drinks instead of two on a weeknight? Crazy.

Jumping off a building.

Maybe, just maybe I needed more crazy.

I closed my eyes and took a deep breath. Then jumped.

The feeling of falling was almost immediately replaced with an intense amount of hot air as wind whipped around me. I managed to crack open my eyes, and then as my stomach dipped, I opened my mouth.

And screamed.

It wasn't pretty.

In fact I'm sure that anyone taking a picture would think I was actually trying to swallow my own head.

And then suddenly.

I slowed.

And stopped.

Just above the ground.

"No splat!" I shouted, pumping my legs back and forth.

"You lived!" Milo shouted. Oh, good, they really were alive and it wasn't a figment of my imagination brought on by the trauma of jumping off a building.

Once I was out of my gear, I waited for Jason, Max, and Reid, who all came tumbling down like it wasn't a big deal at all. They yelled and pushed one another like guys do when they have too much testosterone rolling around their systems.

Reid stopped in front of me and smirked.

"I did it," I yelled.

"Yup." His grin widened.

"Holy shit." Max stuttered to a stop. "Looks like your hair had more fun than you did!"

I reached up and patted my head.

Naturally, only half my hair was in its ponytail; the rest of it was puffed around my face in a rat's nest that out of the corner of my eye looked like horns coming from my ears.

"Stop." Reid grabbed my hands and pulled me into his arms. "It's cute."

I huffed. "I look electrocuted."

"Nah." He shook his head. "You look . . ." He kissed me softly. "Invigorated."

"Yeah?" My voice was a bit breathless—then again, I was kissing Reid Emory, the newest heartthrob to hit Hollywood, the man who had a body like Ryan Gosling on his best day.

"I like it."

*I like you*, that's what I wanted to say. Instead I just nodded like a total lovesick sap and then rested my head against his chest.

"See?" Max came up next to us. "Works every time. Emotional bond secured. You're welcome! Now on to item number two!"

I cringed. "Well, at least we don't have to go on that scary-looking roller coaster thing."

Reid winced.

Max chuckled.

While the rest of the crew started marching back into the Stratosphere.

"Crap," I muttered. "We're doing all the rides, aren't we?"

"Every last one." Reid kissed my head. It was new, this whole kissing my head thing, holding my hand, making sure I was okay. And I hated to think of what would happen when he suddenly wasn't there anymore to give me encouragement.

Encouragement is one of those things you don't think you need until you suddenly have it, and then you wonder how you survived your entire life without it.

That's what Reid was good at. Staying positive, being encouraging. He owned his positive attitude.

And by association it rubbed off.

Because as I walked hand in hand with him and got back into that stupid elevator, all I kept thinking was, *I can do this.*

Because he made me think I could.

Except . . . this wasn't a romance novel, no matter how many times Max joked about it.

Eventually, fame would get to Reid like it got to every one of my clients, and he'd be gone and I'd be stuck watching him on Jimmy Fallon while I ate a tub of ice cream.

Because he was different. I wouldn't be cheering him on while he married some hot model and had ten kids.

I'd be depressed.

"Hey, it's only three more rides." Reid tugged me closer to him. "Besides, after this Max scheduled dinner and drinks."

"As long as we don't have to parachute out of an airplane to get them," I joked.

Max snapped his fingers. "Now there's an idea I'd like to explore."

"Explore this." Reid flipped him off.

Max grinned. "Just look at you two, already joined at the hip. In another life I could have been a relationship expert."

Becca gave him a patronizing pat on his back while she mouthed, *yeah, right* to us.

The elevator ride was again too short.

"Freaked out?" Reid whispered in my ear.

"A bit."

"Hmm." He tugged me back, then quickly turned me around, and his mouth met mine in an urgent kiss. I opened my mouth only to have his wicked tongue slide right past my lips. Shivering, I tugged him closer as his hands roamed across my back, while his tongue drew slow circles around mine.

When we broke apart, the doors were closing again.

Max shoved his foot in between them. "Hurry up, kids."

"What"—I heaved—"was that for? I mean . . . there weren't any cameras."

"There weren't cameras in my apartment either," he pointed out. "And maybe"—his mouth met mine again, his lips peppering me with light, soft kisses—"I did it because I wanted to. Ever think about that?"

"But why?" And seriously why did I care that he was kissing me? He was kissing me!

"I like you." He pulled back.

The doors shut again.

Max's foot wedged its way through as a loud beeping sounded. "Seriously, guys, this is getting embarrassing, you can kiss on your own watch!"

My cheeks heated. "I like you too."

"Great!" Max shouted. "We all like each other. Awesome. Can we go now?"

"Tonight." Reid tugged a piece of my hair forward, then wrapped it around his finger. "After dinner, you and me . . . dancing . . ."

"Just us?"

"No cameras. No publicity stunt. We only have to hit those three clubs, and we can do that tomorrow, right?"

I nodded dumbly.

"Good," he whispered. "Our second date."

"Great guys, real great. Do you realize you can get arrested for this shit? Just holding up an elevator because you can't keep your pants on and—"

"Coming!" Reid called and grabbed my hand as we got off the elevator.

# CHAPTER TWENTY-NINE
## REID

Jordan was a better sport than I expected, even when Max started screaming, mid–roller coaster ride, "I think I heard a clicking noise. Holy shit, we're going down!" Sure, she might have gasped and then clenched my hand so tight I was a bit concerned my bones were going to snap in half and I'd have to wear a cast for the next six months, but the real kicker was when Max convinced her that the bungee that shoots you off the building was the easiest of all the rides because you only go up and then pop right back down.

Not the case.

I had to wonder if Max was the reason Becca switched from bottled to boxed wine. You know, to save money on her own brand of therapy?

By the time we made it back to Aria, it was already dark. Time for dinner and drinks, and, according to our laminated schedule, gambling.

Though only a few tables were Max approved.

Because that's what he did—he micromanaged so much that it wouldn't surprise me at all if he did background checks on all the dealers for the tables he wanted us to go to.

Paranoid freak.

I shared a suite with Jordan and Jason. Colt and Milo were stuck with Max and Becca.

"Odd man out sucks," Jason grumbled once we were back in the room, if one could call a freaking apartment a room. Jason grabbed a beer from the stocked bar and sat on the couch facing the TV but didn't turn it on.

Jordan whizzed by me in a panic-stricken flash. "Be right back."

"Whoa." I grabbed her wrist. "Where you going?"

"Out."

I frowned. "We just got back in."

"Yeah." She fidgeted, then jerked her hand free and patted her hair. "But I forgot hairspray."

"I have hairspray," Jason called out.

"Girly hairspray," Jordan corrected. "I'll be right back. We don't have reservations for another hour or so anyway." Her smile was wide, her eyes unfocused, and I could have sworn she was sweating, but before I could say anything more she was out the door.

"Girls." Jason sighed from the couch. "Think she's really getting hairspray?"

I was still eyeing the door. "Doubt that woman goes anywhere without packing at least three bottles of it. You've seen that wild hair."

"It's sexy." Jason chuckled darkly.

"What was that?" I had half a mind to smack the bottle from his hand, then hit him over the head with it. Repeatedly.

Jason looked up from his beer, his eyes narrowing in amusement. "Someone's got it bad. How long you been sleeping with her?"

Hands shaking, I walked over to the bar and started pouring alcohol, lots and lots of alcohol, in my tall cup. "We haven't slept together."

Another chuckle from the couch. "Is this for lack of trying? Or is your game really that off? Man, never thought I'd see the day where your eyes didn't just magically cause a woman's bra to fall to the floor."

I groaned. "That only happened once."

"Still happened." Jason pointed his beer at me. "Why would you want to let all of that go—over some girl who's probably going to choose her job over you any day of the week?"

I tried not to let his sour attitude get to me, but I was feeling defensive and dejected all at once. Ever since Jason's failed wedding it was like he'd been against any sort of relationship. His glass wasn't half-full, it was half-empty when it came to relationships. I had to remember it had nothing to do with Jordan and everything to do with him.

"We're just having fun," I lied, dumping ice into my drink and stirring with my finger because looking for something to stir it with just seemed like it needed way too much brain power and I was still concentrating on what Jason had said. "Besides . . ." I took a slow sip of the drink and choked—light a match and I could do a pyrotechnics show. "I highly doubt she likes me like that."

Jason put his feet on the coffee table. "Are we in high school? Because I'm pretty sure I said that in high school when Sara refused to go out with me."

"Sara?"

"Or was it Laura?"

"What are we talking about?"

Jason shuddered. "Laura, definitely Laura. Sara gave me the creeps, asked to lick my algebra textbook."

"Because why?" I asked sitting on the opposite couch.

Jason smirked. "Because it had been on my bed."

"Gross." I held up my hand. "I don't know how you and Colt survived high school without getting maimed."

"Oh, we were maimed all right, in all the best ways."

"You do realize you're talking about underage girls, right?"

"Damn it." Jason frowned. "Maybe you're not the only one who's lost it."

"You have to have it to lose it, bro."

"Ass." He tossed the remote in my direction. I ducked in time for it to go careening past my head. "You know what I mean. I haven't had a date since . . . Jayne."

"Let's not count her." I took another sip of my lighter fluid. "You didn't love her, and she lied to you about being pregnant, oh, and I'm pretty sure had I not intervened you'd be sharing a home with her and forced to paint her toes while she watched *Real Housewives.*"

Jason shuddered.

"Honey"—I mimicked Jayne's voice—"remember it's book club night! No, not the cab, grab the merlot! You're so stupid! Hot dogs are NOT one of the basic food groups. Do you even know what's in those chicken wings? Organic! I said organic bananas! No, I won't have sex with you! Did you even shower last night? Baby, turn the lights off, you know I get headaches when the lights are on. Sorry, not tonight, I have a headache."

"You done yet?" Jason winced.

"Baby," I continued, "you never talk to me anymore. What are you thinking? Wait, are you thinking about that slut at the station? Give me her number! You cheating bastard! I saw the way she looked at you over doughnuts and coffee."

"Don't eat doughnuts," Jason interjected.

"But"—I sniffled—"I just get so scared of losing you! Don't leave me. Promise you'll never leave me!" I wailed.

Jason gave me the finger. "Ever think of playing a chick in your next movie? You have that nails-on-the-chalkboard voice down terrifyingly well."

"What can I say?" I shrugged. "Talented and sexy."

"But so very humble." Jason nodded emphatically. "Also, thanks for that trip down memory lane where I ended up in hell and actually for a minute believed it was true—so true that my body still won't stop shaking. Cheers." He lifted his beer into the air and downed the whole thing.

"Go on a date," I offered. "It might help."

Jason licked his lips and eyed his empty beer bottle. "Yeah, maybe."

Silence enveloped the room. But it was the good kind of silence, the man kind, where sometimes a guy just wants to sit, drink his beer in peace, and think about absolutely nothing.

And I mean it when I say nothing. If someone was to take a picture of what was happening in my brain it would be a blank slate.

White.

Nothingness.

Just empty space.

Guys needed that time to decompress, whereas girls used that time to break down and overanalyze every single moment of their day.

"So." Jason broke the silence. "You're sure she's not into you? In a serious way?"

"Look." I leaned forward. "I wouldn't be upset if she was . . . hell, I'd take her however I could get her. She's one of those girls that"—I had trouble keeping the dopey smile from my face—"you just want to be around. I don't know, she makes me happy . . . everything about her, even her—" Jason jumped behind the couch and hid. "What? What's wrong? I didn't even touch my eye!"

He peeked over the couch and grinned. "Sorry, I was just trying to stay out of the line of fire. You have that look."

"No, I don't," I argued.

"You do." Jason pointed. "You can't stop smiling, your voice went all soft, and I could have sworn you started petting your drink with your hand. Your glass doesn't have boobs on it, so stop caressing it or I can't sit here with you. Also, if you get that look in your eyes again while we're alone, just walk away."

I laughed. "Whatever."

"No, no whatever." Jason stood to his feet. "You have the same look Colt wore during my wedding—you know, when he wasn't trying to kill Max. And the same look Max has whenever he looks at Becca, which, let's be honest, he's always looking at her, always touching her. My point is this, you've got it, that thing that no guy wants until they have it and then they can't imagine life without it."

I frowned. "You sound like you're speaking from experience."

"I'm empty." He ran his hand through his dark-brown hair. "I'm going to grab another beer and shower. You should get ready too. You know how Max gets when we're late."

"One time, I was late one time!"

"And he made you sing Boyz II Men at the top of your lungs in Central Park as punishment. Epic moment."

"Stupid YouTube hits."

"Hey, that helped you get that spot in *Phantom*. Admit it, the camera angle with those birds flying around you totally launched your ability to make women think you could be both dangerous and dreamy."

"Stop quoting *USA Today*."

Jason snickered and walked off.

I stared at my drink. I needed to get ready, but where the hell was Jordan? And was Jason right? The smile was back. My face seriously stopped cooperating days ago.

Because every time I thought her name.

I smiled.

And every time I thought about her not being in my life.

My chest felt like it was going to split open and never fuse back together again.

"Shit." I chugged the rest of my drink, and then because I still didn't feel better, I said "shit" again.

# CHAPTER THIRTY

## JORDAN

I pounded on Max's door, my anxiety getting worse by the minute. Reid, Jason, and Colt had decided to go down to the bar while Becca and Milo hit up the slots downstairs. I knew it would take forever to find the girls, and I could only hope that Max had one of their numbers so that I could call them and ask for help. Why hadn't I realized I didn't have anything good enough to wear for a night with Reid?

"Max!" Pound, pound, pound. "Max." Pound, pound, pound. I waited and then—"Max!"

The door jerked open. Max was dressed for battle—dark skinny jeans with a dark V-neck shirt that should have made him look feminine but just showed off his lean body and bright eyes. "You're late."

My hand was still in the air, ready to knock on his forehead. "I'm sorry, what?"

Max checked his watch and sighed heavily. "I expected you five minutes ago." He frowned and looked me up and down. "Hmm, you're all out of breath—clearly your cardio needs work. Maybe join a gym when we get back and stop taking the elevator. Correction, stop taking the elevator once you get that epic elevator kiss. Until then, carry on." He pushed the door open and held out his hand. "After you."

"Where is everyone?" I glanced around the empty suite, feeling stupid for running to Max, of all people, for help.

"Told them I had an important meeting." Max handed me a glass of champagne and took a sip of his. "And I do, now. Sit, sit."

I had no other option but to sit, drink the champagne that had apparently been waiting for me for the past five minutes, and stare openmouthed while Max pointed to the chair opposite me, on which sat a black garment bag.

"Yours." Max yawned. "I hope you don't mind, but before the trip I snatched one of your dresses while you were sleeping in order to get the right measurements."

"Sure, why would I mind that you snuck into my room stalker style and swiped one of my dresses for your own personal amusement? Nothing weird about that."

"Oh, good." Max nodded. "Glad we're on the same page."

Was anyone ever on the same page as Max? I'd really like to know. I made a mental note to ask Reid later.

"Well . . ." Max handed me the bag. "Don't just stare at it. Open."

I set my glass down and excitedly unzipped the bag. It was a gorgeous Dolce & Gabbana dress in my size.

It was lacy and red.

I couldn't focus on anything else other than the fact that something red and lacy—something gorgeous, with a crazy price tag—was within my reach.

"Lace doesn't bite," Max whispered. "But fun fact, it makes Reid want to, so there's that."

"It's . . ." I gulped. The front of the dress dipped really low, low enough that my boobs would definitely be having a good time tonight. The waist was tight while the rest of the skirt spread out in a cute sweetheart style.

All in all, it was something I would have picked for myself had I wanted to spend almost two grand on a dress.

Though I would have chosen black.

And possibly gotten a scarf to cover up.

Or a parka.

"How'd you know?" I gently caressed the lace dress. "How'd you know I would panic and not want to wear anything I brought?"

Max grabbed me by the arms and turned me very slowly to face him. "I have something to tell you."

"Wh-what?" I'd never seen him look so serious, all hints of amusement were gone.

"I'm from the future," Max whispered. "And I've traveled back in time to find you the perfect dress and save the planet from flesh-eating aliens masquerading as bad hair." He grabbed a piece of my hair. "Oh, look." With a tug he pulled it out, then hissed.

I rolled my eyes. "Very funny."

"Or . . ." He smirked. "I've seen your closet. You're Jordan Litwright. Prone to panic. I put two and two together. Oh, and I'm a genius—my mom says so."

"All moms say that."

"Remember." Max released me and ignored my jab. "Your hair is your superpower, making you the Samson in this scenario. So Delilah's going to have a hell of a fascination with your hair. Word to the wise, don't let him cut it." He leaned in. "You may lose your power."

"Power?"

"Magic girl power that has Reid, at this very moment"—Max checked his watch again—"most likely drinking and wondering what the hell you're doing and why the hell it matters."

"You're an odd duck."

Max got a teary-eyed gleam. "I've always wanted to be able to yell, *quack, quack, quack*, without having to use the excuse of watching *Mighty Ducks* one."

I laughed.

"Or two, or three for that matter." Max sighed. "Emilio!"

"Okay." I put my hand over his mouth. "Thanks for the dress, but maybe stop ruining the moment with your words."

I brought my hand back.

Max opened his mouth.

I shook my head.

He pouted and slumped his shoulders.

With a grin I pulled in him for a hug and kissed his cheek, then whispered, "You did good, Max. You did real good."

He hugged me back and whispered. "Only crazy bitches melt at midnight. Don't go doing that disappearing act once things get hot and heavy. My advice is this . . . take it or leave it."

"I'm not sure I want your advice."

"Life," Max said, spreading his arms wide, "is like a box of chocolates."

I rolled my eyes. "I think I know how this ends."

"You buy the box because you think you want variety, but if you're really honest with your greedy little self, all you really want are the caramel ones. But they don't sell chocolates that way, so you do what everyone else does. You follow the crowd and try ones you know you're going to hate. Why?"

I swallowed. "Because you're trying to find the caramel ones."

Max nodded. "Exactly. You think, *maybe this time I'll get lucky*, only you're left disappointed when it turns out to be some weird coconut shit."

"Or hazelnut."

Max nodded. "Or even dark chocolate, which, let's be honest . . ."

"Isn't caramel," I finished. My eyes for some reason filled up with tears as Max put a hand on my shoulder.

"Exactly." He nudged my chin. "I think we both know where this is going."

"Yeah."

"You've found your caramel," Max said softly. "But you've refused to bite."

"But—"

"Biting," Max said with a shrug, "can be scary . . . terrifying, hell, what if you don't even like caramel anymore?"

"RIGHT?" I shouted, half wondering if Max had pumped illegal drugs into the air vents and we were both high on 'shrooms, because, let's be honest, Max actually making sense was scarier.

"There's only one way to find out if he's the chocolate for you," Max said soberly. "I think you know what you need to do."

"Bite," I whispered.

"Louder. I didn't quite get that?" Max cupped his ear.

"Bite," I said, a little louder.

Max frowned.

"BITE THE CHOCOLATE!" I shouted, then thrust my fist into the air for good measure.

"Max," Milo called.

I turned on my heel.

Colt, Milo, and Becca were all standing in the doorway.

"Just don't let him tell you to be the doughnut." Milo nodded. "That translation gets lost really easy."

"Eye of the tiger." Max sighed. "If you listened better you would have had Colt faster. I can't work in these conditions!" Max raised his hands into the air and then, as if remembering our talk, grabbed the garment bag, thrust it into my hands, and nodded. "You got this."

"Okay."

He eyed me up and down, then up again, his eyes watering slightly as he took in my hair.

I patted my head.

"Maybe, just . . ." He tucked it behind my ears. It popped loose. With a curse he tried it again.

This time my hair nearly poked his eye out.

"Damn it!" He flailed back and nearly landed on the couch. "Okay, what if you just let your hair be free. Maybe it's trying to tell you something."

"Well," I said, sighing, "it's naturally wavy and just . . . huge. I straighten it and—"

Max held up his hand. "You *what* it?"

"Straighten," I said slower.

"Aw, it's like you're brand-new." He smiled patronizingly and without taking his eyes off me yelled, "Colt, as a man—though the jury's still out on that one," Max said out of the corner of his mouth, "what say you? Straight hair or fluffy sex kitten hair that goes roar?"

Colt took a step away from Milo and said, "Roar."

Milo charged him.

"Max's fault." Colt held up his hands. "And baby, I love you regardless of your hair."

Milo was midswing when she dropped her hand and kissed Colt on the mouth instead.

"Take that in your bedroom," Max yelled. "Animals."

Becca came up to me and wrapped an arm around my shoulders. "Why don't I help you with your hair and makeup? Max has done enough thinking for one night . . . after all, Rome wasn't built in a day."

"Or was it?" Max tapped his chin.

"Go," Becca directed. "Take a shot of whiskey, put on some cologne, and make sure your hair doesn't look like crap. I won't have you trying something trendy just because we're in Vegas."

Max grinned. "You take such good care of me."

"Take your pills!" Becca directed.

"He's on pills?" I whispered.

Becca rolled her eyes. "Advil. He likes to be preventative when he drinks."

"Ah." I nodded. "Smart."

"As a nail," Max fired back as he nearly collided with the couch, then stumbled up the two stairs and down the hallway.

"So." Becca laughed. "I'm guessing he told you to be a food group?"

"Huh?"

"In order to get your man."

I winced. "Chocolate caramels."

She nodded knowingly. "So let's envision those while we sex you up." She led me down the hall.

"Becca?"

"What?"

"Does it scare you when he starts making sense?"

She shuddered. "Keeps me up at night . . . it really does."

# CHAPTER THIRTY-ONE

## REID

"Where the hell is she?" I smacked Jason because I had to get my aggression out somehow and drinking more seemed like a horrible idea considering I was already feeling my last drink. Besides, this was a date, and I wanted to be able to experience every part of it.

Every part of her.

Water it was.

Regardless of what I was drinking, water, alcohol, I'd still feel drunk off her, the way she moved, spoke. Everything about her was distracting. I always wanted to taste more of her, feel more, share more.

"You're getting that look again," Jason grumbled, rubbing his shoulder and taking a step back while I checked my watch for the tenth time.

"Just go ahead." I sighed. "She isn't back yet and her text said she was running late—"

The door swung open.

So did my jaw.

And Jason's.

I punched him for reacting, the bastard!

He kept staring.

Because who wouldn't?

Jordan, aka the most gorgeous female I'd ever had the pleasure of staring at, was standing in the doorway.

High nude heels.

Legs for miles.

And holy shit, those curvy hips all leading up to a trim waist, and . . . I'm sure there's something more romantic I could say about her breasts.

But being a guy, all I could think was *breasts, tits, breasts, tits,* in that order.

Throat dry, I swallowed as my eyes locked on her face.

Forget her body.

That face.

Her smile was cautious. It was the smile every girl has when she wants her guy to say something complimentary, something epic, something she tells all her friends.

"Uhhhhhhh." I blinked.

Jason elbowed me.

"Uhhhh," I repeated, this time shorter.

"Words." Jason coughed.

"Words," I repeated like an idiot. "Big words."

Jordan's grin grew. "So you like it?" She placed her hands on her hips, and honest to God, my fingers twitched at my sides. They freaking twitched because they were so damn excited to get to hold her hand.

"You look beautiful," Jason said for me, in my place, like a bastard. Should have knocked him out when I had the chance. He kissed her hand.

I let out a low growl.

Jason looked back at me and laughed. "What was that? You think she looks pretty too? Want me to pass her a note or you think you got this, champ?"

"There's a special place in hell for cock blockers," I fumed. "Just saying."

"Ha." Jason grinned. "It's probably right next to Max's cell."

"Truth," Max said from somewhere down the hall, but I wasn't sure if he actually heard Jason or was just used to saying *truth* all the time whenever he finished giving ridiculously horrible advice.

"Jordan?" I held out my hand. "Come here a minute."

"We'll be just outside," Jason called, shutting the door behind him so that we were alone, away from Max's watchful eyes.

"Beautiful," I blurted. "You look beautiful, gorgeous, pretty, cute, breathtaking."

Jordan flushed.

"Mouthwatering." I licked my lips. "Mind-numbing. World altering."

"Wow, that's a lot of words." She laughed.

"I have more, want to hear more?"

She nodded excitedly.

"Heartbreaking," I whispered, tugging her into my arms. "Soul shattering." I kissed her neck and dug my hands into her wild wavy hair and groaned.

"Max said straight hair's for losers. Does that mean wavy is for winners?" she teased, her cute little body arching while I continued kissing down the side of her neck.

"Winning. From here on out, I forfeit, you win. Make a special note of that."

"Deal." She let out a breathy sigh.

"How the hell am I supposed to go out in public with you tonight?" Jordan pulled back, her eyes etched in hurt.

I cupped her chin. "You look good enough to eat. And I'm not the only guy who's going to think that. Holy shit, that's Max's plan! He wants me to go to prison."

"No prison." Jordan winced. "PR nightmare."

"We could spin it." I chuckled darkly and turned her in my arms so her back was to me. My body liked that a bit too much. I'm sure she was well aware of my current situation. "You never know, I may get a part in the next *Mission: Impossible* movie because I kicked someone's ass with a shard of glass, a napkin, and a peanut."

"I'd love to see that trick." Jordan reached her hand behind her. Fingertips grazed the button of my jeans, then moved lower.

I let out a little groan.

The door burst open. "Dude." Max shook his head slowly. "I did not play fairy godmother to your Cinderella so you could sex her all night in the privacy of the suite I paid for." He opened the door wider so everyone in the hallway could see that Jordan was copping a feel and my body was ready to explode. "According to my schedule, we're going to be five minutes late to dinner. Now get a move on before I go all evil stepsister on her ass and rip her dress, steal her shoe, then kill Gus-Gus."

"They don't kill Gus-Gus in *Cinderella*," Jordan pointed out.

"Really?" Max crossed his arms. "I thought Lucifer got that chunky little bastard. Well, I guess I can be wrong once every decade." He shrugged. "Now, let's go."

Jordan pulled away.

"Maybe." I jerked her back. "Keep walking in front of me so Max doesn't think Gus-Gus is my happy word."

"Got it." She laughed.

• • •

Cameras flashed during dinner, and even though I expected it, it still sucked because I wanted more privacy. But I knew after dinner and drinks I would get Jordan all to myself.

"According to the schedule"—Jordan laid her schedule on her empty plate—"we have free time until tomorrow morning."

I stood and held out my hand.

"Wait!" Max stood. "But Ohana means family, and family sticks together!"

"Where the hell did you put that?" Jason grabbed the schedule and turned it over.

In small writing, writing that you'd have to be an Avenger to read correctly, Max had written, "OHANA RULE: if anyone says the word *Ohana*, alone time is hereby revoked and group must stick together. Never leave a man behind. America."

"And again," Milo shouted, "you're Canadian!"

"I'm a dual citizen!" Max fired back. "An alien born in a foreign land." His eyes narrowed. "Besides, I live here, in the States, yo!"

"Aren't we all so glad you do?" I sang and flipped him off.

"Ohana, bitch." Max did a little bow. "Now, off to the club of my choosing. P.S. Make sure you stop for the photo op."

"Photo op?" everyone shouted at once. I groaned into my hands. That was the last thing I wanted.

Max shrugged. "Look, the media wants a piece of Reid and Jezebel. The worst way to feed a shark is to yell, *blood, blood, blood!* So either we panic and bleed all over the cameras, or we seal all over them, feed them without them realizing they're even hungry, then go on our merry little way."

"So now we're seals." Jason tipped back his drink and held up his hand for the waiter.

"Feeding the sharks," Colton added.

"Guys." Max pinched the bridge of his nose. "We give them what they want, then we party like it's 1999."

"Were you potty trained then?" Jordan asked. "Just curious."

"You bastard!" Max shouted in my direction. "Who told?"

"Wait, what?" Jason coughed. "Dude, you would have been like six!"

"OHANA!" Max shouted louder this time, his face red. "Ohana means no tattletales . . . Reid."

"He had a very serious fear of toilets," I said cheerfully, lifting my glass in a salute in his direction.

Max scowled. "Well, maybe you shouldn't have told me that's where bad little boys go when they pee their pants!"

"Nice. Reverse psychology for the win!" Colt held up his hand for a high five while Max started cursing like a sailor.

"Fine." I stood and stretched. "Let's get this over with." Because I knew the faster I did his bidding, the sooner I'd be with the girl in the red dress.

Jordan reached for my hand.

"Are you okay with this?"

"Sure." Her smile seemed forced. "After all, this is why we came, right? I mean, it's about your image, Reid, I haven't forgotten that."

"Funny." I kissed her mouth. "I have."

"Oh, yeah?"

"Yeah." I pulled her into my arms. "Seems a girl in a red dress is taking up all space in my brain these days."

"She sounds hot."

"She's so much more . . . than hot." I kissed her mouth again. "She's everything."

# CHAPTER THIRTY-TWO

## JORDAN

The photo op at Hakkasan nightclub brought me back to reality. Up until now I'd been in the clouds, skipping away, pushing thoughts of my actual job into the crapper while Reid whispered sweet nothings into my ear and Max tapped fairy dust all over my head.

The only positive about my situation was that I didn't have to act. There was no forced emotional attachment because it was already there.

So when cameras flashed and people asked us about our relationship, I squeezed his hand because I felt something. I giggled when he kissed my cheek because he made me laugh.

And when Reid wrapped an arm around my shoulder and kissed my head, I sighed while longingly gazing up into his eyes like he'd just promised me a Kardashian-style wedding with Max as the officiant.

Because let's be honest, Max wouldn't want it any other way.

The club was something right out of a futuristic movie set. Lights—green, red, blue—flashed all over the place, and the entire effect was enough to give me a headache, which in turn made me feel extremely old.

"Up here," Max yelled back at us as we made our way to the fifth level of the club. It was more private and overlooked the main floor. VIP tables were scattered upstairs along with a separate DJ and bar. Everything was blanketed in cool blue and violet colors. We made our way into a semiprivate room.

The colors were even dimmer in that room, blues and whites filling the floor-to-ceiling LED screens.

"You like?" Max turned around in a circle. "We can actually customize the room to look anyway we want."

"Nice." Reid nodded, then checked his watch.

I elbowed him; he winked back.

Oh, dear.

I swallowed dryly and folded my hands across my lap. That lasted all of five seconds before Reid grabbed one hand and placed a glass of champagne in the other.

"What are we toasting to?" Reid asked the group, not taking his eyes off me.

"Marriage," Max shouted. "And real orgasms, none of that fake shit you guys keep trying to sell me every night."

"Huh?" Colton asked. "They perform for you?"

"Not in that capacity, psycho." Max rolled his eyes. "I say we make a toast to Reid's career. If this weekend goes like I think it's going to go, you two kids are one marriage away from an Academy Award."

Reid chuckled, then lifted his glass higher. "So, to success?"

"Success." We all lifted our glasses. The champagne tasted bitter, not smooth. But maybe it was me, I was the problem.

Because every publicist wanted success for their client. You'd be stupid not to—well, stupid and most likely homeless. But that wasn't the point.

Was it so wrong that I wanted to sabotage Reid? That for the first time in my life I wanted my client, his talent, all to myself? Why share him with the world when they would never appreciate the man he really was? And why take the chance that once he was in the public eye—fully in the public eye—they'd ruin him anyway?

"Hey." Reid tilted my chin toward him. "No frowns tonight."

"Sorry." I managed to smile. "Just thinking about work."

"Don't." He set my glass down and reached for my other hand. "Does this feel like work?"

"Well, no."

"Hmm." Without warning he grabbed the back of my head and fused our mouths together, his tongue invading without proper invitation, just dominating me until I felt breathless for more. "And this? Is this work?"

I leaned forward for another kiss. "If it is, can I get overtime?"

Reid smirked, then kissed me again and again, peppering light kisses across my mouth that had me nearly crawling into his lap just so I could get closer, experience more.

"For once in your life," he whispered above the music, "don't overthink . . . this isn't about my career or about yours. Let's make tonight about us."

Max shouted, "Ohana!" above the music, then pointed at both of us as if to remind us that there would be no skipping out.

"And Max." Reid nodded solemnly. "Because if we don't include him, he'll just include himself and then I'm going to kill him and we really will land in a Vegas prison."

I returned Max's point with a wave and sighed against Reid. "Think when he's married he'll cut off the apron strings?"

"If not I'll just burn them," Reid said thoughtfully. "Or maybe just drop him off on a farm so he has space to run."

"He'd like a farm."

"Well, he finally likes animals again, so it just might work out."

"I'm not going to ask." I laughed against his chest. "I'm afraid of every answer where Max is concerned."

The music swirled around us, some crazy techno beat that had Max and Becca bumping and grinding way too close to where I was sitting. The LED screens switched to a dark red that matched my dress; the air felt electric, alive with possibilities.

"You know . . ." Reid whispered in my ear above the music. "I used to be in a boy band."

"I know."

"I was their best dancer."

"Were you?" I bit my bottom lip to keep myself from laughing. "Prove it."

"Thought you'd never ask." He stood and held out his hand, like a gentleman.

Laughing, I took it, thinking he'd swing me around and we'd share a joke about how we're old and don't know how to dance or expend that type of energy anymore.

Instead, Reid started slowly rolling his hips behind mine.

I wasn't sure if I wanted to run away or press against him.

So I did nothing.

Like a real invisible nerd, who'd suddenly been discovered by the captain of the football team, I froze.

Reid placed his hands on my hips, his breath tickling my ear. "Let the music move you."

"Uh." I wanted to ask how. I'd never been asked to a school dance and I'd never actually danced in public. I wasn't that girl, the woo girl who partied on the weekends and stuck her face out of limos and shouted into the night air just because she could.

"Come on." He tugged me harder against him, his lips moving fluidly down my neck as his hips ground slowly into me, moving faster as he lifted my hands into the air and twirled me around.

I finally relaxed enough to let go.

We danced for a few songs while Reid continued torturing me by touching every inch of my body that he could without being indecent. By the time the fourth song ended I was ready to lose my mind.

The teasing had to stop.

"Drinks!" Max shouted, waving us over to the table, where he'd apparently ordered several rounds for everyone.

Control was my thing.

So drinking more than a few drinks in one night seemed . . . well, the exact opposite of being in control. I pulled one of the bottles of water and chugged, only to have it slapped out of my hand.

"No!" Max scolded me. "Girls who wear Dolce don't drink water." He shrugged. "Probably don't eat either, but that's not the point. The point"—he shoved a drink into my hand—"is that part of this night is about you letting go and being awesome. So be awesome."

"The man has a point, Sebastian." Reid lifted his glass into the air. I sniffed the drink.

"What was that?" Max frowned. "Did you just smell your drink?"

"Well, what if you drugged me?"

Max laughed. "First, I would never drug one of my best friends—"

"We aren't best friends," I said shaking my head no.

"Second"—he elbowed Reid—"your innocence is showing. It's impossible to smell drugs in your drink unless you purposely pour NyQuil into the glass, but people who do weird shit like that end up in prison, and you don't want to end up in prison, do you?"

I had no idea how me getting drugged had turned into me going to prison, but I went with it. "Are you there?" I asked sweetly.

Max seemed to think about this for a while, then slowly shook his head. "No, not at the time of your arrest."

"Oh, good, then I choose no NyQuil."

"Aren't you glad I was present during DARE week?" He grinned. "Even won the damn bear because I pledged to be drug-free for LIFE."

"Yet you're drinking." I pointed at his glass.

"This?" He lifted it into the air. "Amateur. This is cranberry juice. Like I would drink in Vegas when I have to babysit you guys." He knocked his drink back. "It's my gift, take it or leave it."

"I'm confused." I looked to Reid, but his eyes were narrowed in suspicion, so maybe I should be more than confused. Alarmed? Maybe *alarmed* was the better word.

"Chill." Max held up his hands. "My crazy days are over, all right? I just know this one"—he pointed to me, so clearly I was the one—"won't let her hair down, so to speak, because her job is to be worried about publicity and actors not wearing underwear." He lowered his gaze to Reid's pants. "Dude, you are wearing underwear, right?"

Reid didn't answer.

I grinned.

"See?" Max rolled his eyes. "Now, say you two were drunk and Reid started stripping in the elevator—"

"There will be no stripping in the elevator," Reid interjected.

"And his light saber just pops out!" Max shuddered. "Can you imagine the ramifications?"

"The empire strikes back?" I joked.

Colton's eyes got wide as he eavesdropped on my conversation, then steered Milo far away from us.

"Ha." Max cackled. "Good one—ain't nobody gonna be striking with that saber, feel me? At least not in public, that's what you have me for!"

"So let me get this straight." I cleared my throat. "You're not drinking, so you can watch me and Reid and make sure he doesn't pull out his light saber?"

Max frowned into his drink. "Well, it's not like I'm going to watch him whip it out, but you get the picture."

"Great mental picture." Reid groaned. "Really, it's like you're trying to kill sex for me."

"I always had a thing for Chewbacca." I felt my cheeks heat.

*"Aghhhhhhhhhhhhhhhhhh."* Max mimicked Chewbacca, then slapped Reid on the back. "May the force be with you, my son."

"Max—"

"Reid, I'm not your father—"

"Max."

"But . . ." Max handed us both new drinks, apparently I'd sucked mine down during his speech. "I'm more like the Obi-Wan to your Kenobi."

"What's a Kenobi?" I asked.

"It's what happens when his light saber meets your . . ." Max squinted. "Force."

"Good talk, Max." Reid slapped him on the back, turned him around, and then waved down Becca to take him off our hands.

Becca started kissing him, they danced, and I was sure Max forgot all about his weird offer to help.

"It's kind of cute," I said once Max was out of earshot.

"What?" Reid tilted back his drink. Even the man's throat was sexy as he took a large gulp and turned those aqua eyes in my direction.

"Max's protectiveness, his plans, his schemes. I mean, it's cute in small doses."

"And yet, he does nothing in small doses. You should have seen him pre-Becca."

I gaped. "He used to be worse?"

"You have. No. Idea." Reid chuckled. "Now finish your drink. More dancing and then . . . who knows what?"

The rest of the evening was fuzzy . . . I remember a few more drinks, and I remember Jason icing his face because he ran into a door. Milo and Colt called it early, leaving me alone with Reid, Max, and Becca.

Somehow we all ended up at some rooftop bar where scantily clad women were dancing.

Max started chucking dollar bills into the air. I believe his words were, "Make it rain."

Becca smacked him.

And then I ended up with a few dollar bills after I jokingly did a little dance in front of Reid.

He stuffed them down my dress, then yelled, "Another!"

Two hours later we were still dancing, but my heels were officially off. I was walking barefoot down the street—until Reid gave me a piggyback to our hotel.

We'd lost Becca and Max somewhere between Planet Hollywood and the Hard Rock.

"Wow!" I gasped. "Look at the fountain!"

"The Bellagio?" Reid yelled back at me, my body slamming against his back as we picked up speed, then stopped in front of the fountain. "I forgot, you're a Vegas newbie. Pretty cool, huh?"

He talked as if he hadn't been drinking all night.

While I was seeing, like, ten fountains, a unicorn, and Danny Ocean after pulling off the con of the century. Hey, George!

"Something funny?" Reid slowly let me down to my feet.

I kept giggling. "Nothing, just thinking about *Ocean's Eleven.*"

"Hot men who masquerade as jewel thieves make you laugh?"

"It's weird you called them hot."

"Quoting every woman alive." Reid held up his hands. "Just being honest."

"We should swim." I nodded, slowly making my way closer to the fountain.

"Oh, no." Reid grabbed my arm and tugged me back. "Not in the fountain, they frown upon things like that."

"But I want to swim!" I laughed. "Naked."

People glanced over at me.

Reid grinned. "We have a huge tub in our room. I promise I'll even turn the lights off and then give you a flashlight so that it looks like the Bellagio."

"But what about the music?"

"I'll hum."

"Really?"

"Yup."

"*Phantom of the Opera* music?" I crawled up his body, landing in his arms as my legs straddled him. He hefted me up and kissed my mouth.

"Why, Sebastian, I didn't know you were a fan."

"He wears a cape. Who isn't a fan of the Phantom?"

"He's also psychologically unstable."

"Again." I laughed. "He wears a cape."

"You know, for a shrew you sure laugh a lot." Reid's forehead touched mine. "Jordan, I'm happy to announce I think the taming is finished."

"How'd I do?" I joked.

"Well, I think I have one more thing I need to check."

"What's that?" I whispered.

"Come back to the room and I'll show you."

"Where else would I go?"

He sobered. "I hope that's always your answer." Reid set me back on my feet. "Now, crawl on my back like the crab you are and I'll walk us back."

# CHAPTER THIRTY-THREE

## REID

"I don't really hate roses," Jordan said once we were in the elevator. "I mean, I've never been sent roses, so . . ."

I gripped her hand tighter. "That's a shame."

One of her heels fell out of her hand. She bent over to pick it up, then apparently decided standing was too much and just sat on the floor.

"I think that bath may have to wait," I said in a soft voice. "Don't want you drowning or anything."

"I'm not even tired." She yawned, her eyes watering as she gazed up at me with such innocence, such trust that it felt like someone had punched me in the stomach. I felt that look, really felt it, in my soul. I wanted to be deserving of that look.

And I wanted it directed at me every day.

Every freaking day.

The gut-wrenching feeling from earlier suddenly disappeared and was replaced with a revelation.

I was falling in love with her.

Jordan laughed and leaned back against the elevator door. "If you sent me flowers, I'd forgive you for anything . . . well maybe not anything, but close. Isn't that pathetic? All it takes is stupid flowers. But they're so pretty . . . and thoughtful. I didn't mean it. A real girl. A special girl would appreciate flowers on a first date."

Hell.

I was already there.

Mascara was smeared underneath her eyes, and her hair was still growing, pointing in every direction, the crazy waves making me want to dive my hands into the length and just pull.

Like a crazed man.

"And chocolate?" My knees popped as I leaned down and held out my hand. "What if I gave you a box of chocolates?"

Jordan blinked up at me with her wide brown eyes. "Are they all caramel?"

Laughing softly, I shrugged. "Every last one."

Her eyes teared up. "You mean it?"

I had an odd feeling this wasn't just about chocolate anymore. "Yeah. I do."

The elevator dinged once we reached our floor. I helped her to her feet and grabbed the other stray shoe as we made our way into our suite.

When we walked inside, it was quiet, and the lights were low.

"So." Jordan turned to face me and then slowly began taking off her dress. I froze in place. "You said I needed to let my hair down. Does that include my dress too?"

It pooled at her bare feet.

She stepped out.

Wearing only a plunging black corset and a matching black thong.

I gulped and told myself to look away. Nothing good would come from sleeping with her while she was drunk.

My mind flashed the message to my body a dozen times, but my feet still moved toward her.

My hands still reached out.

And my mouth—refused to listen.

So I kissed her.

Branded her.

Picked her up with one hand while using my other to dig into that gorgeous head of hair and slowly walked us down the hall toward my bedroom.

She tasted like the first time I kissed her . . . and I wondered if she'd always taste that way to me, sweet with the tartness of a lime on her tongue.

Her legs clenched around my waist, her mouth opening wider as I deepened the kiss, unable to control my thoughts, my body, anything.

I tossed her on the comforter and pulled my shirt over my head, then hovered over her, wondering if I was making an epic mistake in taking what she was offering when she might not remember it later.

My conscience was screaming at me.

Then again, so was she. The hellcat reached for my jeans. "Reid, hurry up!"

"Sex should never be rushed." I gently pushed her hands away. "It should be savored."

"So savor me." Her eyes were unfocused.

I couldn't do it. Damn it.

"I will . . ." I was going to be aching all night because of that woman, but I needed her to be fully aware of who she was sleeping with—and not just that. I wanted her to scream my name and freaking remember that it was me who gave her pleasure. Me. And it would only ever be me who would make her feel that good. "But why don't we take a short nap so we don't get tired?"

She snorted. "That's a stupid idea." Another yawn.

"I'm just full of them tonight," I lamented to myself as I pulled her against my body and kissed her neck. "Just a quick nap."

"But I'm not even tired," she argued.

Her hair smelled like honey.

Body heavy, she slumped back against me.

"Jordan?"

Good thing we didn't sleep together, because I was pretty sure no matter how I rocked her world—she would have fallen asleep midrock.

"I think I love you," I whispered.

She let out a little mewl and turned her head in to my neck.

Ha, the taming of the shrew. What a joke.

Why tame what's already perfect in its own wild, crazy way? I chuckled as a piece of her hair tickled my face.

I'd risk it all for her.

And I wouldn't regret it for a damn minute.

# CHAPTER THIRTY-FOUR

## JORDAN

"Wakey, wakey, chicken shakey!" a voice yelled.

The bed started shaking.

"Earthquake!" I gasped, and then fell onto the floor in a heap of blankets. The minute I thudded I almost wished something would fall on my face. My head was pounding. What did Max put in those drinks last night? I let out a small groan and was met with another loud noise.

"Aw." Max tugged the comforter from my face. "Get in a fight and lose last night, slugger?" He winced. "Damn, that hair could have its own Twitter following. I think I'd hashtag it #thething."

"Why?" I croaked.

"Well, it kind of resembles the Thing, or is that Cousin It?" His eyebrows drew together in thought.

"Not why would you name it that, just why, why are you in my room? Speaking."

"Well," Max said as he took a seat on my bed, "Reid ordered room service and he knew you'd want actual Starbucks, thus he took the elevator down to the main lobby to acquire his lady's favorite drink."

"Why are you speaking in a British accent?"

"I said *acquire* and *lady* in the same sentence. It's what the Brits do."

"Says the Canadian," I grumbled.

"Isn't it fun how both countries get me?" Max grinned. "Now, for real, I'm doing you a favor. No wars have been fought or won over a chick after she wakes up still drunk from the night before, and you have actual eyeliner in your hairline. Somehow it went from here"—he pointed to my eye—"to here." He pointed to my forehead. "And it's not your best look. Plus . . ." He helped me to my feet. "You smell like cheap liquor and prostitutes."

"Your fault. You shoved dollar bills in my hands," I said weakly.

"I was under the impression you wanted to participate." With a heave, he had me in his arms. And was walking me toward the bathroom.

"What's goin' on?"

"Fairy godmothers don't get time off, though I think we really should talk to the union for better benefits. We have to pay for our own fairy dust—take it from me, that shit's expensive."

It was too early for Max.

"All right." He set me on the counter, then turned on the shower. "Now, I won't cross my brother by tossing you in there naked and scrub-a-dubbing you until you bleed. But you have around four minutes"—he glanced at his watch—"possibly seven, if I can stall him at the elevator."

"Before?"

"He gets back and sees this." Max turned me to the mirror.

I gasped in horror.

"You're welcome." He winked. "Now, hurry up. Oh, and it's hot as hell out, so wear shorts."

"Max," I called.

"Yeah?" He turned around in the bathroom doorway, his muscled body flexing. I wondered if he even worked out for that body or if he gave God so much flack that God was finally like, *chill, you want it, just take it; I can't deal with you anymore.*

"Thanks," I said in a small voice.

"Anything for my new sister-in-law."

I rolled my eyes. "We aren't really getting married."

"Yeah, okay."

"No, really."

"Fine."

"Max! Stop agreeing with me!"

He held up his hands, then nodded. "Um, no?"

"Better."

"Three minutes."

"Damn it!" I jumped off the counter onto wobbly legs, then started stripping. Max smartly closed the door behind him while I made quick work to get all the crappy makeup off my face. It was the fastest shower I'd ever taken in my life.

I just finished brushing my teeth and adding some mascara and lip gloss when Reid knocked on the door.

"Jordan, you decent?"

"No."

"Uh."

"Reid, you've seen me naked, does it matter?"

"It matters if you're going pee. Girls hate when guys watch them pee."

"This is the most romantic moment of my life," I gushed. "Now Max said you have coffee." I pulled open the door. "Pay the toll and you may enter."

He thrust the hot cup in my hands. "I figured you'd need a venti. You were in rough shape last night."

"I'd say I know, but I don't really . . . know."

"Oh, wow." Reid frowned. "You mean you don't remember . . . anything?"

Nervousness started making its way down my spine. "No." I gulped. "Why?"

"Wow, I don't know how to tell you this."

"Reid, just say it!"

"We had sex, lots and lots of mind-blowing sex."

"Oh." I glanced at my flushed face in the mirror.

"And you just kept saying over and over again how amazing I was. How big my penis was. What an amazing body I had. I mean, you went on and on and on about just one pec."

"Did I?" Why didn't Max just smother me with a pillow?

"Yeah, and then you begged me for more. Then you may have tweeted out to all of my new followers that I was the best sex of your life. Oh, and the hashtag #ReidEmoryisasexgod has been trending for around six hours. So . . ."

I slapped my forehead.

Then glanced at Reid's reflection in the mirror.

His smile was huge.

"You bastard!" I yelled. "You lying bastard." I set my coffee down, then smacked him. "I believed you!"

"What can I say?" He took a sip of coffee. "I'm a great actor."

My eyes narrowed. "So what happened?"

"You wanted to swim in the fountain."

I groaned. "Please say you didn't let me."

"Didn't let you." Reid nodded. "I'm all for CPR, but I didn't want you to puke vodka all over me once I revived you . . ."

I winced. "And then?"

"I carried you back to the hotel—you walked barefoot, by the way. Maybe when we get back to New York, do a blood test to make sure you didn't catch something."

"Wow, it just keeps getting better."

"And then you stripped in the living room and tried to take advantage of me . . ."

I gulped. "And how did that go?"

"Really well. I was super into it until I felt guilty and told you to take a nap, which you did. At one point you did wake up and call me Phantom, but I think that's just because the sheet was over my back and you thought it was a cape. It took me a good ten minutes to settle you down after that since you literally thought the Phantom was in your bed, but things got progressively better once I sang you back to sleep."

"You what?"

"Sang you," he whispered, "back to sleep."

"What song?"

"'Music of the Night.'"

"Damn it!" I stomped.

"Hey, hey." He chuckled. "There's more time for that later, don't worry. It's not like you have to get drunk for me to sing to you."

"Really?" I perked up, giving myself away completely, but not really caring since he'd probably seen me at my worst.

"Really." He took two steps, then three, then pressed me back against the counter. "Also, two glasses."

"Huh?"

"Of wine." He nodded. "Then I'm cutting you off, because this"—he kissed me softly—"is happening, and I want you to feel me when I kiss you, when I fill you. That a problem?"

"No," I whispered.

"Good." He kissed me again. "Now do something with that hair, it's freaking me out."

"It's fine."

"It's growing." Reid pointed with his coffee. I huffed and took a look in the mirror; the brown edges were slowly starting to puff up by my ears. How? Seriously? "Also, I have eggs and Advil waiting for you." He turned to walk out of the bathroom.

"Hey, Reid?"

"Yeah?"

"It's not pretend anymore . . . is it?"

"It hasn't been pretend for a while, Jordan."

"But." I gulped. "The media and—"

"Screw the media." He shrugged. "This is about us."

"I trust you." I swallowed more coffee, needing the distraction. It burned all the way down my throat as I choked out, "I trust this."

"Good." He nodded. "Jordan, I would never hurt you."

With that he walked off and I was left praying what he said was true. Because I wasn't so sure I would recover from the type of heartbreak Reid Emory would leave me with. If he left, if he hurt me.

He was the type of guy you compared every other guy to.

There was no going up.

There was no getting better.

Only worse.

# CHAPTER THIRTY-FIVE

## JORDAN

I had scheduled two appearances Saturday, both of which would have people speculating about a possible wedding.

Granted, we weren't going to take it as far as to leak a picture of us at a chapel, but I figured if people saw us shopping together, they'd get the idea. It helped that the few places we visited were all draped in wedding paraphernalia. It didn't take a genius to put two and two together, which was what I was hoping for. We could dupe everyone by simply being in the right place at the right time.

Our dinner that night was even supposed to resemble a rehearsal dinner. It was a private party at the Border Grill, which ended up being more like a loud fiesta where Max made Reid wear a sombrero.

Every time Reid tried to take it off, Max shouted, "Ohana!" Somehow the word had developed new definitions and it now just meant *what Max says goes.*

I tried to choke down my fajita, but it was useless. I was so nervous about my night with Reid that I couldn't even focus on the fact that his

Twitter following had more than tripled since our first night out when he'd serenaded me at the restaurant back in New York.

Ren sent me a text saying that Reid's team had been so pleased with his PR that they had a few more actors they were sending our way.

Which meant more money for Ren.

And most likely a promotion for me.

It's not that I wasn't happy, I was elated, but everything was going too well. And that freaked me out.

Because when things were that good, something had to hit the fan, right?

Max stood at his end of the table. "Shall we make toasts to the happy couple?"

Colt chuckled. "It's not really a wedding, so—"

"To my brother from another mother, Reid." He sighed happily. "Because let's just clear the air. Ain't no way we both came from the same person."

"Hear, hear!" Reid lifted his glass.

"I love you, Reid. I think we both know how epic my toasts can be. But I'll just say this. I'm so happy you've finally found your crab." Max grinned at me. "Yes, he told me the story. Don't be ashamed, Sebastian. Under the sea is better . . . it's wetter, take it from me."

I groaned. "Please stop singing."

"Anyway." Max lifted his glass higher. "To the happy couple. Don't have kids first."

"Wait, what?" Reid asked.

Max shrugged. "Let me be first, bro. I gave up sex for you and Jezebel, so the least you can do is let me show Father our firstborn."

I kicked Reid under the table.

"Fine," he spat, and he narrowed his eyes at me while rubbing his shin.

"I, too, would like to say some words." Jason stood. "You know, considering the last wedding I was at was my own and I wasn't able to actually make a toast. Then again, I was blind in one eye, intoxicated, and marrying a vampire—"

"I knew it!" Max pounded the table with his hand.

Jason ignored him and lifted his margarita in our direction. "Jordan, I'm happy to welcome you into our crazy family. Keep Reid away from sugar-free gummy bears, walk in front of him when he sees a grandma, and if he suddenly bursts into tears for no reason, it's probably because he smells Bengay. ChapStick makes him piss his pants, and if you go anywhere near an old people home, be prepared for lots of rocking back and forth and shouting."

"Thanks," Reid croaked. "Great toast, man."

"Well, I tried." Jason flashed him a grin.

Colt and Milo both stood together, holding hands. Milo lifted her glass. "To the girl who's marrying into crazy."

"So very true." Becca winked from her seat.

"Reid," Colt started. "Never thought I'd see the day where you and your eyes settled down, but I think I speak for men everywhere when I say, thank you."

Reid winked at Milo.

She giggled while Colt shot daggers in our direction.

"Now"—Max stood—"if everyone will please bring their attention to the schedule, I think you'll be pleased with what I've written in."

"'Free time,'" I read aloud. "Really?"

"Go wild." Max laughed. "Though not too wild, maybe like half-wild, not full spring break." He reached for Becca's hand, then kissed it. "What say you? Mandalay Bay?"

"Yes!" Becca shot to her feet. "It will be like reliving the island together!"

"Yay." Max pumped his fist lamely. "Fish."

"You'll be fine." Becca grabbed his hand, then waved good-bye to everyone.

"Well," Jason said with a nod to Colt and Milo, "you guys still wanna see that show?"

"Yup." They left quickly.

And I was alone.

With Reid and his hypnotic eyes.

I toyed with my straw.

Reid watched me, amusement evident on his face as his mouth curved up into a smirk. "Nervous?"

"Nope."

"Good." He pointed to my straw. "Also, can I just say how relieved I am that you got all that biting aggression out on your straw before we made it to the bedroom?"

I glanced at my straw, which looked like it had been through a war zone as teeth marks marred every inch of it.

"That could have been you." I pointed.

Reid shuddered. "Gentle, let's practice being gentle."

"Sex should be savored," I whispered.

"Ah, so she does remember."

"I remember that part." I sighed. "I'm glad I did."

Reid stood, then offered his hand. "Let's go."

"Okay."

The walk back to our hotel was too fast.

By the time we reached the elevator I was fidgeting with my hair, twirling it around my finger, and I'd developed an inability to carry on a logical, normal conversation. I was just about to ask Reid if he thought the weather was nice, desperate for any sort of conversation starter, when he gripped me by the hips and pushed me up against the wall.

"Stop." His lips teased mine in a beckoning kiss. "You're overthinking this, like you overthink everything."

"Maybe." My lower lip quivered. "I'm a girl; it's what we do."

"I'm a man; want to see what I do?" He chuckled darkly, and then his mouth descended in all its spicy wildness, taking me from a simple elevator ride straight into the most epic kiss I'd ever received.

His body slowly pressed me backward until my butt connected with the wall. His tongue moved slowly in and out of my mouth, drawing out the kiss, making me lean forward, eager for more, anticipating the tingling sensation that would occur when his mouth connected with mine again. Reid's hands pressed on either side of my head; his hips glided against mine as the elevator hiccupped, causing enough slight friction that I moaned aloud.

One hand moved from the wall and trailed down my hips until he reached around and squeezed my butt, then dug his hand into my thigh as the elevator hiccupped one more time. Reid's hands had me more hot and bothered than was probably socially acceptable in public, but I couldn't help it.

He was a master kisser.

Placing kiss after hot, searing kiss against my lips until they buzzed with his taste.

The elevator doors opened to our penthouse suite.

Reid stepped back. "Still nervous?"

"Yes." I blinked. "No." Reid's eyes zeroed in on my face, slowly lowering until his gaze stopped at my lips.

"Don't be. You're perfect."

Nobody had ever called me perfect before.

He made me feel like it was true.

Like I wasn't invisible.

I shivered uncontrollably as all of my past insecurities surfaced and then, with one sultry look from Reid Emory, dissipated.

Shoulders straightened, I lifted my head and whispered, "I like it when you look at me like that."

"I can't help it." His aqua eyes flashed with hunger. "It's your fault I look at you this way, all your fault."

"Guess you'll have to punish me." I stepped past him, giggling, as he swiped my hand, then slammed his mouth against mine. This time there were no slow languid movements of his tongue or his lips—no, this was possession, domination, and although I'd always booed the submissive type of girl, I was ready to get on my hands and knees and beg him to kiss me like that again and again until my lips were bruised.

My legs flexed, then clenched together as he deepened the kiss, then with one hand swiped the key card over the door handle.

We stumbled into the room.

The card fell to the floor.

Along with Reid's shirt.

And somehow mine.

I looked down. "How'd you manage that?"

"Magic hands." His smooth voice was just as enticing as his mouth. I laughed as he crooked his finger at me, then kissed me again, this time lifting me into the air and twirling me around a few times before setting me back on my feet.

"What was that for?"

"Overcome with excitement." Reid nodded breathlessly. "Felt the need to do a little dance with you in my arms. Why? Didn't you like it?"

I giggled. "I loved it."

"I love—" His fingers dug into my sides as he looped his hands into my skinny jeans and slowly slid them down my body, his mouth following down the valley of my breasts to my belly button and stopping there. "This, this spot right here."

"Oh, yeah?"

"You little rebel, tell me you used to have a belly button ring and I'm going to tattoo your name on Max's ass."

"Not yours?"

"Mine's too pretty."

"Fair." I shuddered as his hot breath teased my stomach. "And yes, I thought it would make me cool."

"Did it?" He blew across my skin.

"Huh?" I blinked down at him. "Did what?"

He licked a circle around my belly button as I dug my hands into his hair and pushed his head down so he would keep going.

Reid chuckled darkly, then glanced up, his piercing blue eyes making me dizzy with longing. "Did the belly button ring make you cool?"

"No." I swallowed. "And I wasn't brave enough to show it off, so it was pointless."

"That's too bad." He started unbuttoning my jeans. I wanted to tell him to stop as nerves started to creep up on me again, but his eyes, those eyes were so adoring, so trusting that I let him. I let him slide my jeans all the way down my legs.

And when they got caught on my feet and I felt like an awkward turtle who'd just gotten pushed on its back, he slowly lifted one foot and tugged then lifted the other.

Being that close to a man, where he could see every single dimple in my skin, every single scar, every single mark, was terrifying to say the least.

But something about his touch, the way he held me, the way he explored, relaxed me.

"This isn't a onetime thing." He glanced up. "You know that, right?"

I nodded slowly.

"This—" He gripped my butt, then tugged my hips closer to him as he placed an open-mouth kiss across my lower stomach. "This isn't a fling. This isn't something that stays in Vegas. I need you to understand that right now."

"I understand." My voice shook. "And I wouldn't want it any other way."

"Good." He winked.

And then my underwear was suddenly pooling at my ankles.

He stood, his grin devilish as he reached behind me and with one hand unhooked my bra.

"Talented." I raised one eyebrow.

"Sebastian," he teased. "You have no idea."

"So show me," I taunted.

Eyes hazy, I watched him beneath my lashes as he slowly cupped my face and whispered, "No complaining when you get dehydrated and are in desperate need of food. I'm locking us in the room until I'm satisfied, until you're satisfied, and then I'm going to do it over and over again. If you want out, you better say something now, because once we start there will be no stopping."

"Kinda bossy, aren't you?"

"You love it." His mouth fused against mine as he lifted me into the air again, as if I weighed nothing, and he plunged his tongue between my lips, tasting so warm and sweet.

"I do," I admitted.

I hadn't realized that we were already in his bedroom. Or that he had shut the door, or that he still had jeans on.

What? Had I blacked out or was he just that good?

It had been years since I'd slept with anyone.

And the first time I decide to jump back into the sack, so to speak, I jump back in with the king of sex.

The room was dim, and in that moment, I was very much aware why he was cast as the Phantom. There was something dark about him, something so seductive that my heart was racing as if I was in danger, but the good kind, the kind that you run toward even though you aren't sure you'll survive it. Like surfing a wave that could kill you.

Or standing outside during a hurricane.

His masculine beauty was both terrifying and intriguing. My body responded and arched beneath his touch like I was an instrument and he was the musician.

"Phantom," I whispered. "Too bad you didn't bring props."

"Ah, so she wants the cape."

I nodded.

"Next time." He winked, dropping his pants to the ground, then tossing them in the corner.

Well, just another thing to be amazed about.

The man didn't wear boxers.

Or briefs.

Or anything.

"So you never wear underwear?" My breathing picked up as he pushed me back onto the bed, his face a mask of pure concentration and lust.

"Nope."

"Ever?" I squeaked.

"Nope."

"Oh."

"That bother you?" He smirked as he slowly hovered over me, his bronzed chest such a ridiculous distraction I had to blink a few times before I answered.

"Nope."

With an amused chuckle, he placed a feather-light kiss across my temple and then down the side of my neck. "Relax."

"I am relaxed," I argued.

"You're freaked out." Another kiss. "Overanalyzing." His mouth descended to one of my breasts. I hissed out a breath. "And figuratively zipping up that skirt again."

I whimpered as he sucked. "What was that?"

"There we go." He blew across my skin.

I gripped the sheets as I tried to keep myself from leaping from my current position and tackling him. Why the torture?

"I love how responsive you are." He paid attention to the next breast while his hand moved south.

"Uh . . ." It came out in a gurgle as I tried to clench my legs together and scoot away. "So, sex, that should happen."

"Nope." Apparently his new favorite word. "You aren't ready for me yet. Believe me, that's not ego talking, that's truth."

I looked down.

And paled.

"Wow, how exactly did they give you a penis enlargement? Your doctor does great work, really, but that's not happening."

"Calm"—his mouth brushed against mine—"down."

"Says the Viking."

"Viking?"

"Getting ready to pillage with his giant—" Reid licked my hip as I stuttered out, "Sword."

"You do realize I'm trying to make this good for you, yet you keep distracting me with your talking. And do you even comprehend how freaking gorgeous you are? Or the hellish amount of self-control I need to keep myself from just straddling you and sinking into you? Hmm? Do you?"

I opened my mouth, but only a croak came out as my cheeks heated with embarrassment. Did he just say *sink*? Out loud? Apparently I was also a prude. Great.

"Sex should never be embarrassing . . . though I'm sure sometimes it is, because life is. Sex shouldn't alter the way you feel about someone; it happens because you can't imagine waiting one more minute." He whispered, "One more second, without physically sharing the most intimate part of yourself with the person you lo—" He looked away. "The person you care for."

Did I hallucinate, or had he been just about to say *love*?

"We need ground rules before . . ."

"Damn, you don't make things easy, do you Jordan?"

Rhetorical question? The silence got awkward, but when I opened my mouth, he placed two fingers against my lips.

"No talking." He nodded. "The only words I approve of are, *more, Reid, yes, Reid, harder, Reid, Reid, Reid, Reid, Reid, Reid*, and if you didn't get it the first time, you can say my name, only my name. There will be no thinking about PR, no thinking about Otis, or your stupid plant, or the fact that I bring roses because that's how my mom taught me to date. There will be tasting, lots of touching, and very close inspection of the most intimate parts of you. No pushing me away, not unless I'm hurting you, and you will not close your eyes. Ever."

"But why would I—"

"Just keep your eyes open, so I can watch you watching me, so that you're present, so that I can make sure you know exactly who's making you feel this way."

He didn't give me any warning.

His hands moved between my thighs.

I closed my eyes.

And received a swat on the side of my hip.

I jerked my eyes open and glared.

"Feisty," he teased. "I can work with that."

And he did.

He so did.

There was no use fighting him as he played me like an instrument, and after about two seconds I was trying to figure out why the heck I was fighting him in the first place.

His hand left.

I leaned up on my elbows.

Just as his head lowered.

"Reid!" I shouted.

"Hmm?" He glanced up. "Sorry, kinda busy, so you're going to have to use one of the preapproved words."

He licked my thigh.

Then bit.

"Ouch."

"Fail!" Reid snickered. "That wasn't Reid approved."

His tongue twirled dangerously close to my core; it was like his mouth was flirting with my leg.

My leg liked it.

Every part of me liked it.

"Reid!" I bucked off the bed. His hands moved to my hips and held me down. "More!"

He looked up and winked. "Love that phrase."

"Reid." I let out a little moan as I tried desperately not to float away and pet the unicorn currently flying overhead. Look, a butterfly! I wondered if Reid would be insulted if I took a picture of that wicked mouth of his and burned candles in front of it, you know, to pay tribute. His tongue swirled.

And then his breath was hot on my inner thigh again, raining kisses down my leg, then back up the other leg. My entire body was hot, then cold, then hot again as his mouth bit and nibbled places I didn't even know existed.

He was going to be the death of me.

# CHAPTER THIRTY-SIX

## REID

She was going to be the absolute death of me. It was like she was embarrassed by how easily her body responded to my every single touch. It was a huge turn-on, making my current situation so difficult I was pouring sweat, and I hadn't even started on the main course yet.

I was still appetizing.

Her body shuddered.

It arched, it shuddered again, then melted against me.

It was freaking gorgeous—watching her take pleasure without me having to give her permission to do so.

"Take it," I whispered. "Come on, Jordan, stop thinking."

"But your mouth was—"

"—making you feel good," I answered gruffly as my body hummed with awareness of all things her. Hell, her taste was out of this world.

Without any sort of warning, she grabbed my head and jerked my mouth to hers.

Her greedy tongue fighting mine, trying to dominate. I groaned as I fell on my back and pulled her on top of me so her body was straddling mine.

I reached into the nightstand.

And came back empty.

Jordan, clearly enjoying herself way too much to pay attention to my panic, just kept kissing me, thrusting her body all over me in the best of ways.

My hand searched again.

What the hell?

"Hold on." I sat up, and Jordan fell back, her face flushed.

"What's wrong?"

"I had a box of condoms right here." I pointed to the drawer.

"Someone was confident."

"Safe," I corrected. "Someone was safe and now—"

I let out a growl as I picked up the empty box and pulled out a sticky note that said, "Stick it, get it? Like as in stick it to her? Ha-ha, I kill myself. Also, payback's a bitch. Now we're even for you signing me up for that stupid show. Oh, also, note the picture." The picture was of a stick figure holding a bag of peas to its middle, maybe its balls? Oh, and he wrote it in blue crayon. The sick bastard.

It would take me at least five minutes to run down to the main lobby. I tossed the box at the wall and glared.

Jordan let out a soft laugh.

"Not funny." I sighed, my body still having other ideas as it tried to unite with her without my damn permission.

"It kind of is." She wiggled on top of me.

I gripped her hips. "Keep moving and it won't be. Seriously, Jordan. I've been putting this off for years."

"Sex?"

"With you." I grumbled. "Okay, so it hasn't been years, but it feels like it and I really, really, really . . ." I sighed as I took in her pert breasts and perfect curves. "Where was I again?"

Jordan moved.

I hissed.

"I know your medical history." Jordan winked. "And I'm on the pill . . ." She moved again. I groaned as my head slammed back against the headboard. "You're welcome."

"Shit, you feel good." I grabbed her hips and moved her exactly where I wanted her. "Are you sure?"

"No."

I jerked back my hands.

"Kidding." She winked.

"Am I laughing?"

"If you were, that means I was doing it wrong," she said in a teasing voice. "And I don't want to do it wrong."

"Impossible."

"Possible."

"Jordan?"

"Hmm?"

"Shut up." With one lift I had her in the air and swiftly thrust into her.

She stopped talking.

I stopped breathing.

And then, very slowly, moved in and out, thinking it wasn't real, nobody could actually feel that perfect.

But she did.

I picked up my pace, sweat pooling at my temples as Jordan leaned over me, and then with a move I'd only ever seen in the movies, she flipped onto her back, taking me with her.

"I think I love you." I chuckled.

She winked while I thrust harder, deeper, then pulled out and flipped her onto her stomach, pulling her back against me so she was almost in a sitting position.

"Damn, this is going to be over too quickly." I tugged her ear with my teeth as I tried to slow down, but every part of me was ready to explode into oblivion.

Her body tightened around me.

I held my breath, trying to prolong the moment.

She arched.

"More, Reid!"

I cupped her breasts and clenched my teeth. "Love that phrase."

I'd like to think her next scream was because of me, and when she found her release and said my name three times and then a fourth, I decided that I was never leaving her bed. Ever.

I held out as long as I could.

Which was about one more second.

Spent, I leaned my forehead against her back.

"Reid?" Her voice was hoarse. Did I do that? Was that me? My chest puffed up.

"Hmm?" I kissed her salty-sweet skin.

"Next time I want to yell *Phantom*."

I slapped her ass, then burst out laughing. "You and every other woman in existence."

"Hey, some like Raoul."

"Raoul can suck it!" I laughed.

"Mature." She slowly crawled off me and leaned back against the pillow, her face flushed. "That was incredible."

"That"—I leaned down and kissed her nose—"was just round one."

# CHAPTER THIRTY-SEVEN

## REID

A pillow was covering my face. The sheet had somehow been ripped from the bed and was dangling halfway across one of the lamps in the corner and Jordan was asleep, shivering, in the middle of the bed, naked.

I laughed and covered her with the comforter, then kissed her head and walked out of the room.

It was morning, though I wasn't sure how early, nor did I care after that marathon last night.

Forget round one.

Round two included ice cubes.

Round three featured a bit of standing and maneuvering and a pulled hamstring.

Round four took place halfway off the mattress.

Round five was a good idea, but we decided against it when neither one of us could keep our eyes open long enough to kiss.

I was wiped.

In the best possible way.

It was impossible to hide my smile as I made my way into the kitchen in search of some coffee.

"So," Max said from behind a newspaper. How was he already dressed? He turned a page. "Either you just gave me a little niece or nephew or, bummer, you had to go down to the lobby last night. But by the sounds of it, I don't think it killed the moment at all."

I lowered my middle finger over the page.

He pulled the newspaper back and grinned. "Hey, at least we're even now. No going behind each other's backs and doing anything crazy. Right? The war between brothers ends, right here, right now?"

My eyes narrowed. "How do I know you're going to keep your word?"

Max sighed. "I thought you might ask that." He reached into his front pocket and placed a key on the table, sliding it across the granite. "It's yours."

"What is this?"

"They key to the Seattle house." Max sighed. "I promised you I'd give it to you if you could stay in a committed relationship for longer than a week, and by my calculations"—he checked his watch—"wow, almost eight days! Well done."

"I'm confused." I pocketed the key. "I'm not in a relationship."

Max's eyebrows furrowed. "But Jordan?"

"I mean"—I scratched my head—"we haven't labeled it or anything, at least not yet. I don't know, man."

"But you slept with her," Max pointed out. "By the loud screams and banging, she could be carrying Reid Jr. and you're not sure about it?"

"Max—" I really didn't want to have this conversation now or explain my fears that Jordan was going to bail on me the minute I wanted to turn things serious. "We're having fun. That's all that matters, all right?"

Max's mouth formed an *O*. "Fine, but the house is still yours. A bet is a bet. And like I said, it sure sounds like you won last night."

"Four times." I puffed out my chest while Max held up his hand for a high five.

"Knew you were my brother." He laughed. "Now, make the girl breakfast. It's the least you can do after all you've put her through."

"Right." I eyed the fridge. "You gonna help?"

"Sorry." Max made a face. "I'm busy doing anything but that. Besides, all I managed to grab at the little store in the lobby were a few protein bars, so you probably need to order room service." He yawned. "And our plane leaves in four hours, so get the girl up."

"Right." I snatched the room service menu and padded back to the room.

Jordan wasn't in bed.

Frowning, I went to the bathroom and knocked. "Hey, we need to order some breakfast, you know what you want?"

Her reply was muffled. "Um, just order me some oatmeal with fruit or something."

"You sure you don't want something more substantial? We had a long night last night . . ."

"No!" She shouted. "No, that's . . . it's fine. That's fine."

"Are you showering?"

"Yeah."

"Want me to join you? I can—"

"Actually, I just finished, sorry. I'll be out in a minute."

"Oh." I licked my lips. "Okay, I'll just grab your oatmeal then."

"Thanks."

I walked off, a bit confused, but then again, women were usually weird after sex, right? And she was probably just doing what Jordan does, which is overthink every damn thing. I made a mental note to ask her if she was okay. I typically didn't do that thing where the guy talks to the girl afterward and makes sure everyone's on the same level.

But for her I would.

Because I cared for her.

Because I saw myself with her.

Not just next week.

But years from now.

The smile was back full force as I made my way back into the main living area and grabbed the phone to order breakfast.

Max. Huh, I had to hand it to him—despite his insanity, he kind of brought us together.

Not that I'd ever thank him.

Because thanking Max would be admitting he was right—and I didn't want to do that. Ever.

So for now, I'd just mentally give him a significant nod and pat on the back.

It's all he was going to get.

# CHAPTER THIRTY-EIGHT
## JORDAN

I wiped the tears from my eyes, but they just pooled with water again! I fanned myself over and over again, then reapplied my waterproof mascara.

Stupid. Stupid. Stupid.

I kicked the tiny metal trash can in the corner, then crossed my arms as my body convulsed with hurt.

A bet.

I was part of bet between the millionaires. How stupid could I be? I never saw it coming, maybe because Reid really is that great of an actor.

I could get over that part, if he maybe explained to me the reasons behind it.

But when Max asked him about us and he didn't say anything? He made it sound like I was a conquest.

And that there were no feelings behind our night together.

I'd heard the entire conversation. I wasn't one of those girls who got so hurt she ran off before she heard the guy defend himself or defend her. Read that book, watched that movie.

So like an idiot, I stood in the hallway and waited in painful silence. I waited for Reid to correct himself. I waited for him to say something romantic. I waited for him to defend our relationship.

I waited and I waited.

And he made a joke about owing me breakfast.

And that was it.

There was no admission of feelings.

There was nothing.

By then, tears were streaming down my face, and I had no choice but to pretend like I was showering when really I was bawling my eyes out and trying to calm myself down.

He was a lying bastard. A lying, cheating, horrible, bastard son of a bitch! I had a very vivid daydream about stabbing him with my hair pick but knew the plastic wouldn't do the damage he deserved. Plus, kicking him in the balls seemed like a more painful option.

But the problem?

He was my client.

Still my client.

I needed him.

He needed me.

I gripped the countertop. "You can do this," I said to my reflection. "You're a professional. Act like it."

That was my pep talk.

Over the next hour, I chatted with Max and Reid like there was nothing wrong. But when Reid touched me, or put his hand on my thigh, it took every ounce of strength I had not to stab him with my fork.

Or just burst into tears.

For one night.

Twelve hours.

I hadn't been invisible anymore.

And it had been the best twelve hours of my life. The sexiest man I'd ever seen was kissing me, holding me, loving me. And I felt it—what other people probably feel on a daily basis.

Wanted.

Desired.

Visible.

He wanted my eyes open, he wanted me to be present, he said, and I was, I was so present.

The sick part? I wouldn't take it back. Even knowing what I knew . . . because even though he was a horrible human being to use me in that way, he still gave me a gift.

It wasn't the sex.

Or even the way he touched me.

It was the way he looked at me, for just one brief moment in my existence, like maybe I wasn't the girl the guy passed over, but the one he searched for.

• • •

"Hey, you okay?" Reid nudged me once we found our seats on the plane. I'd just spent the last ten minutes smiling through my teeth while cameras flashed in our direction and the paparazzi asked if the wedding speculation was true.

"Yeah." I swallowed the lump in my throat. "Just really tired, long night." My smile was weak.

"You can lean on me," Reid offered as he put an arm around my shoulder.

"Nah." I fake yawned. "It's okay. I'll probably drool or something equally embarrassing. Why don't you check your e-mails and make sure everything's good for postproduction this next week? I think you got all your shots in last week, but hey, you never know."

"Work," Reid said slowly. "You want me to work?"

"I'm sleeping." I shrugged. "What else is there to do?"

His eyes heated.

I quickly looked down and yawned again. "Well, night."

"Jordan—"

"Dude." Max turned around in his seat. "Dad's thrilled his eldest finally grew up. All's well that ends well. The ruse is up. Thank God. I'm locking Becca in the apartment tonight. P.S. Wear the earplugs I gave you."

Becca let out a snort. "Sorry to burst your bubble."

"No!" Max shouted. "There will be no bursting of any kind!"

"But," Becca laughed, "I promised my mom when we got back I'd spend the night at their house and go over bridal shower ideas. And she hasn't seen me in a few weeks because of school."

Max was silent.

I heard them kissing, but kept my eyes closed.

"Fine," Max grumbled. "But tomorrow night, you're mine."

"Deal."

More kissing.

It was nauseating.

Sort of.

I clenched my eyes shut.

"Out like a light, huh?" Max commented.

Reid sighed. "Like I said, it was a long night, no wonder she's tired."

"Yeah, well," Max sighed, "At least someone had a good night. Oh, also, I looked into that new complex that we acquired in Chelsea. There are a few openings, still want me to move her stuff out?"

My stomach sank. What the hellfire? When did Reid decide he was going to pack me up and ship me out?

"Yeah." Reid nodded. "It's probably for the best. Her stuff is shit anyways, you know? I can't imagine her wanting any of it, but just in case."

Rage pumped through every blood vessel in my body. It was like he was a completely different person.

"All right." Max sighed. "Maybe you should tell her?"

"Nah, it will be a surprise."

A surprise? Was he high!

The rest of the plane ride, I stewed like a woman scorned. He'd slept with me, made some sort of archaic wager with his brother over being able to stay in a relationship—and let's be honest, a week is so not a relationship—and now he was kicking me out, and what? He's just going to say, "Surprise!" when the guest room is packed up and my pillows are already in my new apartment?

He's probably going to want me to thank him.

Like hell.

I kept choking on the lump in my throat as stupid tears stung the back of my eyes. I would not cry.

Not in front of him.

He didn't deserve the tears.

Or the ego kick he'd get at seeing how hung up I really was on him. Good thing I wasn't in love with him.

Good thing.

My heart pounded painfully against my chest.

Yup. Good thing I wasn't in love.

# CHAPTER THIRTY-NINE

## REID

As luck would have it, the minute we landed, my agent called and said I was needed on set for one last scene. The kissing scene, the same one I'd been having trouble with that I nailed last time.

The director wanted one more take, this time with it raining.

Of course.

Nothing more romantic than a kiss in the rain, or so I've been told.

"Hey." I checked my watch, then nudged Jordan. "I need to run to set really quick and shoot a scene. I'm not sure how long it will take, but—"

"No worries." Jordan flashed a completely fake smile; her eyes didn't crinkle at the sides and her left eye started that weird twitch thing again. "I have some work to catch up on too."

"Great." I leaned in and pressed a kiss to her cheek. "I'll see you later, all right?" I turned to leave, then stopped and ran back. "Help yourself to some wine while you work. Also, Max is going to need your key."

"My key?" she repeated, her face paling.

"It's a surprise. Promise you'll love it."

"I'm sure I will," she said weakly.

"Hey." I gripped her shoulders. "Are you sure you're okay?"

"Yeah." Her eyes filled with tears. "I'm just stressed." She wiped at her eyes. "And you know . . . allergies."

"In the airport?"

"Yup, it was a thing." She nodded and wiped at her nose. "It was on the news, mold in JFK. I'm allergic to mold so . . ."

"Right." Something told me to stay. But being a man, I ignored that something, because what reason would she have to be upset? We'd just spent an amazing weekend together. And when I got home that night, I was going to ask her to move in.

Because the very idea that she would potentially find an apartment and leave me?

Made me want to throw up.

I wanted her.

Forever.

# CHAPTER FORTY

## JORDAN

I cried the entire way to Reid's apartment. My stuff was still nicely placed in his guest room.

But I knew it wouldn't last.

I poured myself a healthy glass of wine.

Chugged it.

Poured another.

Patted Otis on the head.

Then walked over to Max's apartment, key in hand. I knocked twice before he answered.

"Hey." Max leaned against the door frame. "What can I do you for?"

I dangled the key in front of his face.

He frowned but didn't take it.

I grabbed his hand and slammed the key into his palm and tried walking away, but he snatched my wrist and pulled me back. "Have you been crying?"

"No."

"Drinking?" He sniffed the air around me. "That merlot's been on his shelf for five years. Pretty sure it costs around five grand."

I shrugged, not really caring.

"Whole bottle?" Max sighed.

I shrugged again.

He patted my head, then jerked me into his apartment and slammed the door behind him. "Well, I don't want to say I told you so, but yeah . . . I told you so."

"I know." I stared at my feet. "But you had a part in this, don't deny it!"

Max huffed. "Of course I had a part in it! A part in bringing you two kids together! You should thank me!"

"Thank you?" I screeched, my eyes greedily searching for an object to chuck at his head. "You made a bet! Over our relationship!"

Max frowned.

"And then he got a house! A FREAKING HOUSE!" I grabbed one of his throw pillows and tossed it in his general direction. He ducked. "And when you asked Reid about us he didn't even say anything!" I chucked another pillow, which this time hit Max square in the face.

"Whoa, whoa, whoa." Max shook his head. "What the hell are you talking about?"

"I'm moving!" I shouted loud enough for Otis to hear back in Reid's apartment.

"I know," Max said slowly. "But I thought it was a surprise!"

"Ha!" I grabbed another pillow. "You're evicted!" I laughed bitterly. "Surprise!"

"Wait, Reid's evicted?" Max held up his hands in surrender. "That's impossible, I own the building."

"Me!" I dropped the pillow and kicked it with my foot. "I'm evicted, because I'm moving!"

"Right." Max said slowly. "In with Reid."

"I live with Reid!"

"That's what I'm saying."

"And now I'm evicted!"

"Women confuse me." Max scratched the back of his head. "Seriously, what was God thinking?" He glanced up. "One day we'll have that talk . . ." He marched over to the kitchen and poured himself a shot, tossed it back, then faced me again. "Why don't we start at the beginning."

"He didn't claim me," I mumbled.

"From the sounds of it, he did more than claim you . . ." Max said under his breath. "But I digress . . ."

"And don't play stupid; you guys found me a place."

"For your things."

"Exactly!"

"Which upsets you because you don't want to keep your soiled couch and table from Ikea?" Max went back into the kitchen and grabbed the bottle, then held it out to me like I was going to grab it and slam it over his head.

I took the peace offering but didn't drink. "It upsets me because he slept with me and now he's evicting me, going behind my back and finding me an apartment, and, and, and—" I started pacing. "He saw me, Max! He really saw me! And we had one of those damn elevator kisses, and you were so right. It was amazing, epic, everything I could have ever wanted in a kiss. And now? Now it's over with and we're over with and I got too invested. And I'm working with him and now it's going to be awkward and I hate awkward. I do not do awkward well."

Max grinned. "Neither does your hair."

I groaned and sat on the couch, setting the bottle of whiskey on the table. "Sorry, and here I am, coming over to your place, doing exactly what you said I'd do, losing my mind."

"I said other things too. You seem to recall I prophesied a big misunderstanding?"

"Stupid, stupid, men." I ignored him. "I hate men."

"Whoa, there." Max burst out laughing. "Hey, I have an idea. Let's get back at Reid."

"Huh?" I perked up a little.

"Serves him right for going behind your back, making all those big decisions without you! And he expects, what? You to be waiting for him at the apartment? Pining over him. Wearing sexy lingerie and wishing he was with you? I say, hell, no!"

"Hell, no!" I stood and thrust my hand into the air, suddenly liking Max a whole lot more. "You're right!"

"I'm always right." Max's grin grew. "That jackass needs to know what he's missing! Why don't you stay in my guest room and give him something to panic about? Mess with his mind a bit before he goes and evicts you. Bastard!"

"Bastard!" I repeated.

"Great." Max rubbed his hands together. "Why don't you just get ready over there and I'll help you pack up your stuff? That way it looks like you left him and not the other way around."

"That actually makes sense." I nodded. "Then it's like I get the final say."

"You deserve the final say." Max nodded emphatically. "You're a strong, independent woman."

"I am!"

"R-e-s-p-e-c-t, find out what it means to me!" Max started singing and dancing around.

"What are you doing?"

"Sorry." Max stopped dancing. "Got caught up in the moment."

"No more dancing. It's making me dizzy."

"So you did drink the whole bottle."

I held up my fingers. "All but this much."

"So all but a half inch? Why not all of it?"

"I felt guilty." My shoulders slumped. I was emotionally exhausted.

"Aw, little slugger." Max wrapped an arm around me. "Why don't you go down the hall, first door on your right? Sleep it off. I'll go pack your shit."

"Really?"

"Sure, what are Maxes for?"

"World domination," I offered.

"I knew I liked you the moment I met you, Jordan."

"You didn't call me Jezebel!"

"Caught that, did ya?" He winked. "Off you go. Oh, and by the way, I'm leaving Otis. Hades doesn't like dogs."

"Hades?"

A goat was somehow summoned and began prancing down the hall full speed. A gecko masquerading as a cowboy rode on its back.

In a saddle.

"Kids," Max said in a low voice, "I said bedtime. No more *Phineas and Ferb*. Hades, I'm disappointed—you know what that does to Little G! He gets nightmares."

Hades, the goat, hung his head while the gecko stayed completely still on his back. Was it dead?

Max rolled his eyes. "Kids, am I right?"

"Am I high?" I asked in a weak voice while the goat shot a bored look in my direction.

Max coughed out a laugh. "Please. Hugs, not drugs."

I pointed, "But there's a goat and a gecko."

With a shrug, Max made a little sound in the back of his throat, and Hades walked slowly back down the hall with the gecko on top.

"That may be the strangest thing I've ever seen," I mumbled.

"Hell, you should have seen them at Halloween. Hades wanted to be a lizard. Little G wanted to be a goat. It was funny as hell—a bit awkward, though, when a lady goat came to the party. Poor Little G was so confused."

I frowned.

"Well." Max slapped me on the back. "Off to bed. Don't worry, I've got this."

Too tired and emotionally drained to argue, I waved good-bye and managed to stumble into the guest bedroom. The last thing I thought of was that I should have locked my door just in case the goat decided to interrupt my sleep.

# CHAPTER FORTY-ONE

## REID

It was nearing midnight by the time I finally made it back to the apartment. A part of me was hoping Jordan would still be up, but I knew she had to be exhausted—besides, she'd been acting strange the entire day. Sleep was more necessary than a deep talk where I blurted out my feelings and asked her to live with me.

Two weeks after meeting me.

It sounded crazy.

It was crazy.

I knew it.

And she'd probably laugh in my face.

But I wanted her. I wanted her close. I wanted her damn hair. I even wanted her dog. Waking up without her neurotic coffee drinking just seemed like a horrible way to start any day.

The apartment was dark, which was strange considering Jordan had a ridiculous habit of keeping all the living room lights on even if she was in her bedroom sleeping.

Her bedroom.

Soon to be vacant, because I was moving her ass into mine.

My body trembled at the thought. Was I crazy? To want her to live with me? To want more than just a fling for the cameras?

Sighing, I set my keys on the counter just as Otis barreled toward me, his little body shaking with excitement.

"Hey, Otis, where's your mom?"

"Not here." Max's voice echoed in the large room, bouncing off the ceiling and driving straight into my chest. "She's gone, Reid."

"Max?"

A light flicked on, revealing Max as he sat on one of my couches, smoking a cigar and drinking my finest whiskey, the ass.

"Not Max," he said slowly. "I'm the ghost of Christmas present."

"Max, listen to me very carefully. Did someone offer you a cookie that tasted funny? Furthermore, did you actually eat it?"

"Who is this Max you speak of?" He stood. "I am here to tell you your present while also predicting your future."

"All right then." I rolled my eyes. "Of course you can't do things normally and just send me a damn text."

"Ghosts don't have phones."

"I'm sure a real ghost could find one."

"Real ghosts have no need for technology!" he hissed.

"If you're a real ghost, that means I can punch you in the face and you won't feel a thing."

Max's expression wavered.

"Ah, the ghost is getting a bit . . . scared of its own shadow?"

"Ghosts don't have shadows, dumbass."

"Max."

"She's gone." He yawned. "Boxes packed, all because somebody decided to be an absolute ass."

"Gone?" I repeated. "But she's moving in with me. We moved her damaged shit into the warehouse, right? She's . . . there's no way. Why would she be pissed?"

"Men." Max took a long swig of whiskey and slammed the glass down on the counter. "They never listen! Only thinking with their dicks and refusing to acknowledge a woman's need for a little bit of attention after a night of sex!"

"What?"

"See!" Max shouted. "You're all the same! ALL OF YOU!" He paced in front of me. "Did it ever occur to you that Jordan may have needed a bit of, oh, I don't know . . . encouragement after your wild night of passion? More than a slap on the ass and a thanks-for-the-good-time note on her pillow?"

"That's your thing, not mine." I held up my hands.

"Women like to be appreciated in Hallmark form." Max shrugged. "Besides, Becca loves my notes."

"Becca's also a ghost in this scenario?" I took a seat. Conversations with Max were like all-day marathons where people needed to stock up on Gatorade and protein bars if they were going to make it to the finish line.

"Please." Max grinned smugly. "Becca, a ghost? What are you? Five?"

I pressed my lips together and damn near sat on my hands to keep myself from strangling him.

"She heard our conversation." Max's eyebrows shot up. "And now she's gone."

"What conversation?"

"Oh, you know." Max bent down and picked up Otis and began petting him in the same manner Dr. Evil pets his cat. "The one where you said you two were just having fun, oh, also, the bet was mentioned . . . right, so she probably wants to run you over with a golf cart."

"Where. Is. She."

Max kept petting Otis. The little traitor licked his hand and let out a groan. "It's going to take more than your Carmen Sandiego skills to find her; I'll tell you that much. This girl, she doesn't do well with you going behind her back and making decisions. She's not the type. So now, you have a choice. Prove your love . . . or die alone."

"Harsh."

"The ghost of Christmas future was always the scariest one, Reid. Always."

"But you said you were Christmas present."

"Now I'm future. I changed like two seconds ago when I picked up Otis and my voice even got gruffer."

"Hmm, didn't catch that."

He deepened his voice. "I am the ghost of Christmas future, and you're screwed. Better?"

I groaned into my hands. "Max, stop, just tell me where she is so I can fix it."

"Nope." Max set Otis back down on the ground. "But I'll tell you tomorrow once you give me your plan."

"My plan?"

"To seduce the shrew." Max winked. "After all, that's how this all started, right? Seduce the shrew, make her believe that true love conquers all? I mean, the press is convinced. I'm convinced. Hell, I think even you're convinced, but Jordan? Well, she just might need more convincing. After all, girls like that rarely believe in happily ever after."

"Girls like that?" I fumed, clenching my fists.

"The invisibles. The ones who spend their life cast as streetwalker number one or dancer number two. After so many failed auditions, they just come to expect the fact that they're going to be a chorus girl."

"She's not a chorus girl; she's the main attraction!"

"Oh"—Max held up his hands—"you don't have to convince me of that . . . but Jordan?" He slapped my shoulder. "Good luck with that. I'll be waiting for your text. And Reid? I suggest you stay up all night and plan. A girl like that doesn't happen twice."

"I know." My chest constricted painfully at the sound of Max's footsteps as he made his way to the door and slammed it behind him.

Otis pranced around my feet doing his potty dance. I glared at him. My apartment felt empty, too big.

"C'mon, Otis. It looks like we got some planning to do."

As much as I wanted to seriously murder my brother—he was right. My stomach clenched with nausea the more I thought about what Jordan might have overheard back in Vegas. I thought I was helping by not telling Max all the details of what I was thinking—I mean, it's Max. I might as well have taken out an ad on every billboard in America. The man didn't do secrets well.

The man didn't do secrets well.

Damn it, why didn't I just torture the information out of him? I was just about ready to run over to his apartment and give him hell when Otis barked.

"You're right," I sighed, irritated that I was talking to a dog, and a bit alarmed that his bark made sense. Maybe I was the one who ate the funny cookie? "She deserves more than that."

Another bark.

"Something that sweeps her off her feet and proves once and for all that she's not invisible."

Two more barks.

"Any clever ideas, Otis?"

One bark.

"I'm not giving her a bone."

Seven barks later and I had a plan that would, in fact, most likely end with . . .

A cape.

And roses.

# CHAPTER FORTY-TWO

## JORDAN

I opened my eyes and yawned, then nearly had a heart attack as a green gecko stared at me from the nightstand.

"Hey, there," I said in a groggy voice.

The gecko didn't move.

Were geckos a bad omen? Because my pounding head and hurting heart both kicked into overdrive as I gained my bearings and glanced around the room.

It was as if Max had moved me into his apartment in the middle of the night. A few duffel bags sat in the corner and two garment bags hung on the door.

So why the gecko?

"Jordan." Becca's voice sounded on the other side of the door; she knocked and then walked in. "I see Little G gave you a nice wake-up call?"

I frowned at the gecko. "Does he often do that? Just roam around wherever he pleases?"

Becca snorted. "He's like Max in gecko form. What do you think?"

"That thought alone makes me want to sleep with the lights on at night."

"Me too." Becca grinned. "And I sleep with the man."

"Knife under the pillow?" I asked, genuinely curious.

"Nah, but I do keep fruit snacks next to the condoms just in case he has a nightmare."

"Because fruit snacks stop nightmares?"

With a shrug Becca made her way around the bed and sat. "According to Max."

The gecko did a little hop. Becca held out her hand; he walked onto it, slowly, and then lay down. I'd never in my life seen such a thing, a domesticated gecko. Then again, if you could domesticate lizards, why not the tiny ones?

"So." She cleared her throat. "Max said something about an emergency on set."

I grunted.

"An emergency involving Reid."

I licked my lips and looked down at the comforter, silently counting to keep myself from bursting into tears.

"And"—Becca nudged me with her elbow—"I know that this is a rough time for you, but you still need your job, right? And as his publicist, it's in your best interest to spin things."

"So why do I need to spin the emergency on set?" I asked, curious. "What? Did he lock himself in his trailer or something and then put aluminum foil in his microwave? Press would eat that up. Reid Emory—idiot."

"No." Becca stifled a laugh. "But he did have a nervous breakdown."

"I'm sorry, what?"

"Nervous breakdown." Becca winced. "And not the typical *I'm an artist*, blah, blah, blah nervous breakdown where the actor just freaks out on the director and drops a lot of f-bombs."

Dread pooled in my stomach. Yeah, I'd had a few of those actors, but Reid never fit that bill. Which made me wonder, what was his definition of a nervous breakdown?

"He, uh"—Becca leaned forward and whispered—"he's saying he's Batman. At least that's what the Twitter hashtag is, though, honestly, I think you can spin it so he can audition once Ben Affleck's time is up, you know?"

"Batman." I repeated. "As in the caped crusader?"

"The very one." She grinned. "So suit up, Jordan. You've got an actor to save."

"And if I don't?" I argued, already getting out of bed.

"Who knows, maybe you'll lose your job?" Becca offered. "I'm not really sure how those things work."

With a grumble, I forced my legs to walk over to the garment bag, which I unzipped, then grabbed the first and only dress available.

"Uh, what's this?" I pulled out the white lingerie-looking spectacle. The lacy corset flowed down into a see-through skirt and was covered with a lacy wrap that looked like anything but normal daywear. More like I just woke up in a historical novel and the only thing I have to wear is a night rail.

"That"—Becca pointed—"is Max. Believe me, it's best to just wear what he has for you and ask questions later."

"Screw that." I went to the duffel bag.

It was filled with Teenage Mutant Ninja Turtle fruit snacks.

Cursing Max, I stomped over to the next duffel bag. That one was filled with poker chips. Great.

One duffel bag left. "Do I even want to know?" I asked aloud.

"Probably not." Becca burst out laughing.

The bag wasn't very heavy. I unzipped it and sighed. See-through glass shoes sparkled from the middle of the bag. "My shoes, I take it?"

"For the outfit." She nodded.

"You're in on this." I sat down on the floor and sighed. "Whatever this is."

"Yup." She winked. "It's always best to just do as he says. I stopped fighting long ago. Now put on the silly outfit, go out in public, and you just may be surprised what happens."

"Is Reid really having a breakdown?"

Becca pulled out her phone and tossed it to me. It was open on her Twitter page. With a groan I scrolled through all the hashtags: #ReidisBatman #gothamissaved #capedcrusaderreal #batmanandtheshrew.

Several pictures of Reid were tagged.

And in all of them he was wearing a black cape.

And a white mask.

Batman didn't have a white mask, but whatever. I groaned and shoved the phone back into Becca's hand. "I guess I have work to do. And why can't I just wear normal clothes?"

"Max's idea of PR genius." Becca shrugged. "You show up like you're in costume while Reid is already in costume and it looks planned and not like he's actually off his rocker and about five seconds away from talking to himself and feeding a dead pet bird."

"Great," I croaked. "I guess it semi works since we're in this together, until I publicly shame him and then eat a pint of ice cream in my new apartment he found for me without telling!" I yelled the last part.

Becca winced. "Trust me, it will be fine. Just get through today."

"That"—I pushed to my feet—"is going to be my mantra for the day."

# CHAPTER FORTY-THREE

## REID

Ren, Jordan's boss, was ecstatic when I called him first thing in the morning, although he said Jordan wasn't a fan of surprises or public displays of affection.

I told him it was all I had.

After a lot of silence and then a healthy amount of cursing, he'd told me it better go over well with the media or he was going to hang me by the balls and sprinkle me with birdseed.

And watch.

I was trying to figure out why he was so upset, but then he explained that if things went wrong it wouldn't just be Jordan's job but his firm's reputation at stake.

I shivered and checked my watch. Becca texted that Jordan was on her way. The crew had torn down most of the set, but I didn't need anything other than the park and my girl.

Well, that and a stage, props, and a few friends from Broadway.

Hell, I'd said *good PR* so much that day I was pretty sure it was going to become my new catchphrase: *As long as it's good PR.*

"Well." Max crossed his arms. "Our work here is done. It's all you, kid." He slapped me on the back. "Don't screw up."

"Already did." I put the mask back on. "And thanks for trending the whole Batman thing on Twitter."

"Dude, what else are brothers for? All I needed to do was put it on my blog. Seriously, you guys need to read my blog. I have millions of followers."

"You have a picture of a goat, a gecko, and a snake as your background. I still don't understand how people even take you seriously."

"Because I'm awesome." He frowned. "Thanks for your vote of confidence. Now go get your woman."

I attached the mask and nodded just as a cab pulled up and Jordan stepped out.

Performances had always been easy for me. I'd never been the nervous type. Acting was in my blood. Even if the audience hated me, I was in my own world when I was on stage.

Except now.

Now I was bringing her into my world and praying she wouldn't stomp all over my heart, then shoot me.

"Showtime." One of the PAs spoke into his headset just as the lights hanging on the trees flashed.

It was overcast.

And starting to rain.

Which was perfect, because it made the lights stand out.

I waited for Jordan to turn the corner.

Max held his phone up so he could do the live feed. Now that we had our own YouTube channel, our subscribers were able to actually watch this take place.

Worldwide.

No pressure.

Talk about sinking my career if it didn't work.

The *Phantom* overture began to play through the hidden speakers as Jordan made her way toward me, her eyes narrowing.

I held out my hand.

She stared at it.

"Music of the Night" started.

And I began to sing.

"Nighttime sharpens, heightens each sensation, darkness stirs and wakes imagination. Silently the senses abandon their defenses . . ." I crooned, twirling her in to my body so I could sing in her ear. "Slowly, gently, night unfurls its splendor." I could play the Phantom in my sleep. But I wasn't playing the Phantom.

I was acting out a part.

And making sure she knew that she was the main attraction.

The main everything.

"Close your eyes and surrender to your darkest dreams, purge all thoughts of the life you knew before."

Jordan's eyes were wide with shock as I continued singing. A crowd gathered around us as I twirled her with my hand and gripped her hips, tugging her against me.

I walked her backward toward the stage.

Where an entire orchestra was sitting and playing the song. The music crescendoed as I sang one of the highest notes of the song.

"Only then," I whispered, "can you belong to me."

She gasped as I lifted her into my arms and carried her onto the stage. The crowd swayed in front of us as I kept singing, then gently lowered her into the boat.

"Let the dream begin! Let your darker side give in!" I sang. "The power of the music of the night!"

Cymbals crashed around us as I reached into my cape and pulled out a single red rose.

"You alone can make my song take flight. Help me make the music of the night."

The music ended as I slowly caressed her face with the rose.

She was breathing hard, her eyes filled with tears. Gently, I wiped them away with my thumbs. "You told me you liked capes."

Jordan nodded. Damn, she was beautiful. Her white dress looked exactly like the one Christine wore in the movie.

"You aren't really a shrew. You never were." I sighed. "Just like you've never been invisible, not to me. You're vibrant." I swallowed the emotion in my throat. "Just like this red rose, you stand out among the rest. And I'm sorry for not telling you that sooner. I'm sorry for trying to keep my feelings private. I'm sorry that I never got the chance to tell you how desperately I need you in my life. I think it's finally time to tell the truth."

"Reid, wait!" She gripped my hand.

I addressed the crowd and looked directly at Max, who held the phone higher. "It was never Jordan that needed taming. It was me. It's always been me. She turned me from a man who was afraid of commitment, who thought that roses were the way to a girl's heart, into a man who'd be willing to do anything, even sacrifice his own career . . . in order to tell a girl he loves her."

She gasped.

The crowd simultaneously ahhed.

"I'm the shrew." I smiled wide. "But I'm happy to say this woman here has turned me into a man no longer afraid to take that big step. But a man who can't wait to leap."

Tears streamed down her face as I lifted her into my arms. "I wanted to buy you roses, lots and lots of roses, but someone said roses are lame."

"I love roses," she blurted. "I've always loved them." Big tears streamed down her cheeks, meeting her lips.

"Well," I chuckled. "I figured since I gave you a rose in the Phantom costume, you'd give me a free pass."

"I think the Phantom costume counts as a free pass for anything," a woman shouted from the crowd.

"I never meant for you to misunderstand my intentions." I kissed her softly on the lips. "I moved your furniture into storage because I want you to stay with me. But I did tell Max to keep it a secret, since he has a big mouth and apparently a blog with over five million followers."

"Huh." Jordan's eyebrows knit together. "You mean you weren't kicking me out?"

"No." I chuckled. "The exact opposite."

"But Max said—"

"Exactly." I shook my head. "Though, had he actually told you last night, we wouldn't be here now, making PR history, hmm?"

"So is it all about the PR?" Her eyes narrowed.

I dipped her back, kissing her soundly. "No, you should know by now. It's all about you. You deserved the big gesture. Screw the media."

Jordan burst out laughing as she fingered the cape. "Batman, my ass."

"Shh." I kissed her cheek. "It was all I could come up with, otherwise you would have known my plan."

"Your plan to seduce me by song and cape?"

"Did it work?"

She grinned. "I don't know. You may have to bring the cape back to the apartment."

"Still rolling." Max coughed. "Wrap it up, kids."

"Wrap this." I flipped him off.

Max gasped while the crowd chuckled.

"You should know," Jordan sighed in my arms, "I'm a terrible cook. That's why I make you fix breakfast. I can do coffee. And I can buy pastries. That's the extent of my cooking."

"I know."

"And I'm messy."

I laughed. "Believe me, I know that too."

"And I hate turning off lights!"

"My power bill is very much aware of this sad reality."

"Still want me?" She smiled shyly.

"Hell, yes." I kissed her soundly, twirling her in the air, my cape fluttering in the wind, making me feel more Batman than Phantom.

"Anything I should know about you?" she asked once I set her on her feet again. "You know, other than your sad fascination with *Star Wars*, your inability to seduce without using those aqua eyes, and your aversion to asparagus?"

"Just one thing." I grinned.

"Hmm?"

I licked my lips, then whispered gruffly in her ear, "I'm Batman."

# EPILOGUE
## JASON

I stared down at my phone and tried really hard not to panic. I'd taken a week off work to attend Max's wedding, thankful that he was finally going to be distracted enough not to meddle in my life like he had everyone else's. At least now his focus would solely be on his new wife and he'd forget I was even in the picture. During his bachelor party he'd drunkenly pointed a finger in my direction and slurred, "You're next."

I prayed to God that the burning sensation I felt in my chest was heartburn and not an actual curse taking root. My friends and family might allow Max his . . . control, but I kept a wide berth and wanted to keep it that way.

My text alert went off for the third time during the reception. When I finally read it, I nearly fell into my cake.

She's back.

Two simple words.
Words that should have absolutely zero effect on me.

But they did.

Because I knew exactly who *she* was.

And she, as far as I was concerned, could go to hell.

"Everything okay, man?" Colt slapped me on the back, then took a long swig of beer, his gaze falling on the waves as they crashed against the beach. We were in Bora Bora for the destination wedding, and I should be relaxing, not having a panic attack that felt a hell of a lot like a premature heart attack.

"Yeah," I croaked. "Just . . ." I lifted my phone into the air. "Work."

"Hmm." Colt eyed me over his beer. "Unless someone's actually bombed the town or a Mafia hit man is hiding out in the bushes, work wouldn't be texting you on vacation." He swiped my phone from the table before I could grab it, then paled and slid it right back to me.

"And by she . . ." Colt nodded slowly. "I'm guessing—"

"We should be celebrating a wedding and not talking about the chick who broke my heart, then freaking left with our best friend."

"Still can't say his name."

"Doesn't deserve to be said," I snapped.

"Easy." Colt held up his hands in surrender. "So what are you going to do?"

Max and Becca made their way to our table, and they both looked so damn happy I wanted to puke. I used to be that happy. Once upon a time, before the love of my life basically ran over my heart with her Honda Civic.

"Nothing." I shrugged. "It's America, she can live wherever the hell she wants."

"But the rest of the text said . . ."

"I know what it said!" I yelled. I rarely yelled.

Colt stood and walked off.

I didn't mean to snap at him. I just didn't want to acknowledge the texts or anything else about my past life.

And I really, really didn't want to know that she'd had a kid.

And that he looked exactly like her.

Or that she was asking about me.

"Everything cool?" Reid slid in a seat next to me. "Colt seems pissed."

"He's not having sex." I nodded. "Max is exhausting all his groomsmen."

"I hate Max," Reid said in a bored tone, lifting his beer bottle in the air in a fake salute to his brother. "But I do love free trips to Bora Bora."

Jordan ran toward us, her feet kicking up sand as she launched herself into Reid's lap and whispered something in his ear. His laughter grated my nerves. I was officially surrounded by wedding cakes and engagement rings.

At least Jordan and Reid had been slightly normal—they'd moved in together shortly after the whole Phantom episode and had been inseparable ever since. Her four-carat engagement ring caught the sun just right, nearly blinding both my eyes. I pulled down my sunglasses and crossed my arms. Reid's movie, with her help, was a blockbuster hit and they still did a weekly YouTube relationship talk that had over ten million followers and growing.

Max had made several appearances as a guest.

As had Hades.

I'd never been invited—then again, what would I have to offer?

A black eye? Because as of right now that was my MO . . . the accident-prone family member who almost married a girl because she tricked him into thinking she was pregnant.

I'd dodged the bullet.

But now I was alone.

My mind went back to the text message. I tried not to think about it. Instead, I focused on the conversation between Reid and Jordan about their next YouTube webisode.

The group laughed about something—I'd tuned them out again.

I tried to join in the laughter around the table as everyone sat down and continued drinking.

But all I could think about.

Was the girl with curly red hair.

And the annoying pang in my chest that went along with it.

# ACKNOWLEDGMENTS

As I was going through the edits for this book, I just kept repeating to myself, "Is this my life? How did this happen?" I don't even have the words to express how grateful I am that I get to wake up every day and do something I love. I know that's not the norm, because I lived the opposite of that for many years before finding my passion.

I want to thank God who is forever first in my life and gave me this passion for writing to begin with. I swear there were so many days I was like, *What am I supposed to be doing with my life?* And now, I know, all those crappy rundown broken roads, somehow, gave me a story to write. I guess you could say even the bumps life gives you are important because they create your story—and every story, no matter how crazy, is a beautiful thing.

My husband, Nate—ugh, you are just . . . I can't even. You're incredible. My hero, our son's hero. And every day you inspire me to want to be a better person. Thank you for being you and for not getting mad when I ignore you while I write. You do such a beautiful job parenting; you're an amazing daddy, an incredible partner, and my best friend.

Thank you to my AMAZING agent, Erica. She has to be so tired of all my frantic e-mails but she just . . . gets me, as if she's a mind reader, which I'm still convinced she is!

Skyscape, thank you for believing in this story and not telling me it was crazy to do a slapstick rom-com where the main characters have weird quirks! You guys have been so fun to work with, and it's been a true honor to go through this process with you!

Readers. I'm obsessed with you. ALL OF YOU. I can't get enough of your encouraging messages and all-around amazingness! The Rachel's Rockin Readers fan group, thank you for letting me bounce ideas off you guys and not going, *Oh here she goes again asking us for more feedback!* You guys truly do "rock."

Bloggers, I HATE making this giant blanket statement to all the bloggers who help out and post on Facebook/Twitter/Instagram; I feel like it just seems so vague, but I truly appreciate each and every one of you! It's such a thankless job, yet you do it because you LOVE books. Thank you for constantly helping authors get out there, and thank you for your support. I know I wouldn't be where I am without you!

I hope you guys enjoyed Reid's story! As always you can find me procrastinating on Facebook in my fan group Rachel's New Rockin' Readers . . . and I do have an Instagram obsession; follow me @RachVD to see my writing adventures!

Hugs!

—RVD

# ABOUT THE AUTHOR

*Photo © 2014 Lauren Watson Perry, Perrywinkle Photography*

Rachel Van Dyken is the *New York Times*, *Wall Street Journal*, and *USA Today* bestselling author of Regency and contemporary romances. When she's not writing, you can find her drinking coffee at Starbucks and plotting her next book while watching *The Bachelor*. She keeps her home in Idaho with her husband, adorable son, and two snoring boxers.

Rachel loves to hear from her readers! You can connect with her on Facebook at www.facebook.com/rachelvandyken or join her Facebook fan group, Rachel's New Rockin' Readers. Her website is www.rachelvandykenauthor.com.

Want to be kept up to date on new releases? Text MAFIA to 66866!

Made in the USA
Middletown, DE
12 July 2017